MOTHERS, WITCHES AND QUEENS

ALBERT JOYNSON

MRS D'S PUBLISHING HOUSE

COPYRIGHT

Text Copyright © [2024] by Albert Joynson

All rights reserved. No part of this publication may be reproduced, distributed, or transmitted in any form or by any means, including photocopying, recording, or other electronic or mechanical methods, without the prior written permission of the publisher, except in the case of brief quotations embodied in critical reviews and certain other noncommercial uses permitted by copyright law.

This is a work of fiction. Names, characters, places, and incidents either are the product of the author's imagination or are used fictitiously. Any resemblance to actual persons, living or dead, events, or locales is entirely coincidental.

First Edition Published by Mrs D's Publishing House
ISBN: 978-1-7384833-3-4
Cover design by miblart

ACKNOWELDGMENTS

Once more, I must thank my mentor, Emma and my editor Steven, who made my writing (somewhat) intelligible.

Of course my parents, Jane and Simon, and my brother Henry and my fiancé Jake. You all showed me so much love and grace whilst I persisted with this writing business. Even when there was very little evidence that I was ever going to get anywhere with it. For believing in me even when I didn't. Without you I'd never have published anything, especially you Jake, since you really did most of the publishing for me. I don't know what I'd do without you but I'm sure it'd be rubbish.

For this book especially though, Mum I must give you special credit. This is a story about just how inspiring and powerful a mother can be. You showed me that, and I think must take some of the blame for my enduring obsession with women in fiction. Before I knew them, I had you.

And to all my fictional heroines, Mary Poppins, Galadriel, Esme Weatherwax, Gytha Ogg, Catherine Earnshaw, Lorelai Gilmore, Piper Halliwell, Marmee March, Moira Rose and far too many more to mention. You aren't real, but the effect you had on me was.

Thanks a lot ladies.

PART I

WATCHED

1

"So, be honest with me, what did you think of that one?" asked Mum, as we trundled down the street towards home at last, after another fairly uninspiring university open day visit. I frowned, trying to think of a way to tactfully explain how much I didn't want to go there.

"Put it this way," I said, "I can't really imagine spending the next three years of my life there."

"Perhaps not at first, but you've got to admit, the student halls were much nicer than we were expecting them to be," said Mum, clutching at straws.

"They were nicer than we were expecting because they look like a prison from the outside, and on the inside, they only seem like a halfway house," I replied.

"Alright," Mum conceded. "I admit, they did look a bit bleak. Why do they make them look so uninviting I wonder? Got to admit though, seven uncles and aunts and my boy will be the first in the family to go uni." I couldn't help rolling my eyes.

"Mum, Daniel was the first to go to uni," I said. "I'll be the second."

"Yes alright," said Mum, "but still, my boys are the first. Gives me something to show off about in the Christmas cards."

"Well, that's the main thing," I said, giving a half-hearted laugh.

"You don't think he'll mind, do you? Only that Mini is parked in our spot," said Mum, as she parked up in front of Mr Davies' drive.

"The other day, I saw him park on a pedestrian crossing. We're doing everyone a favour by blocking him in," I said as we climbed out of the car.

"True enough," said Mum. "Now, back to the matter at hand… halls."

"To be honest, Mum, I don't know if I even want to live in student halls if I do go," I said.

"When you go you mean, and where else would you stay besides student halls?" said Mum, not-so-subtly continuing the war of wills we'd been waging since the UCAS application had first reared its ugly head.

"I mean if," I replied, "and I was thinking maybe Adrian and I could get our own flat somewhere. After all, Adrian won't be living in student halls, will he?" Adrian had dropped out of Starkton sixth form shortly after we returned from Easter break. It seemed a bit pointless for him to carry

Mothers, Witches and Queens

on, what with all his prior education having been in the fay forest. He had barely understood any of what went on in class.

"But how would you pay for it?" asked Mum.

"Well, I'd have my maintenance loan and Adrian has his mushroom money," I replied. Mum gave a snort of laughter.

"We really have to come up with a better name for it than mushroom money," she said. "It makes it sound like he's a drug dealer or something."

"Could you imagine it, Adrian dealing?" I said. "No one would ever underpay him because they couldn't bear to see the disappointed look on his face." The grin that was spreading across my face faltered as I felt something electric on the back of my neck; that tingling feeling you get when someone is right behind you. I turned my head and my eyes fell on the green Mini parked in our spot. There was a woman with long, curly dark hair in the driving seat and a balding man in overalls sitting next to her. They were engrossed in an A to Z, although I couldn't shake the feeling they'd been watching me.

"Maybe they're lost," said Mum, following my eyeline to the car, before strolling on over and tapping on the window. They all but jumped out of their skin.

"Sorry, did I make you jump?" Mum yelled through the window, before they had a chance to lower it.

"N-no bother at all," the man stuttered.

"Are you lost, Lovely?" Mum asked, almost poking her head all the way into the car as the window rolled down.

"No, thank you!" said the woman, a little too quickly and a little too loudly as she started the car.

"S-see you," stuttered the man, the car already speeding away before he'd even got the window up.

"That was weird," said Mum with a shrug, as she made her way to the house.

"Very," I agreed, as I pushed the key into the lock and let us in.

"We're home!" Mum called, chucking her puffy coat on the pile in the entrance hall. There was the faint shuffling sound of slippers in the distance, and then the kitchen door swung open. There was Adrian, in his powder blue dressing gown and pink fluffy slippers. I grinned, taking him in, before he sniffled, and my stomach dropped. His eyes were red and there were tear streaks down his cheeks.

"Adrian, what's wrong? What happened?" I asked, crossing the hall in a split second, then wrapping my arms around him and pulling him into my chest. He hadn't had one of his nightmares about Merlin in weeks. I thought he'd been doing better. I stroked his hair as I held him, and he mumbled something muffled into my chest.

"Sorry, I couldn't quite hear you," I said, loosening the hug just a little.

"Prue died," he mumbled, letting out a little shaky sob, sending my heart racing out of my chest.

"What did he say, Love?" Mum asked, peering around us awkwardly as we took up most of the kitchen doorway.

"He said Prue's died. Who's Prue, Adrian?" I asked, fighting the panic out of my voice. Mum snorted again.

"He means Prue Halliwell, from Charmed. He must be at the start of season four, poor love," said Mum, patting him on the head as she squeezed past us into the kitchen.

"I'll pop the kettle on," she said as she went. I felt my chest loosen and relief washed over me.

"Is that true, Adrian? Were you watching Charmed again?" I asked. He sniffled and nodded.

"They were just having the funeral and demons attacked again and Piper smashed up a vase," he said, his voice still a little shaky. I chuckled and ruffled his hair.

"Oh dear, well, that sounds bad, but at least you're okay. You scared me half to death when I saw you in the doorway like that," I said, leading him through.

"Sorry, I didn't mean to scare you. How was the open day?" Adrian asked, wiping his eyes on the fluffy sleeve of his dressing gown as we made our way into the kitchen.

"Uninspiring," I replied.

"Oh, it wasn't that bad, they had some nice big trees on Campus, Adrian, you'd have liked it," said Mum, handing us both a cup of tea.

"We have trees here, Mum, we literally live next to a forest, I'm not gonna move to uni just for trees," I said.

"No, I'd hope you'd also go to class," Mum bristled.

"Obviously," I bristled back.

"Phoebe goes back to college to get her degree in season

three," said Adrian, in a somewhat obvious attempt to diffuse the tension.

"Do you think maybe you're watching too much Charmed?" I said, chuckling.

"I don't think so," said Adrian, "I can't really explain it. I just keep finding stuff to do with witches. First it was those Terry Pratchett books, and now Charmed. I just find it fascinating, all this magic stuff."

"Adrian, you're literally a water nymph," I said, barely stifling a laugh.

"I know that, but Piper can freeze time and Phoebe sees the future. Imagine that," Adrian said, taking my hand and leading me back into the living room.

"So how was your day, then?" I asked, attempting to steer him away from Charmed for a moment.

"Uneventful really," said Adrian. "I popped into The Fun Gi but they didn't need me for anything, so I just dropped off Mr Davies' order on the way back here. Other than that, I've just been chilling."

"Sounds nice," I said, plopping down on the sofa.

"Well, there was one other thing. Someone rang the doorbell, but when I answered it there wasn't anybody there," said Adrian, as he plopped down in my lap.

"Probably just a prank," I said.

"I guess, just felt a bit... off is all," he said absentmindedly. He pressed play on another episode of Charmed.

"I'll keep an eye out," I said, wrapping my arms around

his waist. I'd started to feel a bit guilty about leaving him home alone so much recently.

"Okay," he said, leaning up and kissing me on the cheek.

"Oooh, this is a good one, they're gonna meet Paige," said Mum, sinking into the armchair and passing us the chocolate digestives.

"I hope I meet a witch one day," said Adrian.

"Try the admissions desk at some of these open days," said Mum, giggling. This time it was my turn to give a snort of laughter.

2

"Adrian, you're going to have to let me borrow that blousy thing of yours one of these days," said Linda, as I made my way downstairs. I perched myself next to Michael, who was halfway through getting dressed at the kitchen counter. She'd been very jealous of my work uniform ever since Marshie had given it to me. It consisted of a silky green blouse top, the object of most of the jealousy, and a pair of baggy brown trousers, which I'd been reliably informed by Alex were "pazoozoo pants" or something like that anyway. Alex had told me I was giving very earth mother vibes, whatever that meant.

"I don't have to go into school today you know. I could skip it," said Michael, as he pulled on a sock with a hole in it big enough that it barely qualified as a sock anymore.

"No, you could not, Michael Tombs, now eat your

breakfast," said Linda, placing a bowl of cereal in front of him so forcefully that most of it ended up on the kitchen counter. They'd been bickering more and more lately, the debates about university were getting more tense by the week.

"I'll be fine, don't worry," I said, giving him a peck on the cheek as he struggled with his tie.

"Well, I'm keeping my phone on," said Michael, "so if you get any more mysterious knocks on the door or something doesn't feel right at work, just call me, okay?"

"Will do," I said.

"Promise?" he asked.

"I promise," I said, wrapping my arms around his waist and taking a deep breath as he enveloped me, placing a kiss on my forehead.

"He'll be fine. You're going to be late," came Linda's muffled voice from the world outside of Michael.

"I'm going, I'm going," said Michael, releasing me as he made for the door.

"Love you!" I called.

"Love you too," came his voice from the other side of the door.

"I'd best be off too, Adrian love, you have a nice day at the shop," said Linda, as she finished off Michael's cereal and plucked a coat from the pile on her way out the door.

I had one more cup of tea in the sudden peace of the empty house, before setting off for The Fun Gi, Starkton's number one - and only - boutique mushroom emporium.

Mothers, Witches and Queens

Summer was well and truly upon Starkton now, so I was glad of my billowy uniform as I walked into town. Starkton was, at the best of times, what Linda would call "a bit dingy" but for some reason, recently I'd been enjoying it less than usual. Maybe it was the young men who, at the first sight of the sun, had seen fit to whip their tops off and had quickly transmogrified from milky pale to painful pink. Or perhaps it was the general unpleasantness of hot tarmac. I wasn't quite sure I'd put my finger on it yet, but something wasn't sitting right. Before I could ponder this quandary any further, screeching breaks and a car horn ripped me out of my thoughts.

Looking down, I found myself standing in the middle of a crossing with a slightly funny looking green car already halfway pulled across it.

"Sorry! I was in my own world!" I called, as I embarrassedly scuttled across the road. I still hadn't really gotten used to actually having to walk to where I was going. In the fay forest you just sort of got there, as long as you were invited of course. Luckily, The Fun Gi was only five minutes from Michael's house.

The bell tinkled as I stepped over the threshold and I took a breath. The Fun Gi was the only place in Starkton where you could really smell the fay forest. The shop floor was characterised by several long, dark, wooden troughs that ran almost the length of the store. Each was filled with loamy soil, bits of old tree stump, moss, and of course, mushrooms.

"That you, Adrian?" came Marshie's voice from the back of the shop.

"'Tis indeed. Marshie," I replied, stepping behind the counter and into the backroom, which contained rows and rows of soil beds absolutely bursting with mushrooms.

"Nice morning, Adrian lovely?" asked Marshie, poking their head out from behind a particularly impressive toadstool. Marshie was, in their own words, "three feet on a good day, four on a bad one." They had a button nose, straggly green hair, big brown eyes and an infectious smile which was almost perpetually stamped on their face, regardless of the fact it only contained three sporadically placed teeth.

"Not too bad, Marshie," I replied, "only nearly got myself ran over once."

"Must be a record," Marshie joked, plunging their hand into one of the soil beds as we spoke.

"So, anything you need me for today?" I asked, as a collection of tiny pink mushrooms sprang out of the side of a particularly juicy looking piece of tree trunk.

"I've got a few things that could do with posting and a little job that only a water nymph could help with if you wouldn't mind," said Marshie, plucking the tiny specimens' stems and placed them delicately into a little brown box.

"What do ya need?" I asked, as I grabbed the hose and started filling the paddling pool Marshie kept for just such occasions.

Mothers, Witches and Queens

"Oh, you know, I keep the soil nice and moist for my little friends, but you really can't beat the stuff in the fay forest. Do you think you could infuse it again for me, Lovey?" Marshie had a way of asking for favours that made it seem as if they were asking for the world on a silver platter and seemed to feel terrifically guilty about it. Despite it being the only thing I did at The Fun Gi that was of any value. Not to mention, Marshie was a member of the fay council nowadays, elected to represent non-royal gnomes. So really, they had every right to order me about, not that they exercised it much.

"No trouble, Marshie," I said, slipping my shoes and socks off as I hopped into the pool. I closed my eyes and let the water run into me, filling me up before I gently pushed it out of my fingertips, with just a little of me going with it.

"That's the stuff," said Marshie under their breath as I formed the water into a globe in front of me and then, with my hands, split it into little streams, each snaking their way to one of the various soil beds.

"Thanks, Adrian, the parcels are all just behind the—"

The tinkle of the doorbell cut Marshie off.

"I'll go," I said, hopping out of the pool and heading back to the shop floor.

"Anything I can help you with?" I asked our lone customer, as I stepped out from behind the counter.

"N-no nothing, thank you," he said. He was just a little shorter than Michael I'd guess, bald, wearing overalls and pale as a sheet. You'd think I had two heads and a tail from the way he looked at me.

"Well, let me know if you need anything," I said, offering my friendliest smile in hopes I didn't scare him off. He didn't reply, just sort of shuffled round the shop, gingerly touching the mushrooms. Every now and then I was sure I saw his eyes flicker to me, if just for a second.

"No shoes," he said eventually. For a second I wasn't entirely sure what he meant, then I remembered.

"Oh yeah, I forgot to put them back on, I took them off out back," I said with a little laugh, out of awkwardness as much as anything.

"They'd never let us do that at the garden centre," said the man.

"Oh, you work at the garden centre?" I asked.

"What? No. I mean… I've got to go!" he said all but sprinting out the door, sending the bell jangling loudly as he went.

"Did he pinch anything?" came Marshie's voice from behind the curtain.

Marshie didn't have much for me to do, so once I'd put my shoes back on, I left with the parcels for the post office. Since I'd started working for Marshie, I'd learned that fancy foodie types will pay an arm and a leg for a particular kind of fungus called a "truffle", and Marshie grows them in their sleep. Turns out, the profits from The Fun Gi were where Olivier was getting the human money for the agents

Mothers, Witches and Queens

working on finding new charges, like I used to. Now, the profits mostly just go to helping any champions that were choosing to go back to their lives in the still world, and me of course.

The post office was just down the road from The Fun Gi. Since I'd started working there, I must have been to the post office every other day. The walk was short, familiar and unremarkable, but today something was different, somehow tense. Before stepping inside, I had a look around. Nothing stood out: a few parked cars, a man walking his dog and a lady with curly dark hair reading a paper on a bench.

"Nice day for a walk aye, Adrian," said the lady behind the glass window as I stepped inside the post office. She'd told me her name ages ago and I'd forgotten it, now it was far too late to admit that.

"Lovely. You should get out in it," I said, handing her the packages.

"Usual stuff?" she asked.

"Oh yeah, nothing out of the ordinary," I replied.

"Right, well you're all set then, Love," she said, whoever she was, as I tapped the company card against the scanner.

"See ya," I said, waving goodbye as I stepped out the door, just in time to see a green car speeding away from the post office at an alarming rate. I took a step onto the pavement and remembered stepping out onto the crossing, the car horn of the funny looking green car blowing at me. I squinted down the road, but the speeding car was already gone.

"It's probably nothing," I told myself, trying to ignore the chill running down my back. I walked back to the house as quickly as I could without breaking out into a jog.

3

I was sure Mr Moore was saying something. His lips were moving, which was a dead giveaway. It might have even been interesting, but there was no way to know for sure. To say it was in one ear and out the other was too generous. None of it went in anymore. Sitting through English lessons without Adrian had become, by far, the worst part of my day, which was saying something.

Whatever it was he was saying, he must have finished it, because everyone started packing their books away. I'd never been an academic exactly, but recently school was starting to feel increasingly pointless.

"You alright, Michael?" asked Jess, pulling me out of my head as I shoved Wuthering Heights into my bag with less respect than it probably deserved. She had her hair up in its signature school look - a ridiculously tight bun - as per usual, and her tie was tied about as thick and short as it could possibly be without undoing itself.

"Living the dream," I replied, setting off for PE.

"Missing Adrian?" she asked.

"Is that a bit pathetic?" I asked, slumping against the corridor.

"Maybe a little, but it's sweet too," she said. "Where are you headed?"

"I've got PE," I said.

"Wanna skip?" she asked.

"More than anything," I replied.

"Sixth form canteen it is then," she said. "By the way, what do you make of the new kid?"

"Oh… erm Jude, right? I've not really spoken to him properly. Why?" I asked her.

"Well, you fell in love with the last new kid," Jess said, grinning.

"I'm still in love with the last new kid, thank you very much," I said, trying to ignore the unmistakable sensation of my cheeks beginning to burn.

"Which is lovely and all, but the new one can't seem to take his eyes off you," she whispered, her eyes flicking over my shoulder.

I stretched, yawned and looked for myself in one faux casual motion to see what she was talking about. There Jude was, looking at his shoes, although I'm sure I just about caught him glancing away as I looked over. He was tall and skinny with pale skin and jet-black hair that made his skin look paler. He seemed fascinated with chains and skulls based on all the ornaments dangling from his bag.

"I don't think I'm his type," I said as we set off for the canteen.

"Yeah, that's probably why he spent so much time looking at you. I find once I see someone that's not my type, I just can't take my eyes off them," she teased. I rolled my eyes in lieu of a reply and did my best to pretend that my silence wasn't because I couldn't come up with anything clever to say back.

"Michael, Jess, over here!" Alex waved from a table in the corner of the canteen. He'd been a bit lonely, what with Jack still being off school.

"What's the gossip?" Alex asked as we sank into our chairs. He always sat with his back to the wall on a table in the corner. He never said why, but I suspected it was because it was the best seat for people watching.

"We were just discussing how the new boy is definitely falling in love with Michael," said Jess, setting my cheeks off again.

"Can we maybe stop saying that?" I begged.

"Well, you'd best keep an eye out," said Alex.

"I heard some very interesting things about a certain Jude Warren."

"Of course you did," I replied, planting my face on the table in surrender. If you wanted gossip at Starkton sixth form, Alex was the one to give it to you. At the moment, I didn't particularly want gossip, but I doubted very much that Alex was going to let that stop him.

"Apparently, he left his old school one town over because of some nasty rumours about him," said Alex.

"Which you intend to spread here?" I asked. Jess gave me a gentle elbow to the ribs as her not too polite way of telling me to shut up.

"Not at all," Alex said, "I'm just telling you two. If it spreads, you'll only have yourselves to blame." I rolled my eyes with my face still down on the table where I could be safe in the knowledge Alex didn't see it.

"So come on, spill it," said Jess impatiently.

"Well, apparently, he was into sort of satanic stuff. Big black pentagrams started turning up on the walls and people were finding animal skulls in their lockers and stuff," Alex whispered.

"That's kind of cool to be fair," said Jess under her breath.

"Well, I have to agree to be honest, but there was one rumour that was a bit creepy to do with…" Alex's voice tailed off.

"To do with what? Come on, tell…." Jess's voice tailed off too. I looked up from the desk, they were both looking past me. I turned and saw was Jude at the opposite end of the canteen, unmistakably pretending he hadn't been looking at me.

"Well, that's creepy," Jess hissed.

"What was the rumour?" I said under my breath, turning

Mothers, Witches and Queens

back to Alex, suddenly feeling like it wouldn't hurt to know as much as possible about my... admirer?

"You know how biology classes do dissection occasionally? Like a frog or a sheep's eye or whatever?" asked Alex. Jess, and I both nodded in unison.

"Well apparently some of the bodies? Corpses? Specimens? Whatever you call them, some of them went missing from the store cupboard. They never proved it was him, but someone swore blind they saw him with bloody fingers behind the bus shelter," said Alex.

"So, what was he doing with them?" hissed Jess, wide eyed.

"Who knows, messing around with their insides or like...." Alex's voice trailed off.

"You don't think he was eating them, do you?" asked Jess, looking horrified.

"Well, I didn't until you said that," said Alex.

"It's probably just gossip," I said, trying to convince myself as I ignored the feeling of his eyes boring into the back of my head, which was probably just my imagination playing tricks on me. Not that I could bring myself to turn around and check at this particular moment.

"Yeah... probably," agreed Jess, sounding as unconvinced as I felt.

"I'm gonna invite him to sit with us." I heard the words leave my mouth before they'd fully formed in my brain.

"You're going to what?" Jess squeaked, looking at me like I'd started speaking in tongues.

"Oh, this is going to be fun," said Alex, who was now grinning like a Cheshire Cat.

"Come on, it's probably just mean girl gossip and rubbish and we're freaking ourselves out over it," I said. "And he's the new kid. He is probably lonely. This is our chance to be nice."

"Well, apparently today is the day I start being nice," said Alex.

"I'm going over," I said. It came out like more of a declaration than I had intended, as I set off for Jude's table trying to avoid the little voice in the back of my head telling me he'd been eating sheep's eyeballs behind the bins and next he'd be eating mine. Jude must have noticed me heading his way because his eyes were so firmly glued to his phone, you'd have thought it was sucking him in.

"Hey, do you want to come sit at our table?" I blurted out. Conversation at the surrounding tables fell silent. I'd accidentally all but yelled at Jude. Nerves make me loud apparently. The silence hung in the air like a bad smell. I could feel eyes on me, the people sitting in the vicinity, and beyond. As the silence spread, more were drawn in, until it felt like everyone in the cafeteria was staring at me, staring at Jude, and he still hadn't said a word.

"Never mind," I squeaked, this time quieter than intended as I speed walked back to Alex's table and the hum of conversation resumed.

"That was good," said Alex, grinning at my agony.

"No, it was not," groaned Jess, who was cringing about half as much as I felt was appropriate.

"Maybe you're not his type after all," Alex teased, obviously enjoying this too much.

"Not anymore anyway," said Jess.

"That's what I've been saying all along," I said, burying my face in my hands.

"Well, I've got to leave now, or my skin might get up and crawl away without me," said Jess, standing abruptly.

"Where ya going?" asked Alex in a singsong tone.

"To find Sam and tell her exactly what just happened here in excruciating detail," said Jess.

"Oh good. I was worried more people wouldn't hear about this," I replied, with my face still hidden in my hands. I let the darkness close in on me until a minute or so later, when I felt a tap on my wrist.

"Can I ask you a favour?" came Alex's voice, only something was off. He sounded sincere. Alex never sounded sincere. I looked up, and he was leaning almost all the way across the table, his eyes fixed on me.

"Sure, anything Alex, what d'ya need?" I said.

"Do you think you and Adrian could come round to visit Jack tonight...?" Alex's voice had dropped to a whisper.

"Is he still having nightmares?" I asked. Jack hadn't been coming to school since the kidnapping by the mirelings. Oliver and the gnomes had made sure the kidnapping victims didn't remember anything, but Jack still wasn't doing very well.

"Yeah, he says there's a woman in his dreams that reminds him of Adrian. I'm not sure it'll do any good, but he said he really wanted to see Adrian." Alex gave a resigned shrugged of his shoulders, as a jolt of nerves shot through me. I'd have bet money that the woman that looked like Adrian, that Jack was dreaming about, was Nimueh. It was Adrian's text tone that finally pulled me out of my panic as my phone buzzed in my pocket.

"Oh, speak of the devil," I said, grateful for an excuse to avoid this conversation.

"Oooh, what's he said?" asked Alex, scooting around the table to hover over my shoulder.

Adrian: Hey don't panic or anything, but I kind of feel like I'm being watched.

"Creepy," said Alex, reading from over my shoulder.

Me: *What, why?*

Adrian: I keep getting this feeling like there is someone right behind me.

Adrian: And this weird guy came into the store.

Adrian: And there was this weird green car that kept turning up.

The image of the woman in the green mini parked in mum's spot thundered to the front of my mind as Adrian texted me and my stomach flipped.

Me: Was it a Mini?

Adrian: What's a Mini?

"How doesn't he know what a Mini is?" asked Alex, still hovering over my shoulder.

Me: It's a type of car. It doesn't matter. Are you okay?
Adrian: I'm watching the road from your window.
Me: Okay, have you locked the doors?
Adrian: I think it just drove down the street.
Me: I'm coming now. Don't answer the door to anyone.

"Alex, I gotta go," I said, already storming out of the building, my heart thundering in my chest as I went.

4

Knock, knock!

I almost jumped out of my skin as the knock on the door echoed around the house. Half of me wanted to run for the door, the other half wanted me to creep along the corridor like a spy. I ended up doing some weird sort of jog thing and almost tripped over myself heading down the stairs. I held my breath, slid the key into the door, and unlocked it.

"Hey are you okay? I heard you'd had a bit of a scare," said Jack, standing in the doorway. His hair was twisted into tight dark curls. He was smiling, but he looked tired with big bags under his eyes, and he'd lost weight since I'd seen him last.

"Oh… erm, sorry, how did you know?" I asked, a little confused. I'd been expecting Michael, or maybe a stalker, but not Jack. From what I could tell, Jack had been hibernating a little since we'd got him back from the forest.

"Alex texted me. He was looking over Michael's shoulder when you texted him." Jack gave a nervous little chuckle.

"Oh, well, come in, come in. Thanks for checking on me. I'm probably just being silly. Rattling around the house on my own was making things worse," I said awkwardly, fiddling with my fingers as I led Jack into the kitchen and flicked the kettle on.

"Hey, never can be too careful, just look at what happened to me," said Jack, as he took over tea making duties, much to my relief.

"Oh yeah, still got no memories of what happened?" I asked whilst fetching the milk, knowing full well he had no memories. Olivier's mushroom tea had seen to that.

"Still nothing, but I have been having some weird dreams," he said, a jolt of nerves shot through me as he poured the tea.

"What happens in the dreams?" I asked, hoping they weren't bringing up anything that might be tricky to explain.

"Well, there are these scary little green guys gnashing their teeth at me, which for some reason I always want to call goblins. It's all a bit murky once I've woken up to be honest, but there's definitely water, maybe a beach? I'm not sure. There's a woman though, a beautiful blonde woman, with amazing blue eyes. She kind of looks like you, actually." He had a distant look on his face as he spoke, almost as if he wasn't fully there, like his mind was elsewhere, back in the dream. Scratching at it, trying to reach, to remember.

Mothers, Witches and Queens

"Don't let Alex hear you saying I remind you of someone beautiful. We'll never hear the end of it!" I laughed, and hoped he didn't notice the sweat beading on my brow the moment he started describing Nimueh.

"Oh, he already knows about all this. I think he was gonna try to arrange for you to come visit, but I thought I'd just come over. D'you recognise the woman? From the description I mean?" he asked, looking at me now. His eyes were greenish blue and red around the edges, watery almost and intense, tired but focused.

"Nope, afraid not," I said, gulping down my tea to avoid holding his gaze as I lied to his face.

Knock, knock!

"You okay?" Jack asked, as I all but jumped out of my skin, splashing tea up my nose, before coughing and spluttering it all over the counter.

"F-fine, fine," I said, choking.

"I'll get the door. You just keep inhaling that tea," said Jack, chuckling as he headed towards the entrance hall.

"Oh. Hey, Jack, what are you doing here?" I heard Michael's voice from the entrance hall as I blew the tea out of my nostrils on some kitchen roll.

"Alex texted me that Adrian was home alone and feeling spooked. So, I thought I'd check on him, since you were at school," said Jack as I pushed the door open to the entrance hall. Michael was just stepping into the hallway and kicked his shoes off. He was a little red in the face, with his fringe plastered to his brow with sweat.

"Did you run home?" I asked, as a smile crept across my face at the sight of him.

"Thank goodness you're okay," said Michael, ignoring my question as he crossed the room and pulled me into his arms.

"I'm fine now. I think I'm overreacting," I said, wrapping my arms around his waist as he stroked my hair. I breathed him in, his sweat, his smell, warm and familiar and safe.

"Right, looks like you've got things handled Mike, so I'll head off," said Jack, still standing at the door.

"You sure?" asked Michael, letting me go to face Jack.

"Yeah, I've gotta get back, or my parents might think I've actually gone to school." He gave a half smile.

"Thank you for coming to check on me. It was really good of you," I said, peeking out from behind Michael.

"No problem, feel better Adrian," he said, as he slipped out of the door. Michael locked it behind him, before leading me back into the kitchen to put the kettle on.

"I think Jack wanted to talk about his dreams. They seem to be freaking him out a bit. Does he look tired to you?" I asked.

"A little, but I think it's probably normal after what happened to him," said Michael, glaring at his phone.

"You're probably right," I said, trying to peek over and see what he was looking at.

"Did the car look like this?" he asked, showing me a picture on his phone.

Mothers, Witches and Queens

"Yes, but way dirtier. How did you know?" I asked.

"This is a green Mini. I saw one parked outside the other day. When you said there was a green car, I just got a bad feeling." Michael looked worried, his eyes flicking from me to his phone, as if the picture of the Mini could reveal some clue.

"Who was driving it?" I asked.

"Erm, I didn't really get a good look at them, a lady with dark hair, I think, and a bald guy in overalls," said Michael, as my breath caught in my chest. "What's wrong? You've gone pale... paler." He took my hands in his. I looked up into his warm amber eyes and tried to focus on them, to ignore the squirming in my stomach.

"There was a man in overalls in the shop today," I said. "He seemed skittish... almost like he was scared of me."

"That's it, you're not walking to and from work on your own anymore, no way. I'll walk you before school and pick you up after, or Marshie can walk you home," said Michael, pulling me into his arms again.

"You're trembling," I whispered, stroking his back.

"I'm scared someone's gonna hurt you," he whispered back, lifting me off the ground. I wrapped my legs around his waist and snuggled my head into his shoulder.

"I'm fine. You don't need to worry about me. And hey, what about you? Who's gonna walk you to and from school?" I asked, as he carried me into the living room and sank into the sofa.

"They're not following me, they're following you, and

if they do follow me, I'm not worried," said Michael, giving me a wink.

"Oh no, whys that then?" I asked.

"Cause I'm a big, strong champion of the fay forest with a shining silver shield and a massive hammer," said Michael.

"That you are," I said, trying not to let my eyes wander to Michael's arms as he not so subtly flexed.

"You're blushing," Michael said through a grin.

"You're showing off!" I said, poking his chest accusatorially.

"Am I?" Michael asked in mock shock, flexing even less subtly as he made his chest pop where I'd poked it.

"I'm gonna wipe that smug look off your face," I teased.

"How ya gonna do that then?" Michael asked, grinning so wide I could almost see his molars.

"Like this," I said, starting to lean in, a smile curling my lips as Michael's amber eyes grew wide, drawn into mine. I could feel his breath growing shallow as I inched closer. One hand rested against his muscular chest, the other behind his head, entwining my fingers in his hair. Michael's hands snaked to my hips, holding me close, our lips milometers apart.

"Right, best get you upstairs and out of the danger zone," said Michael, letting out a shaky breath as he stood, lifting me off the sofa as my legs wrapped around his hips and he carried me upstairs.

"Where are we going?" I asked, my eyes locked on his.

"To hide from stalkers under the bedsheets," said Michael with a wink, before planting a tender kiss on my lips.

5

"Do you think she'll be pleased to see me?" Adrian asked, as he pulled on his fay robes. It'd been a while since I'd seen him in them. A loosely fitting robe of light blue, I think it was silk, but I wasn't sure. It had green embroidered detailing of trees and leaves and a cloak which dragged a couple of inches on the floor, in a darker blue. He looked beautiful, but I never got the sense he was comfortable in it, like when he put on the robes it reminded him of who he used to be, and everything that came with that person.

"Of course, they will be pleased to see you. Why wouldn't they be?" I asked, as I struggled my way into the strappy leather armour that Nimueh had provided months ago. I'm not sure I really needed to wear it anymore, but it was worth it just to see the look on Adrian's face when he saw me in it. Plus, somehow it was nice to feel like I had a place in the fay forest.

"Because I gave up all my responsibility and ran off to the still world with the most powerful champion of a generation and left them to clean up after the whole war business," Adrian huffed as we stepped out of the house, heading for Mr Davies's conveniently large oak across the road.

"After you negotiated peace and deposed a dictator for them," I said, taking his hand in mine and giving it a little squeeze.

"You deposed Merlin. I just stood there like a potato," said Adrian, glancing both ways before pulling me through the tree with him.

"You mean you stood there like a chip, and also, no, you didn't. You convinced everyone to believe in you, to go against Merlin. You inspired people," I said, following him through the tree. When I came out the other side, he was looking at me with those big watery eyes of his and my heart skipped.

"You really think I inspired people?" he asked. His voice was small. In amongst the great creaking trunks of the fay forest Adrian seemed smaller, but here I felt bigger, like I was a part of something more.

"I know you did," I said, lifting his hand to kiss it, grinning as he turned a shade pinker.

"I love you," said Adrian, grabbing me by the waist and pulling me into a hug, or rather, pulling himself into me, burying himself in my leather clad chest.

"I love you too, Inspiring-Former-Leader-Adrian," I said, giving him a quick squeeze.

"Right, well, let's get going," said Adrian, pulling himself together as he took my hand and set off down the winding yellow path of the forest.

"Doesn't it make you feel kind of magical, being here?" I asked, as wind whistled through the trees and dancing light pierced through the leaves, bathing the world in green.

"It makes me feel like I need to turn on a lamp," said Adrian, chuckling. He picked one of the wildflowers growing along the side of the path and handed it to me.

"This smells like… vanilla?" I guessed, taking a deep sniff of the flower.

"Yep, don't forget to stop and smell the flowers. Before you know it, you'll get to your destination without enjoying the journey," said Adrian. He stopped to smile at me and suddenly my mouth was dry, I'd forgotten where I was and I was smiling so broadly my cheeks ached.

"What are you smiling at?" Adrian asked, as his pale dimpled cheeks got pinker still, his blond hair tumbling past his glittering eyes.

"Just my boyfriend," I whispered, leaning down until we were at eye level, inches from each other, a broad smile peeling back, showing his soft lips and white teeth.

"Me too," Adrian whispered back. I could feel him breathing, the rise and fall of his chest. His collar bone peeking through the top of his robe in that way I liked even though I don't really know why I liked it.

"Did you two need something? Or did you just come here to stare dreamily into each other's eyes in plain view of my cottage?" Olivier's matter-of-fact voice pierced our world.

"We came to talk. You're sitting in your garden?" Adrian asked, turning to Olivier, who appeared to be doing paperwork on a bench.

"Well observed, what did you come to talk about?" she asked, lowering her spectacles to the tip of her nose.

"Adrian is being stalked. We thought you might know something," I said, following Adrian into her garden.

"You're being stalked?" asked Olivier, getting up and pulling Adrian into a hug. She was smaller than him, but she was stocky and she had him in a tight squeeze.

"I am, and you're working in the garden. You never used to work in the garden," said Adrian, apparently distracted by garden benches.

"Oh yes, well, I got the idea from Linda's garden, actually," she said, shooting me a smile and a wink.

"Oh, she'll love that, I'll tell her," I said, getting distracted by garden benches myself.

"I find so many people come to see me these days," said Olivier. "It's easier if I'm outside. I think it makes people think I'm available."

"Well, I guess you've got me to thank for that, Mrs Leader-Of-The-Water-Nymphs." Adrian gave a nervous giggle, which didn't mask how obviously guilty he felt over the whole thing.

Mothers, Witches and Queens

"Yes, I suppose I do. That was quite the letter you wrote," Olivier smiled, a kind smile, a smile that said she wasn't upset with Adrian. I hoped he could see that.

"I didn't plan it, I just …" Adrian dropped his gaze as his voice trailed away.

"Adrian, I'm not cross at you. It was a good letter," she said, craning up to give his shoulder a little squeeze.

"You're not?" he asked, giving a long breathy exhale. You could see his whole body releasing something.

"I'm not," she said, cracking a smile at Adrian's relief.

"I told you she wouldn't be," I said, draping my arms over Adrian's shoulders from behind, crossing them across his chest.

"You know, you could have dropped it off in person, there was no need for the cloak and dagger," said Olivier, sounding mildly amused.

"But Cherry got it to you alright?" asked Adrian, still sounding slightly anxious.

"Cherry?" asked Olivier.

"Yes, Cherry, the elf, bright red hair, he said he'd give you the letter," explained Adrian.

"Hmmm strange, don't think I know a Cherry," said Olivier, "the letter was just on my desk in my cottage when I got home." I must admit I was surprised. Olivier seemed like the sort of person who knew everyone.

"Oh, well, he's very nice," said Adrian, offering another sheepish smile.

"Now. You said you were being stalked?" Olivier asked,

remembering why we were there better than we did, although the trip had already been worth it for Adrian's relief.

"I am, and we thought you might be able to help, or well, Michael thought it'd be a good idea anyway, to come, that is," said Adrian.

"I thought you might be able to help, and I thought you'd want to know," I explained, shifting behind Adrian slightly as Olivier fixed me with her ten ton gaze.

"By mirelings?" she asked.

"What, sorry?" I replied, suddenly dry mouthed and nervous.

"Is he being stalked by mirelings?" Olivier asked again.

"I'm being stalked by a green Mini," said Adrian.

"A what?" Olivier asked, confused.

"It's a car, but I mean, he's being stalked by two people in a car," I said.

"Human people?" asked Olivier.

"As far as we can tell, human people," said Adrian, nodding.

"Not Nimueh?" she asked, looking suddenly serious.

"No, they didn't look like Nimueh anyway, and if Nimueh was disguised, Michael would see through it," Adrian pointed out. I could feel his breathing growing rapid and shallow, and held him tighter against me.

"Why are you asking about Nimueh?" I asked, my body tensing as images flashed through my mind of her towering over Adrian and of Mum, held captive by the lake.

"We never found her," Olivier said gravely.

"How's that possible?" I asked.

"She probably snuck off into the mireling lands once she knew that her betrayal wasn't a secret," said Adrian. He'd gone rigid in my arms, and I could tell he was battling to keep a wobble out of his voice.

"Don't worry, we've not got any reason to believe she's been able to access the grove. I just thought I should check, since you said Adrian specifically was being stalked," said Oliver.

"Like Adrian said, I'd have seen through any disguises. They didn't look like fay to me. Just people," I said.

"In a green Mini," Adrian added, his breathing getting a little closer to normal.

"Then I'm not sure how I can help," Olivier said, looking confused.

"Well, can't you like, cast a spell or something, to find out who it is?" I asked, suddenly aware I hadn't really thought this plan through all that well. An awareness which was only made worse by Olivier's now quizzically raised eyebrow.

"I'm afraid I cannot. If there was such a spell, I think we both know the only man who'd have known it," she said, taking an ominous tone.

"Oh well, never mind," said Adrian, quickly trying to move the conversation along.

"Couldn't you speak to the police? I believe this sort of

thing is more their area, correct?" asked Olivier, her eyebrow still alarmingly raised.

"I did think about that, but the problem is I'm worried they might try to look into who Adrian is," I explained.

"Would that be bad?" Adrian asked.

"Well, if they look too closely, they might find that records of yours that should exist might be missing," I said.

"What like?" Olivier asked.

"Like the fact that he was never technically born, or has never been to the doctors or a hospital or a primary school or—"

"I take your point," said Olivier, mercifully lowering her eyebrow.

"So, what do we do then?" Adrian asked.

"You've got a whispering stone. Keep that with you all the time, at least that way if you ever do feel in danger, you can reach me and Michael quickly," said Olivier.

"And you've got your phone. Maybe for now we just keep an eye on things, and I'll keep walking you to and from work," I said. I couldn't help feeling like I was letting him down a little, although Adrian did seem less worried.

"Well, I've got a meeting of the fay council to get to, but do keep in touch you two, and Adrian, try not to worry too much. We'll find Nimueh," said Olivier. Adrian nodded and waved as Olivier set off down the yellow path deeper into the forest.

"Are you okay?" I asked, watching as Adrian sunk onto Olivier's bench. I joined him, placing my hand over his and

Mothers, Witches and Queens

knitting our fingers together. I looked down the path to watch Olivier go, but she'd vanished. I'd missed it. I wanted to watch the moment people arrive at where they're going in the forest, but I'd not caught it yet.

"I think so," said Adrian.

"I'm not sure what I was expecting coming here for help," I said. "I just... I wasn't sure where else to turn."

"It's okay. I don't think it would be fair to expect you to magically have the solution to me being stalked," said Adrian, as he reclined across the bench, resting his head in my lap. As he looked up at me his golden hair fell back in waves.

"Sometimes it is hard to know what magic is and isn't the solution to," I said, stroking his hair back out of his eyes, as a shaft of pure light peaked through a break in the canopy, catching his face so that he almost glowed.

"In my experience, it's the solution to very little," said Adrian with a chuckle, his eyes little slits of blue as he squinted into the light.

"I think I've been hoping it could be the solution to everything," I said.

"What do you need solving?" he asked, taking my free hand in his and holding it to his chest.

"I think, if I'm being honest, it's been really hard going back to the normal non-magical world when I know about all this," I said, looking around us. When you really look at the fay forest, it's hard for your eyes to find a place to land. There's so much to see. They might set on the flowers of every colour, growing up as tall as a full-grown man, with flower heads as big as pie dishes. Then be drawn to an iridescent butterfly, bouncing through the air on wings the size of your hand. Or you could look up into the canopy of green that stretches on as far as the eye can see in every direction. Or to the ground, with the web of roots that cover the floor in every direction, like the veins of the forest. It made Starkton feel grey.

"Is that why you've been fighting with your mum over university so much?" Adrian asked, opening his eyes fully as the shaft of light vanished behind a waving branch high above us. Enveloping me in his bright blue globes, I gulped and nodded.

"I think so," I said. "I don't think I even realised that was what was wrong at first, but maybe subconsciously." I sighed as the tension in my chest, that I didn't even know I was holding, started to release.

"You've not been enjoying school either, have you?" Adrian's voice was soft and gentle and full of kindness, and when he spoke it made my eyes sting.

"I've missed you," I whispered, struggling to speak around the lump in my throat.

"Maybe we should tell your mum you don't want to go to university," said Adrian, sitting up. He gently pulled me down to lie facing him, with my head in his lap. His fine fingers running through my hair felt warm and tingly and made me never want to move again.

"I don't want to disappoint her," I whispered. A tear

running down the side of my face fell into my ear, which tickled.

"Well, we don't have to do anything right now, but it's an option," he said, placing his free hand on my chest.

"Thank you," I whispered, as another tear tumbled down my cheek.

"What for?" he asked, smiling as he wiped my tears away with his thumb.

"For noticing I was struggling, I don't think I could have said it on my own," I said, letting out a shaky breath as the lump in my throat dissolved away. I don't think I even really knew.

"You're welcome," said Adrian, leaning down to plant a kiss on my forehead.

6

"Are you sure you want to go to this?" I asked, slipping out of bed and pulling on one of Michael's hoodies. The bottom of it dangled just above my knees. It had become my preferred form of what Linda liked to call lounge wear. I liked it because it smelt of Michael and it was cosy.

"Don't worry, it's the last uni open day trip and then we're done, I think maybe once we've finished these I'll talk to mum, at least that way we can say I gave them all a chance before I made up my mind," said Michael, fiddling with his tie in the mirror before turning around to face me. A smile stretching across his face as he did so made my cheeks burn.

"What are you smiling at?" I asked.

"You!" he said, pouncing on me, wrapping his arms around my waist to lift and spin me. I chuckled as Michael's bedroom span around me, making me dizzy.

"Come on Michael, time to go!" Linda's voice called from downstairs.

"Come on then," said Michael, dropping me over his shoulder as he left the room.

"This is making my tummy wobbly," I said, bouncing off his shoulder as we went.

"Needs must," Michael chuckled as he bounded down the stairs.

"Michael, you'll give the poor boy a stomach ache!" Linda protested from the front door where she was already bundled up in coats.

"You'll be okay, won't you?" Michael asked, setting me down at the door to the entrance hall. "You'll keep the doors locked?"

"I will, I promise," I said into his chest as I hugged him back.

"The sooner we're gone, the sooner we're back," said Linda, tapping her foot at the door.

"Right, see you soon," said Michael, leaning down to kiss me before heading out the door.

I waved from the window as Michael and Linda drove off, then flopped down on the sofa and wondered what to do with myself. Which quickly led to me rooting around for the next DVD in the Charmed boxset that Linda had lent me.

I'd just set myself up with a pot of tea, a pile of chocolate biscuits, a blanket and had season four of Charmed all loaded up and ready to go, when my phone rang.

"HELLO, ADRIAN? CAN YOU HEAR ME? AM I

Mothers, Witches and Queens

DOING THIS RIGHT?" Marshie's rather bewildered voice shouted through the phone at me.

"Marshie, I can hear you stop shouting," I said, stifling a giggle, imagining Marshie screaming down the phone from the back of their shop. Michael had taught me to use a phone. I'd found it pretty simple, but Marshie seemed to be mostly self-taught and evidently hadn't been a particularly brilliant teacher, or student.

"Is this better?" Marshie all but whispered back.

"Just speak normally," I said, hoping Marshie couldn't hear me grinning down the phone.

"Okay, how about now?" Marshie asked, finally speaking in a nearly normal tone.

"Perfect, did ya need something, or just fancied out trying out your phone voice?" I asked. When Linda spoke on the phone, she started elongating all her words and making funny shapes with her mouth. She even stood up straighter. Michael said it was her phone voice.

"I was hoping you could come and watch the shop for me. Emergency back in the forest, council business, can't be missed, I'm afraid," said Marshie.

"Erm, I suppose…" I said. My stomach churned. I didn't want to let Marshie down, but the image of that green Mini was flashing through my mind. I'd promised Michael I wouldn't leave the house.

"I know it's your day off, so sorry Adrian, it's just I've got no one else I can ask, I won't be long." Desperation was seeping into Marshie's usually chirpy voice, and I could feel their guilt stabbing at me as they asked for what was really only a very little favour.

"Don't worry about it, Marshie, I'll be there soon, I'll just get dressed," I said, swallowing my nerves and making a silent plea to Michael to forgive me.

"You're a star, thank you, thank you, thank you Adrian!" Marshie positively beamed down the phone before hanging up, which did make me feel a little better as I jogged up the stairs and pulled on my uniform.

It was sunny in Starkton but not hot, and windy. Michael's favourite weather. He said he liked watching the wind mess up my hair. I didn't mind it either, I liked to let it catch my fringe. It made me feel dramatic, even more so when the wind whipped at my eyes until they watered. Although I realised I probably looked a bit mad to onlookers. Luckily, the streets were quite quiet. By the time I'd reached The Fun Gi, I'd crossed the path of a postman, seen a curly haired woman with sunglasses, sitting across the street reading a paper and some pigeons fighting over what looked like flaky pastry.

"I'm here Marshie!" I called over the jingling of the bell as I stepped into the shop and let the smell of the fay forest fill me up, chasing away the dusty tarmac smells of Starkton.

"Oh Adrian, you're a lifesaver. I'll be back as quick as I can. Shouldn't take long, mushroom caves, gnomes feuding, that sort of thing. You know how it is," said Marshie, slipping out the backdoor to the large tree they'd cultivated in

Mothers, Witches and Queens

the yard behind the shop, where they vanished into the forest.

I watched them go, then headed back inside, tying on an apron over my green silken blousy thingy and brown pazoozoo pants. I amused myself for a while by reading the guides to various mushrooms that Marshie kept in leaflet form on the counter. Emblazoned across the front of each one was Marshie's favourite joke: "Every mushroom is edible, just some are only edible once." Followed by "A 'What's good to eat?' guide can be found inside". I was reading about the difference between black and white truffles when the doorbell jangled.

"Oh, hello there. Let me know if there's anything I can help you with," I said with a smile, as a tall, skinny young man stepped into the shop. Dressed in black from head to toe, he had jet black hair that didn't look quite natural, pale skin and was dripping in chains and little decorative skulls. I couldn't quite make up my mind over whether he looked scary or not.

"Thank you," he mumbled, not looking up from his shoes as he drifted towards one of the troughs of mushrooms that ran across the centre of the store. I made an effort to smile and stepped out from behind the counter, but he still didn't look up at me. Instead, he knelt by the trough as if studying the mushrooms. As I watched him, an uneasiness took over me. He seemed nervous and it was making me nervous too. There was tension in the air, as though something was about to happen.

I almost jumped out of my skin as the bell rang again, and a lady stepped inside. She was the lady from the bench with the curly brown hair. Her skin was slightly wrinkled, she had a warm olive complexion and looked as though she sat out in the sun a lot. Up close I could see she was covered in bangles and necklaces dangling with little gemstones and feathers, and her clothes were drapey and colourful. Purples and yellows, scarves and cardigans blending comfortably together. She was still wearing her sunglasses. I supposed perhaps she'd forgotten to take them off.

"Let me know if I can help you with anything," I said, trying not to sound nervous as my eyes flicked back to the boy in black.

"Thank you, Dear, I certainly will." I couldn't quite workout if she actually sounded sinister or if it was my nerves getting the best of me.

"Actually, could you explain this to me?" asked the boy, speaking at last. He'd gotten up from his hunched position and was pointing to a piece of dead wood with some mushrooms growing out of it on a shelf against the back wall.

"Of course, follow me," I said, leading him to the back wall, a little relieved he'd finally asked for something.

"Do you guys erm... sell these?" he asked, in a sort of hesitant voice gesturing broadly to the display.

"Do you mean the mushrooms or the dead wood because—" Michael's ringtone cut me off, along with a little pang of guilt. A reminder that I'd broken my promise to stay indoors.

"Sorry, bear with me a moment. I've just got to take this," I said, reaching for my phone.

"N-no problem," the boy in black stuttered.

"Hey Michael, is everything alrhnng—" My ears thundered as something smacked against the back of my head. I slumped forward into the wall, biting my tongue as I dropped my phone. Sinking to my knees, the taste of iron filled my mouth, and my ears rang. I tried to stand, but my legs wouldn't move. I blinked my eyes, trying to clear my blurred vision. Another impact rocked me and the world went black.

7

"They look like prison blocks," I hissed, already regretting the harshness in my tone as Mum bristled back at me.

"Don't be so dramatic, you've not even given them a chance," she whispered, half pleading, half telling off.

"Why do we even go on these tours if you don't care what I actually think?" I hissed, my tongue running away with me as we trudged behind the rest of the crowd following the campus tour guide around the university housing. I was about to say something else I'd regret when I paused. A bald man in overalls had caught my eye, or rather it seemed as though I'd caught his. He was walking past our crowd in the other direction. I was sure he'd been looking at me, but the moment I'd spotted him his eyes were on the ground. Or maybe they'd always been on the ground and my mind was playing tricks. Ever since Adrian had told me about the man in The Fun Gi, I'd been on edge.

"Because I'm trying to find somewhere you might actually like." Mum almost gave up the pretence of a whisper, as the people at the back of the crowd not too subtly glanced over their shoulders at us.

"Well, you've failed, and I don't want to go to the talk about freshers' week or student life or any other rubbish either," I said, giving up the whisper completely.

"Well please yourself, Michael, but I'm going to them, so you're stuck here until they're all done regardless." Mum huffed, almost coming to a complete stop, letting the tour leave us behind. I glanced over my shoulder distractedly, looking for the man, but I'd lost sight of him. "Michael, are you listening to me?" Mum raised her voice.

"Whatever, go to the talk. I'm not bothered, and I'm not coming," I said, turning round on the spot. That man had to be somewhere.

"Fine!" Mum barked, bustling off after the crowd leaving me alone on the campus, suddenly acutely embarrassed and a little ashamed of myself.

"Well, this is going well," I said to myself awkwardly, as I started walking somewhat aimlessly through the campus, keeping an eye out for overalls. The campus wasn't really so bad. There were blossom trees, which Adrian would have liked. More than anything, the problem was that I could tell how desperate Mum was for me to like the place. As if she thought that if she could find a campus I liked, she wouldn't have to worry about me deciding not to go to uni. That, and I had the unshakable feeling someone

Mothers, Witches and Queens

was watching me. Which was making tours of the newly refurbished gymnasium and halls impossible to pay attention to.

"Excuse me, are you Michael?" said a timid voice from behind me, bringing me out of my daydream.

"Yes, why? Did my mum send you?" I asked, turning on the spot to find a lady in yoga pants and a sweater who'd clearly been reaching out to tap me on the shoulder. She had dirty blonde hair done up in a high ponytail and a nervous look on her face.

"No, she didn't. We just wanted to speak to you," she said, slightly picking at her chipped nail varnish as she spoke.

"Who's we, and how do you know my name?" I asked, standing a little straighter as my hand instinctively drifted to the shard of Excalibur dangling round my neck. She wasn't a disguised fay, I'd have seen through it, but she was still making me uneasy.

"Me and my friend Terrance," she said, looking back over her shoulder. I followed her gaze to a man lingering a few metres back under one of the blossom trees. My chest tightened as I realised who I was looking at and I all but charged at the balding man in overalls, rage filling me up at the sight of him. He was the man from the green Mini.

"You! Why are you following me? What do you want with Adrian?" I barked, grabbing him by his overall straps and pulling him up to within an inch of my face. I was suddenly simmering, my heart racing, thundering in my chest. This was the guy that had been following Adrian, scaring Adrian. I was gonna make sure he never did it again.

"Wait, wait, we can explain, we can explain, please give us a chance!" I could feel her tugging on my arm from behind and the eyes of various passes by gluing themselves to the scene I was causing. I couldn't let go. My fists were tight, my eyes locked on Terrance.

"I-I d-didn't mean to frighten anyone. I'm s-sorry." Terrance stumbled through his words, his voice trembling. He looked terrified, and a little remorseful.

"Please, we want to help. We think you're in trouble. We think Adrian might be in trouble," said the woman from behind me. I still held his straps tight in my hands, but I could see the fear in his face. With a shaky breath, I counted to three in my head and let Terrance go. I stormed away from them for a second, so I couldn't grab at him again, my chest still heaving as sweat beaded on my brow.

"Explain yourselves," I snarled through gritted teeth.

"We will, we will, but first, just tell us, where is Adrian now?" asked the woman, in a lowered serious voice that filled me with icy dread.

"Why? So, you can stalk him?" I jabbed, but my heart wasn't in it. Fear was sapping the fight out of me.

"We think a friend of ours might want to take him," Terrance croaked, finally righting himself, he'd been doubled over panting.

"WHAT?" I barked, my body stiffening as I started rummaging for my phone.

"I don't think she'd really go through with it though. She's not a monster," said the woman, turning back to Terrance. Although I found myself not believing her, she didn't seem to believe herself. She wouldn't have been here if she did.

"You didn't see her in the car, Liz, when she saw Adrian, when we followed him to the mushroom shop. She wasn't herself, there was this look in her eyes…" said Terrance. My legs felt as they were going to give way beneath me. I'd seen them that day, outside our house, and I did nothing to stop them and now Adrian was in danger.

"What do you mean?" I asked, my hands trembling as I hit call on Adrian's number.

"It seemed like… someone else, not Gwen… someone different." Terrance had met my gaze now, and the look in his eyes made my blood run cold. It was dread. Dread that poured out of him and ran through me like ice water as I waited the agonising seconds for the phone to ring.

"Hey Michael," my heart soared, almost jumped out of my chest, relief prickled my eyes, his voice was like bird song.

"Is everything alrhnng—" And then the world turned cold.

8

The world was black and my mouth dry, metallic tasting. My head was slumped forward and pounding, thundering, aching. I didn't open my eyes. I wanted to hide in the darkness. I didn't dare look up, not sure where I was or how I got there. I was sitting, restrained. Suddenly I lurched forward and something went taught at my chest, caught me.

"Bloody cyclists," snarled a voice in front of me out of the darkness. A woman's voice, cruel sounding, strained.

"Careful, he nearly slipped out of the seat. We don't want to hurt him anymore than we have to," said a second voice. It was softer, it sounded like a boy, nervous, or perhaps even scared.

"Yes, yes, I'm being careful," the woman huffed, and I felt movement, a low, slow rumble. We were in a car. I must have been belted up in the back seat.

"The plan wasn't to hurt him at all actually. Did you have to hit him so hard?" said the boy, a mix of frustration and nerves. A memory floated into my head. I'd been in the shop, with a boy and a curly haired woman, and something had hit me in the back of the head. I'd collapsed, and everything had gone black.

"How did you expect me to knock him out gently?" the woman hissed. I squeezed my eyes and clenched my fists and desperately fought not to start trembling as panic started to set in.

"I didn't expect you to knock him out at all. We said we were going to talk to him, coerce him, maybe threaten him. You never said we'd knock him out and bundle him in the back of the car. You didn't even try talking to him," said the boy, raising his voice a little.

"And since when were you suddenly so precious over him? Last I heard, you wanted rid of him so you could have Michael to yourself," said the woman. My chest seized and I bit my lip, stifling a gasp. They knew about Michael. They knew his name. Another memory flashed, I'd been on the phone to him when they'd hit me. He might know something's wrong, he might be looking for me. A little hope kindled in me.

"I want to get him out of the way, but I wasn't planning to hurt him. I knew if I could speak to them, with time Michael would see sense, realise he was meant to be with me. Michael was going to choose me," said the boy. He sounded almost love stricken the way he spoke about

Mothers, Witches and Queens

Michael. It was peculiar. I wasn't angry, more bewildered.

"And what if he hadn't returned your feelings? What if he'd chosen Adrian? What then? You should be grateful I did this. Now we can get him out of the way," said the woman. My heart thundered in my ears so loudly I was worried they'd hear it through my chest, turn around and realise I was awake. I didn't know what they'd do then. I drove my fingernails into my palms, clenching hard to stifle my trembles as a buzzing rang through the car.

"Check who it is," the woman hissed.

"It's Liz again. Should I answer? I don't think she's going to stop calling," said the boy.

"Fine!" barked the woman. The car lurched again, and I slid further in my chair, almost choking as the seatbelt caught me. I winced as my headache worsened. It was like a brick was banging around in there. My stomach flipped, and I thought I might be sick.

"Keep an eye on the road!" the boy hissed. The woman didn't respond, but I could feel her temper bristling without even looking at her.

"Hey, Liz," said the boy, in a mock casual tone that was wholly unconvincing.

"It's Jude, I'm on Gwen's phone... Oh, she's driving, that's why she didn't answer the other times you called." He spoke quickly, doing a poor job of keeping the panic out of his voice. "Erm, nothing in particular, just out for a drive," he said, his voice wobbling.

"I'm not lying to you Liz." Jude's voice heightened as

he lied. "No, my voice always sounds like this," he said as it got higher still.

"Put her on speakerphone," hissed Gwen.

"Fine," said Jude.

"Liz, you're on speaker. Is there something you need? I'm a bit tied up right now lovely." Gwen spoke now in a voice I didn't recognise, soft and warm. She almost reminded me of Linda.

"Gwen, what are you doing? You're not following that boy again, are you?" asked an unfamiliar voice, which must have been Liz. That little spark of hope burned a little brighter. Someone was out there who might know what was happening to me.

"No, we're not following him," said Gwen. I could hear the smile on her face even if I couldn't see it. Like she'd amused at herself, enjoying the deception. Cold sweats were taking me now, dousing the hope. There was something malicious in her pleasure.

"Well, Terrance and I are with the other one," said Liz, my stomach flipped. Did they mean Michael? Did this mean someone had captured him too?

"You're with Michael? What's he like? What's he saying?" Jude asked. He sounded almost feverish.

"He's very worried. He thinks something bad might have happened to Adrian," said Liz. Relief washed over me. It didn't sound like they'd hurt him. Perhaps he was even looking for me with them.

"How did you find Michael, anyway? I thought you and Terrance had got cold feet," asked Gwen. There was that bite in her tone again, almost an accusation. She sounded dangerous, like she was struggling to keep her temper, to keep the mask up.

"Enid saw him in the entrails. She said we needed to speak to him. She mentioned you too, Gwen, mentioned a darkness around you. Are you sure—" The word entrails repeated in my head. Who were these people?

"I'm sure she did, Liz, after all, when is Enid not pointing her crooked finger my way?" Gwen snapped at Liz, cutting her off. All the warmth of softness in her voice was gone.

"Hang up on her Jude," said Gwen.

"No, Jude, wait!" I heard Liz plead down the phone. Panic washed over me, my body tensed, my head pounded and again I was almost sick. This was my chance, slipping away.

"MICHAEL, SHE'S LYING, SHE'S GOT ME!" I screamed as loud as I could, hoping he heard me, or Liz heard me, just that someone heard me. For a third time, the car jerked to a stop and this time I opened my eyes. Jude was looking over his shoulder at me, mouth agape, eyes wide, still holding the phone in his hand, seemingly in shock. Gwen still faced forwards I saw her hands first, gripping the wheel so tightly she'd turned white at the knuckles. In the mirror I could see her face. Twisted into a something between a grin and a glare. It was her eyes that stole my breath away, one a warm chocolate brown, the other scarlet red and blazing with fury.

"You're going to regret that," she said.

9

"D-don't worry Michael, we'll find him, we'll g-get him back." Terrance was stuttering. His voice was somewhere off in the distance, barely registering. In the front of my mind, the same thing kept playing over and over. "SHE'S GOT ME" in Adrian's voice, cracked and afraid. Over and over like a scratched record. Liz had my hand. They were leading me somewhere, but I didn't know where. I couldn't really feel my legs. I just saw blossom trees and people sliding back behind me, as if I was drifting.

"Where are we going?" I asked after I don't know how long, watching almost trancelike as a car park came into view.

"We've got to get to Enid. She'll be able to find Adrian," said Terrance, as he unlocked an old rusty pickup truck with bags of soil in the back. Liz climbed into the back seat while Terrance held the passenger door open for me. I knew

I shouldn't go with them. I didn't know them. They were strangers. Mum would go ballistic with me, but I had to. Adrian needed help, and I didn't know where he was. They said they could find him.

"How?" I asked, desperate for some hope, as I climbed in.

"She's a haruspex," he said, as if it was the most natural thing in the world. I didn't know what that meant and hadn't the energy to ask. I barely had the energy to keep my eyes open. It was like someone had taken my plug out and all my life was washing down the drain. I fell into silence and my eyes drifted to the mirror, to Liz. She was muttering something. She'd screwed her eyes tight shut and had her arms out in front of her, each hand holding the opposite wrist, forming a kind of link.

"What's she doing?" I mumbled numbly, streets and lights and tarmac sailing by around us.

"Have you ever heard of manifestation?" asked Terrance. I nodded. Some girls in school had talked a lot about it around exam time. Based on how they looked coming out of the exams, it hadn't done them much good.

"She's meditating and manifesting," he said.

"Why?" I asked.

"It's a bit hard to explain," said Terrance evasively.

"Try," I barked, finding a little anchor of anger to drag myself back into my body.

"We're erm... we're witches," said Terrance in a small voice. I didn't know whether to laugh or cry. I'd climbed

Mothers, Witches and Queens

into the car with two complete strangers and now it turned out they were barking mad.

"Stop the car. I'll find him on my own," I said, reaching for the door handle.

"We know about the forest!" Terrance's voice rang out behind me, and I froze.

"What?" I whispered, pausing with my hand on the door. They sounded mad, of course. But then, I was a prince type champion and my boyfriend was a water nymph, so maybe I was being closed-minded.

"We've been dreaming about you, in The Hut, fighting, and at Grandfather Tree, when the old man got captured, and in the lake, with Adrian, we've been dreaming about you. All of us have, the whole coven," said Terrance. For a second, the world span around me and I thought I might be sick. My mouth dried up as a shiver ran over my skin. The feeling of being watched, violated even, washed over me.

"The whole what?" I croaked, barely able to speak.

"Coven," said Terrance. "There's a bunch of us, witches I mean, me and Liz and Enid and Gwen and well, I suppose you don't need the whole register. Anyway, we've all been having these dreams about you, and—"

"Since when?" I interrupted. I needed to know how long this had been happening, how long Adrian and I had been being watched, and I also needed Terrance to shut up for a moment.

"It's been going on for months, and around the same time we all noticed our practices were getting a bit more…

impactful." He talked like an excited child at show-and-tell, and it was making me want to shove a sock in his mouth.

"Practices?" I asked. I got the sense he was going to keep talking whether I engaged with him or not.

"Yes, we all have our own practices. I do a lot with plants, you know, using them to check up on people, and Liz does a lot with meditation and manifestation. Like she is right now, see?" said Terrance, pointing at Liz, who was still muttering in the back.

"What is she manifesting?" I asked, craning my head a little to look at her, trying to ignore Adrian's voice as it replayed once more in my head. SHE'S GOT ME.

"Listen to what she's chanting," Terrance said. I closed my eyes and focused on Liz, on the mumbling under her breath.

"Get out of our way, get out of our way, get out of our way," she repeated over and over.

"Is it working?" I asked.

"See for yourself," said Terrance. For the first time he sounded certain, not nervous, perhaps even prideful. I looked ahead to the road, paying attention for the first time. At first everything seemed normal, and then little by little I noticed it. Every traffic light turned green just as we closed in on it, every car changed out of our lane as we approached, every roundabout was miraculously clear.

"It's working," I breathed, my skin prickling as a rush of hope surged through me. If she could do this, maybe their

Mothers, Witches and Queens

friend really could find Adrian. Maybe I hadn't just climbed into a stranger's truck for no good reason at all.

"You see it?" asked Terrance, choking a little on his words as a smile burst across his face, his eyes swimming, pride beaming out of him.

"Its magic," I said, and he turned to me, tears tumbling down his cheeks.

"We're real witches Michael, we're really real," he whispered. I nodded but didn't break his gaze.

"Eyes on the road, we're almost there and for goodness' sake, Terrance, pull yourself together!" Liz's hard, clear voice took me so by surprise that I almost jumped out of my skin.

"R-right you are," said Terrance, abruptly pulling the car into the local park car park.

"Why are we at a park?" I asked, following Liz and Terrance as they got out of the truck and set off into the park.

"Enid likes to fish," said Liz, leading us down the path marked River Ramble by a park sign.

"We don't have time for fishing. Adrian is in trouble," I said, my stomach churning. Everything here reminded me of him. The sight of the river conjured images of swimming with him at our lake. The trees dotted along the bank brought to mind the fay forest. It was as though the world was screaming at me, so that I might think of nothing else.

"Don't worry, Enid can find Adrian," said Terrance. He

sounded confident, I'm sure he thought it was reassuring, but it felt dismissive.

"You still haven't explained why you were stalking us." I lashed out, stress and my temper getting the best of me.

"We, erm… we didn't mean to scare anyone." Terrance shrank away from me.

"We all wanted to understand why our practices were getting more potent. Gwen said that the only thing to do was to find you two and some of us went along with it," said Liz, shooting Terrance the look Mum gave me when I'd done something wrong. Like abandon her at a university open day.

"But I got the impression you were starting to recognise us, so I suggested we stop," Terrance added hastily.

"She didn't like that. She'd been talking about setting up a meeting, but after Terrance and the rest of us started to get cold feet… well, you know what happened next," said Liz, no longer meeting my gaze.

"Keep it down, you'll scare off the fish!" came a voice from a tent set up next to the river a little further down the path.

"We need your help, Enid," said Terrance, looking relieved as Liz broke out into a jog reaching into the tent and all but pulling a diminutive old lady out of it. She had grey hair pulled back and messily stuffed inside a bucket hat and was dressed all in murky green and brown. Everything she wore seemed to contain hundreds of pockets, from her cargo trousers to her lumpy utility jacket.

Mothers, Witches and Queens

"Unhand me!" She huffed, batting Liz away whilst glaring at her and Terrance. It took a moment before her eyes fell on me and peeled wide, her mouth dropping open.

"Can you help find Adrian?" I asked, my voice catching on his name. At first, she didn't say a word, she just stared, and then, seemingly regaining herself, shot a withering glare at Liz and Terrace.

"What did you to do?" she hissed, as she began smacking them both on the arms.

"It's Gwen. She's gone mad. We've told Michael everything. We had to," said Liz pleadingly.

"She's been a bit strange lately, but saying she's gone mad is a bit much," said Enid, pausing her assault for a moment.

"She's kidnapped Adrian, she's more than a bit strange," I blurted out, as heat rushed through me again.

"She's what?" spat Enid, agog.

"She's taken him, and she didn't sound herself on the phone. I think something's happening to her," said Liz worriedly.

"If only I'd thought to check her succulent this morning," said Terrance regretfully. As if that sentence made any sense at all.

"Never mind that now. What do you need me for?" asked Enid, straightening herself as she met my gaze.

"She's got him, she could be taking him anywhere, they said you could find him," I said, a lump forming in my throat at the image of Adrian restrained in the back of that damned green Mini.

"I see, well we'd need—"

"Enid, your rod!" said Terrance, cutting her off. He pointed at a rod that was set up on a tripod and had started twitching.

"Well, that's a bit of luck isn't it," said Enid, reaching down and grabbing the rod as she began to tug and reel.

"We do not have time for fishing," I repeated.

"Oh, you do my boy, believe me you do," said Enid, as she yanked her rod up, bringing a small silvery fish sailing out of the river, flapping in the breeze. In one swift motion, she cast the rod aside and leaped onto the fish, grabbing it and dashing it against a nearby rock with startling agility.

"Knife!" Enid commanded, shooting out a hand which Terrance fumbled to fill with a knife that had been lying beside the tripod. I found myself inching closer, fascinated by her brutality. She slid the knife along the fish's belly, slipped her finger inside and in one swift motion, flicked its entrails along the ground in front of her, where she stooped to study them. My stomach churned at the stench issuing from the glistening vermillion scattered across the grass.

"What on earth is she doing?" I asked.

"Shhh." Liz and Terrance both shushed me in unison. An odd silence fell. Liz and Terrance almost looked like they were holding their breath as they peered over Enid's shoulder.

Mothers, Witches and Queens

"He will lead them somewhere... to a doorway... to a place full of... mushrooms... a shop, I think," said Enid.

"The Fun Gi," I whispered, nerves shooting through me like electricity.

"You know it?" asked Liz, tearing herself away from Enid and her entrails.

"I do, we've got to go, now!" I barked and started back towards the car, a walk turning into a jog and breaking into a sprint as I tore down the path.

"I'm coming Adrian, I'm coming," I called.

10

"J-just tell me what you want from me," I whispered, trembling. I was huddled up as far back into the car as I could get, my eyes locked on Gwen's single angry, ruby red, unblinking eye as it blazed back at me.

"Erm Gwen... what are we doing?" asked Jude, his voice small and uncertain. At the sound of Jude's voice, Gwen's face froze, the cruel, hungry expression melting away. She blinked her eyes hard and when she opened them again, the red eye was red no longer. It was the same chocolate brown as the other.

"They'll be looking for us. We've got to be quick," she said. Her voice was still harsh but cooler, less cruel, less hungry. I didn't say anything, just pulled myself into as tight a ball as I could, hoping to keep out of her reach.

"We want you to take us to your gateway to the fay

world," said Jude after a moment's hesitation, still not quite able to pull his eyes away from Gwen.

"How do you know about the fay world?" I asked, my voice trembling uncontrollably. My body lurched forward as the car started to move again. My head was thundering painfully, my vision momentarily blurry.

"We've had visions of you. We know there's a tree you use to travel. Take us to the tree," Gwen commanded. How they knew about the fay world I didn't know, but clearly they didn't understand everything.

"H-humans can't pass through without a shard of Excalibur, and I don't have any," I whispered, trying to feel out everything they knew.

"You can take them through, though, can't you? You've taken Michael. We've seen him in the forest with you," said Jude. When he spoke about Michael, something in his tone shifted. He became almost possessive, jealous even.

"Don't try to trick us again, just take us to your gateway," said Gwen, threateningly, her gaze still fixed on me in her mirror.

"My head," I groaned, shutting my eyes tight as I clutched my head, stalling to think. There had to be something I could do.

"I told you, you hit him too hard," Jude hissed.

"What else was I supposed to do? We need him to find the gateway," Gwen spat, and suddenly it struck me. They kept saying *the* gateway. That thought there was only one

Mothers, Witches and Queens

tree I could take them through. They didn't realise that I could take them through any tree I chose.

"F-fine, I'll tell you," I whispered. I opened my eyes just a crack, only to wince for real this time as the light lashed at my headache.

"Good boy, you take us through and then all this nastiness can be over," said Gwen, switching with unsettling speed to a softer, kinder tone.

"It's... it's in the back of the shop you took me from," I whispered, remembering Marshie's tree.

"You mean we kidnapped you from the place we need you to take us to?" asked Jude.

"He's obviously lying," said Gwen, in her familiar, colder voice.

"I-I'm not, the shop is a front... its run by a gnome, h-how else do you think we grow so many types of mushrooms so easily, all year round?" Jude and Gwen paused, considering what I'd said. I was desperate to convince them. I couldn't afford for them to think I was lying. There was a chance Marshie would be back from their trip and could help me.

"It does kind of make sense when you think about it," said Jude, feeding the little glimmer of hope in the pit of my stomach.

"Right, we're turning around," said Gwen, driving onto and all the way around a roundabout, picking up speed as we hurtled back the way we'd come.

"Why do you want to go to the forest?" I asked, bracing

myself against the door as Gwen tore through traffic, wincing as my head split each time she slammed on the brakes.

"We're witches, and for some reason, we're connected to the forest," said Gwen.

"And especially to Michael," said Jude, dreamily.

"Michael and Adrian," Gwen corrected as she plunged her foot into the floor, running a red light. An almost alien sense of urgency seemed to have taken over her.

"But why do you want to go there?" I asked, only half registering what they were saying. I knew about human witches, but from what I understood, they were usually harmless and peaceful and not likely to kidnap someone in broad daylight. They were usually more to do with meditation and crystals and setting intentions.

"Well, I thought maybe if we went, Michael might—"

"Power," Gwen snapped, cutting Jude off before he had a chance to lilt poetic about Michael. It was strange. Maybe I should have been angry that he was so besotted with my boyfriend, but all it seemed to inspire in me was pity. I watched Jude for the rest of the drive, distracting myself from the nausea. He couldn't settle. He flitted between anxiously watching the road, fidgeting with his fingers, checking on me, wincing and groaning in the back of the car, and occasionally looking at Gwen. It was as if he was searching for something in her. Some reassurance what they were doing was right and safe.

"We're here," Gwen declared, as I lurched forward,

almost falling from my seat one last time. Within seconds I was being manhandled out of the car, struggling to keep my shaking legs beneath me as I was half-dragged, half-staggered to the door. I glanced around the street, wincing against the light, but there was no one to cry out to, no one to help me.

The bell chimed as we stepped through the door of The Fun Gi and I held my breath, hoping against hope. But Marshie's chipper voice didn't answer it.

"We're close, I can feel it," said Gwen, letting go of me as she strode into the shop. Jude didn't follow, he'd frozen. I followed his eye to the broken display I'd been slammed into, still littered across the floor against the far wall.

"You don't have to do this," I whispered. He froze, still holding onto me, holding me up. His hand tightened around my arm, squeezing it painfully. His breathing was quickening, he was panicking.

"What did you say?" Gwen hissed, wheeling round to face us, one eye blood red and boiling once again. Jude's grip on my arm released as he took a step back towards the door. My legs gave way beneath me and I sunk to my knees.

"Your eye, Gwen… what's happening?" Jude asked. His voice was small, scared. Gwen's eyes fixed on him, and I took my chance subtly drawing trickling paths of water from the loamy soil around us, holding it at my fingertips.

"It's fine, ignore it," Gwen commanded, sweeping across the room towards us. Jude took another step back. His back was now against the wall.

"What's wrong, Jude? This is everything you ever wanted. It's within your reach, to be someone, to be powerful, to be a proper witch. Not a silly little boy playing dress up in his bedroom!" There was venom in her words. Jude didn't speak, just stood, still as a stone. She bent down and grabbed me, yanking me to my feet with implausible strength as she began to drag me, stumbling, towards the back of the shop. The bell chimed for a second time, and she froze. Glancing back, I barely caught sight of Jude running away down the street.

"Coward," Gwen muttered, her eyes still on the doorway. I tensed, held my breath and focused all the water I'd gathered, thrusting it forward, sending the jet crashing into Gwen's face. She stumbled back and her grip on me loosened. I pulled away, falling to my knees. As she crashed into the back wall, I was already scrambling away from her, around the counter and out of sight of her.

"Naughty, naughty little water nymph. One of Nimueh's line I bet," said Gwen. A chill ran down my spine as she spoke. In an unfamiliar voice, cruelty and glee curling out of every syllable. Gwen swept from behind the counter, pushing her soaked curls out of her face to reveal both eyes burning red, wide and mad and full of power. Fear flooded through me anew. This wasn't Gwen anymore. The way she moved, almost floating through the room, her posture so straight she almost seemed to grow before my eyes, every motion and gesture grand and sweeping.

"How do you know th—" My words choked as she

grabbed me by the throat and lifted me effortlessly off the ground with one outstretched arm. Her blood red eyes locked on mine. I wheezed and spluttered, clawing at her hand as I dangled above the ground. I couldn't breathe, my eyes welled up and my head throbbed as though it was going to burst.

"Now, you've led Gwen on a merry run around, but the time for tricks has passed. You're going to walk me through a tree, any tree." She spoke cruelly but calmly as I writhed in her grip, barely flinching as the bell chimed a third time.

* * *

"Put him down!" I shouted. My shard, already a shield, was sailing through the air before I properly took in what I was looking at, but the image burned itself into my mind. Adrian, dangling from that woman's hand, clawing at it, gasping for air, his face turning purple and his eyes bloodshot and bulging. Her, unflinching, holding him effortlessly, one arm outstretched, staring him at him coldly. But that wasn't the worst of it. There was something not fully there, floating just above her like a shadow or shade of a woman, her hair was red, wild and twisting and her eyes blazing.

"A champion… a prince, an Excalibur piece…" The words came from Gwen, but it was the shade of her that turned to face me. The ghost of her lips moving, she raised an arm with her hand outstretched towards the shield as it sailed through the air and Gwen's arm followed.

Panic washed through me. Whatever this thing was, it knew about me and the shield, and it looked like it was about to catch it. I braced myself as the shield connected. Gwen's arm crumpled with a sickening crunch as the shield slammed through her fingers and crashed into her side, sending her flying into the shop counter. Adrian hit the floor with a thud, wheezing and panting. He lurched, grabbing the shield. It popped back into a small piece of jagged shiny green stone as he scrambled towards me. One hand still at his neck, his eyes fixed on Gwen's bloodied body, splayed out across the counter. The shade's eyes still fixed on me, looking almost hungry.

"Are you okay?" I asked, heaving Adrian up and away from her. He trembled in my hands as I held him against me. I could feel him shaking, feel his heart racing.

"D-don't l-let it..." His hoarse voice wheezed and spluttered as he broke out into a fit of coughing, one clammy trembling hand forcing the piece of Excalibur back into my own. I squeezed it and my glittering silver hammer burst into being. I looked down at him, small and sickly pale now as the colour rushed away from his face and my grip tightened around the hammer, my jaw set like granite as I fixed my gaze on Gwen.

"Fragile little body isn't it," said Gwen, as she righted herself. Her voice and her movements were so calm, as though she didn't feel a thing, yet I knew she had to be in agony, I'd heard bones breaking.

"Gwen, what are you doing?" Liz called from behind

me, her voice trembling. The shade turned its neck, a broad grin spreading across its face.

"What is that?" I breathed, watching as it raised its hand. Gwen, in unison, raised hers too, examining the broken, bent back fingers, the thumb almost sliced clean off. Blood streamed down her hand, covering her forearm.

"What do you mean, she's Gwen," Liz hissed.

"I d-don't think she's Gwen anymore," Terrance stuttered in a small voice.

"Gwen isn't home right now, but don't worry, I'm taking good care of her," said the shade. Cruelty oozed through the room as Gwen, mirroring the movements of the shade, dragged her mangled hand through the air, behind it glistening red blood hung in place.

"What the…" Liz breathed, leaving the sentence incomplete. The scarlet liquid began to shift, forming a circle, with more complex patterns spiralling out. My mouth went dry as I watched in stunned silence. Within seconds, a strange pattern hung in the air, composed of floating blood.

"Do you like it?" Gwen asked, the shade's lips moving in unison, its boiling red eyes fixed on my hammer. None of us spoke. We barely breathed as she made her final move, bringing her still intact hand sailing through the bloody pattern. It split and then erupted, something emerging out of the ring.

"I'll be back for that pretty hammer of yours, but for now, I'll leave you a plaything," she said, inching back towards the back door. I wanted to follow her, to stop her for good, but I couldn't move. I couldn't leave Adrian. An arm and a leg pulled themselves out of the ring of blood.

"What on earth is that?" asked Liz, her voice growing higher, fear strangling her.

"Let's not wait to find out," I said, stepping forward, putting myself between it and Adrian. I slammed my hammer into it, but it slipped through as if nothing was there at all. Blood splattered across the walls of The Fun Gi and then began to move, streaking from every corner of the shop, pooling.

"This is bad," I said to myself as much as anything, watching as it formed first legs, then a body, arms and a head. It was a person, but faceless, featureless, like a naked manakin, made of blood. It lunged at me with its arms outstretched. I brought my hammer up, cutting from groin to head, splattering blood across the ceiling, turning my stomach. But the arms remained, gripping tightly to my shoulders.

I watched, horrified, as the scattered blood trickled towards it, already reforming itself. Its fingers stretching, growing, reached towards my mouth. I tore myself away with all my strength, bringing the hammer into the side of the creature, then swiping down through the reforming head, then across again, swinging wildly, splattering every inch.

"It's still coming," Liz whispered as we backed away, moving to the far wall. It was herding us away from the door, cutting off our escape. Again and again, I splattered the thing. I was sweating, my chest heaving, my arms growing heavy. I took a deep breath, closed my eyes tight and once more unleashed a flurry of blows with everything I had, sending every piece of it flying. Then I turned to Adrian.

"What do I do? Adrian, help me," I pleaded, fighting the fear out of my voice as I looked into his bloodshot, teary blue eyes.

"Water... back room... paddling pool..." Adrian choked painfully on his words, but it was enough. I grabbed him, dragging him passed the already reforming body into the backroom, where a paddling pool with a hose in it sat in the centre of the floor.

"Fill it up," I barked to Liz and Terrance as they ran in after us. I left them, taking a step back onto the shop floor, once more splattering the bloody creature across the room before slamming the door to the shop behind me and locking it.

"W-what's this for?" Terrance asked, fumbling with the tap. Liz fed water into the paddling pool, which Adrian had already crawled into, pulling his knees up to his chest as he sat trembling in the water.

"Trust him," I said, with no energy to explain. I watched the water level ever so slowly inch up the side of the pool.

"Will this help?" asked Liz, grabbing a discarded watering can off the floor and dumping its contents into the pool.

"Anything, anything with water," I said, looking around the room frantically.

"A-away from the door," Adrian croaked at me from the pool, pointing at the door behind me. I rotated on the spot and what I saw almost turned my stomach. Blood was seeping through every crack, every gap, dripping around the door, pouring into the room. It was like something out of Stranger Things.

"Adrian, how long do you need?" I asked, backing away from the door, holding my hammer between it and me.

"Just keep it back," said Adrian. He struggled for each word, lying back and letting the water wash over his bruised neck.

"I'll do my best," I said, sweeping the hammer through the legs, already forming in front of the door, splattering them across a poster explaining which mushrooms make the best soups. I took a step back and stumbled. A bloody hand had formed and was wrapping itself around my ankle, and a body was sprouting out of it. I kicked at it, scrambling backwards across the floor as the creature pulled itself up to its full height.

"Smash it, once more!" Adrian gave his strangled command as the creature dove for me, arms outstretched. I yanked the hammer up in front of my face and it sprung into a shield. I pushed off, meeting it in mid-air and crashed straight through the centre of the creature, splattering it to the four walls.

Mothers, Witches and Queens

"What now, Adrian?" I asked, shaking blood off me as I backed away from the rapidly reforming shape.

"Find me a drain," he whispered. I got to my feet and started looking, but Adrian caught my eye. He knelt in the pool, his arms outstretched as water engulfed him, washing him clean before stretching towards the bloody figure, leaving him and forming a bubble around it. A hand reached out of the bubble, but Adrian brought his own sweeping down and the water sliced clean through it, severing the gory appendage. He raised his arms above his head and began to wave them in a circular motion. Slowly at first, the water started to spin, then steadily picked up speed. The blood blended with the water like milk stirred into tea. It became a roiling, foaming, frothing sphere of red that hovered in the air. Adrian was like an orchestral conductor, his eyes iron focused."

"A drain," Adrian whispered, his voice tense. I tore my eyes away from the sphere to really look at him. His face was strained and pale, glistening with sweat.

"There is one here," said Terrance, shoving a potting desk out of the way to reveal a little drain in the corner of the room. Adrian turned his head and with shaking arms, guided the globe over the drain. His movements becoming quicker and tighter as he did. The sphere shifted and stretched, becoming a funnel as he guided it and disappearing down the drain.

Liz, Terrance, and I rushed to the drain, holding our collective breath. We waited, watching for any sign of the creature returning. There was only the glugging sound of a drain emptying. At last, I came away from the drain, dropping to my knees. Cold and wet greeted me as I knelt in Adrian's pool, pulling him into my chest.

"You did it," I whispered, stroking his sodden sweaty hair as I held him. He clung onto me, but only barely. His arms were weak, he was tired.

"You saved me," he whispered. I squeezed him once more and then broke the hug to look into his eyes. They were tired, half lidded, heavy and still painfully bloodshot.

"Are you okay?" I asked, tears prickling as relief loosened my tight muscles. I had him, and he was okay. Whatever the bloody creature and Gwen and the shade were, we'd deal with later. For now, all that mattered was Adrian.

"My head hurts," said Adrian, flinching as he blinked his eyes.

"Did you hit it when she dropped you?" I asked, pulling my hand away anxiously when Adrian flinched as I stroked him.

"Theyhitme," he mumbled, his words slurring together.

"Adrian, look at me," I said. He didn't respond, his eyes were already sliding shut. I pulled back his eyelids as he went limp in my arms. One of his pupils was bigger than the other and when I took my hand away, there was blood on his eyelids. Blood from my hand, blood from the hand I'd been stroking his head with.

"Adrian, stay awake," I whimpered, panic taking over

Mothers, Witches and Queens

me. I gently turned him in my arms and found a sticky patch of red on the back of his head. He was bleeding.

"Adrian, don't go to sleep," I all but commanded. But he was already gone and my breath was short. I wasn't sure why it's bad for people with a concussion to fall asleep, but the movies had always made it pretty clear that it was.

"Help me with him," I barked at Terrance, as tears tumbled down my cheeks. I handed Adrian's limp body to Terrance as I shoved open the door to Marshie's courtyard.

"He needs a hospital," said Liz, as she and Terrance followed me into the courtyard.

"He needs Olivier," I said. I clutched my piece of Excalibur and ran it down Marshie's tree, grabbing Terrance and pulling him and Adrian through with me.

PART II

THE HIDDEN QUEEN

1
———

"What is happening?" asked Terrance, as he looked at the expanse of green in awe. His eyes were so wide I thought they might pop out of his head.

"You said you dreamed about this place. Well, now you're here," I said, snatching Adrian out of his arms.

"The fay forest," said Liz, clattering through the grove behind us, hanging onto Terrance's overalls. There was a similar awestruck tone in her voice.

"I'm not waiting for you," I barked, focusing on the anger so I wouldn't burst into tears. First I was walking, then I was jogging and before long it was all I could do not to sprint down the yellow path of the forest stretching out before me. I could hardly bear to look at Adrian, lying in my arms, unconscious again, hurt again. My heart thundered in my chest and a lump formed in my throat as the image of my hand red with his blood flashed through my mind. For a moment, I thought I might be sick.

"Don't leave me, don't leave me, don't leave me," I whispered over and over, and the tears spilled.

"Michael?" came a startled voice from just ahead of us down the path. I pulled my eyes up to take in Olivier's garden gate just as I was about to run into it.

"Olivier! Adrian needs help. Please help," I said, my hands trembling, still cradling him in my arms.

"What happened?" she asked, looking bewildered as her eyes tracked from Adrian, to me, to Terrance and Liz running up behind me, narrowing to suspicious slits as she all but glared at the haphazard witches panting for breath.

"He was kidnapped and there was a… ghost thing and blood monsters and… Just heal him!" My voice cracked, strangled by panic. Waves of cold sweat poured out of me.

"What? Kidnapped? Blood monsters… and who are they?" Olivier pointed at Liz and Terrance, suspicion and confusion and concern flitting across her face as her eyes darted between us.

"JUST HEAL HIM!" The words rumbled out of me like thunder, The Voice emerging without my bidding. It wasn't my intention to use it, not on Olivier, but my fear for Adrian clouded everything. The sound echoed through the forest and birds scattered in all directions. Olivier's eyes glazed over and she knelt, cupping Adrian's head in her hands as cool water poured out of her, enveloping his wound.

"What was that?" asked Terrance. I didn't respond, I

was too busy watching the colour drain from Olivier's face. Guilt filled me up like ice water.

"Michael?" My stomach flipped as Adrian's beautiful blue eyes fluttered open.

"You're awake," I whispered, blinking away tears as I tried to fight the cracks out of my voice. I lifted him, peppering his cheeks with kisses as a soaring elation rushed through me.

"Where are we?" asked Adrian, his arms wrapping around my neck, pulling him tighter to me.

"We're at Olivier's hut," I whispered, rubbing the wet patch on the back of his head, checking for blood, but to my relief, there was only water now.

Olivier rolled back on the balls of her feet, her drained eyes focusing back to consciousness.

"You used the voice on me, didn't you?" she asked in a surprisingly even tone, which did nothing to stop my stomach churning anxiously.

"It was an accident," I said, cringing internally at what I'd done. "I'm sorry."

"What's the voice?" asked Terrance and Liz in unison. They must have been steadily inching towards each other as the forest impressed itself upon them. By now they almost looked joined at the hip.

"Who are you?" Olivier shot back, ignoring their question. She struggled to her feet and made her way to her garden pond, which she unceremoniously dropped herself into, leaving Liz and Terrance utterly bewildered.

"They're witches," I said, watching with relief as colour started returning to Olivier's face.

"Like in Charmed?" Adrian asked, peeking his head over my shoulder to look at them.

"No, not really, although I did used to love that show," said Terrance.

"Why are they here?" Olivier barked.

I gulped. "Some members of their convent—"

"Coven, we're not nuns," corrected Liz.

"Sorry, coven. Terrance and Liz were worried that some members of their coven, well… might have been about to do something dangerous to Adrian, so they came to warn me," I said.

"And why would these witches do something to Adrian?" asked Olivier, bristling. I could see her protective instincts like a mirror of my own.

"They've been having dreams," said Liz. "Well, we all have really, about Adrian and Michael and the forest and this place and since the dreams started, our spells have got… a bit more tangible."

"We can do magic," Terrance blurted out excitedly.

"Yes, and some of us… well, Gwen mostly, thought that if we met them, found them, or came here, our magic might get even more… tangible," explained Liz.

"You're the guy from the shop, aren't you?" asked Adrian, his eyes on Terrance as he got to his feet with my help.

"Erm yes, sorry about that. We didn't mean to scare

Mothers, Witches and Queens

you," said Terrance, looking sheepish as he withered under Olivier's gaze.

"Anyway, Gwen went a bit… intense, and we got worried, so we went looking for Michael and Adrian. To warn them," said Liz, barrelling on.

"But it was too late. Gwen had already got Adrian," I said, an aftershock of panic rocking as I pulled Adrian to my side and kissed his head gently.

"I think there was something wrong with her. Her eyes kept changing colour, going red, like, scary red," said Adrian, pushing warm feelings into me as I felt him lean against me.

"Not just that, she had this like… ghost woman floating over her, sort of in her. It looked like she was controlling her," I explained.

"What?" asked Terrance, Liz, Adrian, and Olivier at once.

"You guys saw it right?" My question was met with blank expressions and slowly shaking heads.

"I only saw her eyes were red," said Terrance, as Liz's face creased into a puzzled expression.

"Michael, describe to me exactly what you saw," said Olivier.

"Prince champions can see a thing's true form," Adrian breathed, to himself as much as anything, I think. Looking up at me with wonder in his twinkling eyes.

"It was a woman, but it was as if she wasn't quite there, like she was translucent, and she knew things. She knew I was a prince. And when she spoke, it was almost like she was a split second ahead and then Gwen would speak with her."

"She was talking in the third person," said Terrance.

"She said I led Gwen on a merry chase," said Adrian slowly, with a look on his face, like he was remembering something unpleasant. "She wanted me to take her to the forest." A shiver ran through him as he spoke.

"Yeah, she wanted my shield. She seemed surprised when she tried to catch it and it destroyed Gwen's arm, she said the body was fragile," I said. My stomach churned as the crunching sound replayed in my mind.

"Sounds like someone was controlling your friend. Someone very powerful." Olivier spoke slowly. All her anger had gone now. She was thinking, planning.

"Who could do that?" asked Liz, alarm in her voice as she checked over her shoulder nervously.

"An enchanter," said Adrian softly.

"What, sorry?" said Terrance, cupping his ear.

"You saw how Michael controlled me. That is one of the abilities of prince type champion. Enchanters are another type of champion. Magic comes as easily to them as breathing," explained Olivier, speaking quickly, as if the answer to the question should be self-evident.

"Then it's not Gwen's fault?" asked Liz, hopefully.

"And what was this about a blood monster?" asked Olivier, ignoring her.

"Gwen, or rather the shade, made it. She did this thing

with her blood, drew something in the air, a rune or something and it made this man... thing out of blood," I explained.

"Well, that narrows things down," said Olivier, blanching in a way that, if I didn't know any better, would have made me think she was afraid of blood. The fact I did know better only made me more nervous.

"So, what do we do now?" asked Liz, stepping into the garden, determined not to be ignored. Terrance, on the other hand seemed to have been struck dumb by the sight of a dryad walking up the path ahead.

"Adrian, Michael, you go with these two and investigate Gwen's things. Look for signs, notes, anything that seems out of place," said Olivier.

"Like what?" I asked.

"You'll know it when you see it," said Olivier, which elicited a snort of laughter from Adrian.

"And what will you be doing?" I asked.

"I'll be checking the records of the Excalibur system for every enchanter we've come across," she replied. "It won't be a long list. It's not like they're two a penny."

"Sounds like a plan," said Liz.

"And get those two out of here," said Olivier, waving her hand in Liz and Terrance's general direction as she pushed her glasses to the top of her nose and trudged back into her cottage.

"It's nice to meet real life witches," said Adrian as we set off down the path back to the grove. He was putting a brave face on it, but he was clutching my arm so tightly my hand was in danger of losing circulation.

"It's nice to meet you too," said Liz, offering a hand. It was almost imperceptible, but just a split second before he took Liz's hand and shook it, I'm sure I saw Adrian flinch away. All I wanted to do was bundle him up and take him home.

"I'm sorry about you friend Gwen being all possessed," said Adrian, showing a compassion which I wasn't capable of at the moment. I had an overwhelming urge to break her other hand.

"I'm sorry we stalked you. That was wrong of us," said Terrance.

"Don't go lumping me in with you. I didn't stalk the poor boy," said Liz, delivering a quick jab to Terrance's rib as we approached the tree.

"Hold on tight," said Adrian, offering them both his hand as we passed back onto the back patio of Marshie's shop. My phone was buzzing in my pocket the moment we arrived back in Starkton.

Mum: Michael, I'm sorry about the fight. Where are you? Let's go home. We can talk about this.

Mum: Don't ignore me Michael, I'm trying to make up here.

Mum: Answer your phone, Michael!

Mum: Young man, if you don't answer your phone so help me.

Mum: Please, Michael, I'm not angry anymore.

Mum: Michael, you're scaring me. Answer the phone.

A pang of guilt struck me. As I scrolled through her texts, a notification of four missed calls popped up.

Me: Sorry, Mum, I'm back in Starkton, things got a bit scary, I'll meet you back at the house. I'll explain everything.

"Anyone fancy a cuppa?" I asked, ignoring the voice in my head reminding me what a bad son I was.

2

Terrance and Liz gave us a lift back to Michael's house in Terrance's car. It smelt a bit damp and largely of soil. It wasn't much different from Marshie's shop in that respect, just without that hint of fay forest magic. They'd been taking it in turns brewing pots of tea since we got back, I think by way of an apology. Michael would have made the tea himself I'm sure, but the instant he'd sat down I'd climbed into his lap and hadn't felt a compelling reason to leave it yet.

"Michael! I'm home. Where are you?" Linda's voice boomed through the house about an hour after we'd got back.

"We're in the living room, Mum!" Michael called back, sitting up a little in his chair. Liz and Terrance did the same on the sofa, everyone was still a bit on edge.

"How on earth did you get back— Oh hello, sorry, who

are you?" It was hard to tell whether Linda was about to give Michael an earful or have a heart to heart, but whatever the case may have been, the presence of Terrance and Liz had given her pause.

"Mum, this is Terrance and Liz," said Michael, awkwardly introducing them whilst still seated with me on top of him. Terrance and Liz stood and offered Linda their hands in turn.

"And why are they... I mean, sorry, where are my manners? I'm Linda. It's nice to meet you. What are you doing in my living room?" said Linda.

"They're witches," I said, cutting to the chase slightly. By the look on Linda's face, I don't think I'd helped much.

"Like fay?" Linda asked, eventually.

"Oh no, we're human, sorry. You've never taken part in any witchcraft by any chance, have you?" Terrance asked, his handshake with Linda lingering for longer than was normal.

"No, I erm, what?" Linda looked baffled.

"Sorry I was just getting a vibe, anyway... I'm very into garden magic, and Liz—"

"I do a lot of yoga and meditation," said Liz, cutting Terrance off. She seemed quite highly strung for someone who meditated so much.

"I work in a travel agents," said Linda, seemingly so baffled she'd defaulted to small talk mode.

"We've been dreaming about Adrian and Michael," said

Terrance, which elicited the strangest combination of puzzlement and a withering glare I'd ever seen from Linda.

"You make us sound so creepy," Liz groaned, cupping her face in her hands.

"Someone explain please," said Linda.

"There's a bunch of them and they all started having the same dreams about me and Adrian and then they got magic powers and one of them went completely crazy or maybe got possessed, we don't really know. And anyway, they kidnapped Adrian, so Liz and Terrance helped me get him back." Michael barely stopped to draw breath as his arms wrapped around me. He pulled me closer as he nuzzled into my hair and breathed me in. It's a wonder I didn't melt into a puddle there and then. Linda's mouth moved wordlessly for a few seconds. It looked like she was repeating the run-on sentence back to herself, processing, and then her eyes fell on me.

"You poor thing," she said, with so much sympathy in her voice, my eyes started prickling again.

"I'm okay," I lied, my voice breaking as I spoke.

"I'll call Michael in sick for school tomorrow. You two deserve the day, cup of tea?" she asked, as sympathy shifted to a warm, encouraging smile. I nodded as a tear spilled over my cheek.

3

Adrian had big bags under his eyes when we piled into the back of Terrance's car the next morning. He'd not slept well. Tossing and turning all night, waking up sweating and crying and begging the kidnappers in his dreams not to take him away again. I'd not slept much either. When I wasn't awake trying to soothe him, I was waking with a start, to check he was still there.

"Here you go, take this," I said, passing him the thermos Mum had made us that morning before work.

"Thanks," said Adrian, popping his hands out of the too long sleeves of my hoodie before awkwardly pouring himself a cup of tea as we sloshed down the road to the coven's meeting place.

"What's she doing?" he asked, pointing to Liz, who was muttering in the front seat with her legs crossed in a full lotus position.

"Manifesting her way through traffic," I said, unable to resist the grin tugging at my cheeks.

"Cool," said Adrian, as if this explanation made perfect sense to him and didn't merit any further explanation whatsoever.

"So, what are you guys hoping to find?" asked Terrance, as we pulled up outside Starkton community centre. It had to be said, we did make excellent time with Liz on board.

"You heard Olivier, we'll know it when we see it," said Adrian, waving his arms about and doing a pseudo meaningful voice as he rolled his eyes.

"That hit a nerve with you, did it?" I asked, letting out a little chuckle.

"Ugh, she just likes to be mysterious and doesn't like saying I don't know," Adrian huffed, gulping his tea as we climbed out of the car. Starkton community centre looked like it had once been a white building, although now it was murky, and sun bleached. Long strands of green, which I assumed was ivy but didn't really know, climbed over the chipped and yellowing pebble-dashed exterior.

"The ivy is quite witchy," I said, taking Adrian's hand as we entered the slightly damp smelling building.

"It's actually climbing hydrangea. I planted it myself. It's a miracle it's doing so well, to be honest," said Terrance.

"Maybe it's your magic," said Adrian with a smile.

"Oh, my goodness, do you really think?" asked Terrance, suddenly beaming.

"Oh, come on Terrance, don't lay an egg. They're just

being polite," said Liz, leading the way through the entrance hall. We came to a fairly basic composite wooden door that had been decorated to within an inch of its life with crystals and pentagrams.

"The coven meetings happen through here," said Terrance, unlocking the door and leading us in. The room was largish, about the size of a secondary school classroom, with one window running along the wall opposite the door. The floor was covered in mismatched rugs of every colour, with small crystals and stones dotted about. Little glass bottles hung from the ceiling rafters. The strings they dangled from had been stapled to the ceiling panels, which didn't feel especially witchy to me. Colourful blankets, which had also been stapled unceremoniously into the ceiling, covered the harsh overhead lighting of the community centre.

"Who did these?" asked Adrian, making his way over to one of the many cross stitches that covered the walls like a hodge podge attempt at a gallery display. His arms had disappeared inside the hoodie, so the sleeves dangled at his sides, and as I watched him I felt a rush of love run through me. It was all I could do to resist the urge to bundle him up and carry him home to hide under the duvet with me.

"Oh, those are Penny's. She's our very own little Norn," said Terrance.

"Norn?" I asked.

"They weave the skein of fate," said Liz.

"The what now?" I asked.

"It's like they predict the future with what they weave," said Adrian, his eyes fixed on the image.

"Or control it," said Terrance, melodramatically.

"What's got you so fascinated?" I joined Adrian, putting a hand on his shoulder. He immediately slumped into me, in a half faint, and as I stared at the woven image, I understood why. Goosebumps prickled my skin, and a shiver ran down my spine as I took in the scene: a forest clearing, around a bright blue lake, with two people in it. One bigger with warm brunette hair, holding a smaller figure in his arms, with a shock blond hair. They were kissing.

"This is us." Adrian's voice trembled as he spoke, turning to face me. His perfect porcelain skin was flushed faintly pink and his eyes were swimming with tears. I nodded thickly, swallowing around the lump in my throat and a shock of elation ran through me as I remembered the first day we kissed. The day, months ago, when Adrian surprised me in the woods with my very own lake.

"There's more than one of you," said Liz, from a half lotus position on the floor.

"Let's find them," said Adrian, with a smile on his face that I hadn't seen for a while. I nodded, and we split up, scouring the walls.

"There's one of us here standing in front of a massive tree… I think it must be Grandfather. This must be the day we captured Merlin," Adrian called from across the room. I scanned the walls, ignoring a few sunsets and starry nights until my eyes fell upon an eerie memory and my fists

Mothers, Witches and Queens

clenched reflexively. I stared blankly at the woven image of a boy with blonde hair, suspended in a silvery cauldron of murky liquid. I checked over my shoulder that no one was looking and knocked it off the wall.

"Found any yet?" asked Adrian, flitting from picture to picture like a hummingbird.

"Nope," I said, making sure to step on the thing before I moved on to another and another until my eyes fell on something I didn't recognise.

"Oh look, Michael, it's you and me, under the blossom trees," Adrian called excitedly from across the hall.

"I think I might have something too, but I'm not in it," I called as I stared at the image, perplexed. In the foreground knelt a blonde figure with their back to me, beside them a twisted dead looking black tree, which propped up another blonde character. They were both looking towards the background of the picture, which contained a huge, impossibly large mess of twisted, thorny black and brown branches. The stitching of the mass of black had frayed where the weaver had gone over the same threads again and again, building a matted knot of black. At once I knew I was looking at The Hut.

"I don't like it," I muttered to myself, trying to squash down the anxious feeling building in the pit of my stomach. I turned away, following the urge to push the tapestry out of my mind, but Adrian was already behind me. His face dropped as his eyes flickered over the picture. He had nightmares about The Hut. I knew he did. Sometimes he spoke about it in his sleep. He didn't linger long on this picture before moving to the next.

In spite of myself, I turned back, some knot inside me twisting me up and drawing me back, but only for a second. Out of the corner of my eye I caught Adrian's hand shoot out of his sleeve like a viper, snatching another picture off the wall.

"What's that?" I asked, but got no response. He simply shoved the picture under his hoodie and shook his head silently.

"Show me," I said, gently laying my hands on his shoulders. His body was stiff and trembled beneath my touch.

"It's nothing." His voice was tight and small, strangled almost.

"So let me see," I said. My own voice taking on a shrill tone that reminded me painfully of my mother.

Liz gasped from across the room and she glared at Terrance. "You were supposed to get rid of that," she said through her teeth.

"I got distracted by Gwen's succulent," said Terrance, who I only now realised had been silently fussing over a collection of succulents arranged along the window ledge, each one with a name tag hanging off the pot. They were all of them green and flourishing, except for Gwen's, which was a disconcerting shade of blackish purple and drooped listlessly.

"Adrian… it's just sewing. Let me see it. I promise it'll be okay," I said. But how could it be? He was sheet white,

Mothers, Witches and Queens

tears tracking down his face, and he had gone from rigid to shaking uncontrollably in my arms. With one hand, I rubbed his shoulders, and he began to relax a little. With the other, I reached down under his hand and prised the scrunched picture from his clenched fist. I pulled him into a hug as I shook out the image.

It took me a heartbeat to work out what had upset Adrian so much. The little threads showed a blonde boy dressed all in black, surrounded by green leafy forest, draped over something large and grey. I squinted for a moment at the arch of rock before it dawned on me that it must have been a tombstone. Stone coldness flooded me and I squeezed Adrian tighter to me.

"This doesn't mean anything," I said, quickly screwing it up and tossing it aside. Trying not to let the image burn itself into my mind. "Right Terrance? Right Liz?"

"Right," said Terrance, nodding. "Penny has an overactive imagination, that's all. D-didn't you want to look over Gwen's stuff?"

"Yeah, let's do that Adrian," I said. "Like Olivier says… erm, what was it? You'll know it when it's there or something."

"You'll know it when you see it," Adrian mumbled, sniffing and wiping his eyes on his too long sleeve as he relinquished his hold on my waist.

"Her stuff is just over here," said Liz, leading us to a little collection of half burnt candles surrounding a small wooden chest with a pentagram crudely carved into it.

"Do you mind if we look through it?" asked Adrian, sniffling again as he produced his flask from the hoodie pouch. He poured a cup of tea and offered it to me, managing a little smile, although his eyes were still watery.

"Keep it if you like. I'd say she owes you both that much," said Liz, as she apologetically handed me a pack of knock-off Jaffa cakes that she'd produced from God knows where. I still ate them.

Adrian flicked the latch of the chest and it popped open. Inside was a loose assortment of candles, gemstones, and a couple of decks of cards.

"Weird. I've never seen that second deck before," said Liz, peering over Adrian's shoulder. One deck, whilst dogeared and folded in places, had beautiful painted watercolour illustrations. Adrian picked them up, handing them to me to rifle through. The cards had things like wands, pentacles and goblets on them.

"That's her tarot deck," said Linda. "She used to use it all the time, but she sort of seemed to lose interest after the dreams."

"Maybe she was making these," said Adrian, laying out what looked like another deck, only the images on them were hand sketched in pencil.

"I've never seen those," said Terrance.

"Me neither," said Liz, picking one up.

"The Meditator, this looks like me, doesn't it" she said, shoving the card under my nose and then Terrance's. There was a vague likeness.

Mothers, Witches and Queens

"The Enchanter, The Queen of the Lake, The Prince, The Son of the Lake." Adrian read the titles as he laid the cards out. Each bore a likeness, if a little clumsy, to their presumed inspiration, whether it be Merlin or Nimueh or me or Adrian. Although there were some I didn't recognise, like The Maiden, The Crone and The Geomancer. There was one titled Seventh in Seven, which depicted a round-faced smiley lady, with six little stars twinkling around her.

"Let me see that one," I said, stopping Adrian as he flicked past a wild-haired, wide-eyed woman with her hand outstretched into the foreground and a manic look on her face.

"The Hidden Queen." Adrian read the words aloud as he passed the card to me. The sketching on this one was scratchier, more jagged, and manic.

"This looks like the shade," I said, inspecting it.

"It kinda looks like old pictures of Morgana, if you squint a bit," said Adrian, bending the card back to get another look.

"Hello?" came a timid voice from the door behind us. Adrian almost jumped out of his skin.

"Oh, hey, Penny," said Terrance.

Penny looked mid-twenties, with frizzy brown hair tied in an unravelling plait. She was wearing a patchwork dress and a green cardigan that looked like it itched. I watched her eyes peel back wide as they fell on Adrian and me. They were quite blue. Not a patch on Adrian's, but pretty by normal standards.

"Adrian and Michael?" she asked, taking a few tentative steps forward and offering her hand to shake.

"You're the Norn," said Adrian, taking her hand in his, her cheeks flushed slightly.

"I suppose I am, although I wish certain individuals wouldn't call me that," she said, shooting Terrance a look.

"We've seen some of your work," I said gravely, struggling not to hold the effect it'd had on Adrian against her.

"I'm so sorry to hear about what happened to you with Gwen. She's not usually like that," said Penny apologetically.

"How did you hear about it?" I asked.

"We've got a group chat," said Liz.

"It's not very witchy of us, is it?" Penny said, giving a little laugh, which Adrian returned. The sound of his laughter softened me a little.

"Still, the best witches I've ever met," said Adrian.

"You're sweet," said Penny. I could see it happening in real time, like it always did. Adrian had this quiet way of charming people, he made everyone that met him warmer.

"We should be getting back," I said, surrendering to the urge to hide under the duvet with him.

"I'll drive you," said Terrance.

"Do you mind if we take these?" Adrian asked, still clutching the chest and the cards.

"Keep 'em, they're yours," said Liz, giving him a friendly pat on the back.

4

"Adrian, I've got an idea," Michael said, pulling on a black zip up hoodie over his school uniform. Linda had said she couldn't keep calling in sick for him, although she did give us a week of hiding from the world.

We were supposed to be studying Gwen's cards and working out who or what the shade was. This study had mostly taken place from the comfort of Michael's bed or inside the pillow fort we made on Tuesday. The studying in question would have looked to a layperson, an awful lot like canoodling, to use Linda's word.

"What's that then?" I asked.

"Come here so I can show you," said Michael, beckoning me from the bed. Wearing only my boxers and Michael's shirt, which was big enough that it dangled like a dress.

"What are you up to?" I caught Michael's eyes lingering

on me, and warmth bloomed in my cheeks as I slipped out of bed.

"I'm going to sneak you in!" he said, at once wrapping me in his hoodie and zipping it up behind me.

"Nobody will notice a thing," I said, chuckling and breathing Michael in. His warmth tingled my skin, and my breath caught as Michael's hands slipped under my thighs and lifted me up. I wrapped my legs around his waist and my arms slipped under his, holding me fast to him.

"I'll just say I've had a big lunch," said Michael, laughing and pressing his lips to the crown of my head.

"Michael, you'll have to be quick if you want a— oh bloody hell what have I walked in on?" Linda opened and then quickly slammed the door to Michael's room closed again.

"That'll teach her not to knock," said Michael, before he heaved me up tight against him and carried me out of the room towards the stairs.

"Michael what on earth are you doing?" asked Linda, who sounded rather flustered.

"Don't know what you mean, Mum, ready when you are." I could hear the smile on his face and had to stifle a giggle.

"You're being daft is what you are," said Linda, followed by the sound of a zip being pulled down and cool air spilling into my warm, dark world.

"Hello, Linda," I said, giving a sheepish smile as I craned my neck round to look at her.

Mothers, Witches and Queens

"Hello, Adrian," said Linda, who I could now see was doing a rather unconvincing attempt to fight the grin on her own face.

"Oh, my goodness! How did you get there? So sorry, Mum, I had no idea, honest" said Michael, smiling so broadly you'd be able to see his wisdom teeth if he had any. Linda rolled her eyes as she let loose a chuckle and opened the door.

"Put him down and get in the car quick," she said, heading out. I let my legs drop and Michael placed me back on the floor. The cool tiles of the entrance hall sent a shiver up my back.

"Will you be okay?" Michael asked, playing with my messy blonde hair as he spoke to me.

"I'll be right here when you get home. I'm not going anywhere, I promise," I said, fixing his deep amber eyes with mine. I knew he didn't like to leave me. We'd been stuck together like sugar on a bun since the tapestry with the gravestone. Which we both had silently agreed never to mention. Although it did manage to force its way into my head and fill me with icy dread at inopportune moments, like this one. As it turned out, there were very few moments that were opportune to be filled with icy dread.

"Just hide under blankets and watch Charmed and drink tea and I'll be back before you know it," said Michael. The softness in his voice almost made me wonder if he knew what had just forced its way into my head. He sighed and turned to leave, then paused and span around on the spot, slid his hand to the small of my back as he dipped me and delivered a kiss so smoothly it felt choreographed, sending my stomach into a flutter.

"What was that for?" I said, staring up into his handsome face as he held me. He was smiling, his cheeks flushed, his hair dangled tickling my cheeks, but there was a sadness in his eyes. For a second, all I wanted to do was burst into tears.

"Just wanted the last kiss until the next kiss to be a good one." His voice sounded almost regretful as he straightened up, squeezed me tight, and stepped out the door. "I'll see you soon," he said, waving as he went. I nodded and waved back but couldn't muster a word as I watched him disappear down the path into Linda's car. Once they'd driven off, I took a deep, shaky breath, closed the door, set the new deadbolt Linda had installed and let myself slump onto the cold tiled floor.

"I don't want you to go," I whispered, as the emptiness and the loneliness rolled a tear down my cheek.

5

I craned my neck back as we drove away, watching as Adrian waved us off and went back into the house. Then I counted the seconds, guessing how long it would take him to have all the doors locked. I went round last night and made sure all the windows were properly closed, although I'm not sure what good it would do if Gwen turned up, I don't think a yale lock would pose much of a challenge.

"Are you alright Michael?" Mum asked, placing her hand on mine, which I now realise was a balled fist.

"Can we go back?" I said. I finally turned my eyes away. We'd driven far enough that you couldn't see the house anymore anyway. Mum's face fell a little, which usually preceded a no.

"Michael, you can't just drop out of school and spend every waking moment of every day with Adrian, its healthy to have a bit of separation, you know?" she said, attempting a convincing smile.

"You know I'm not asking just because I'd rather be with him, right? It's not like I just can't be bothered with school anymore, Mum. We're not just love-struck dumb teenagers," I said.

"I didn't say you were Michael, but even so," said Mum.

"Even so, what? The last time I left him he was kidnapped, like really, full-blown hit on the back of the head, knocked out, kidnapped. And the person that did it is still out there, and somehow, I'm supposed to go to school and focus on A levels when I know he's home alone and he's scared, Mum," I said.

"The house is all locked up though. He's not going to go out again, is he? He'll be right where you left him when you get back," said Mum.

"They know where we live, Mum, they'd been following him. They know where we live and they're not normal, they're magic. What if he's not there when I get back? What if something else happens to him? I don't think he could…" I stopped short, my eyes dropped, and I held my head in my hands. I couldn't finish the sentence. I didn't want to have the thought at all.

"Michael?" Mum asked, sounding worried as we pulled up outside the school.

"It's nothing, Mum, forget it," I said, setting my jaw as I climbed out of the car and set off for school.

"Love you, have a nice day." I heard mum call from the

car, but I didn't turn back. I don't know what I'd have done. I felt as though if I opened my mouth again there was no controlling what would come out, stress or anger or tears or a rage or guilt.

"You're back. I texted you last week, but you didn't reply," said Jess, who had taken up walking alongside me. I didn't respond. I barely even looked up. It didn't seem to slow her down much.

"Jack is here too. He started a couple of days ago. Now we've got the whole gang back together," she said as she accompanied me happily into the sixth form canteen, where everyone was waiting to file into their respective form rooms. Jess led me to a table in the corner occupied by Alex and Jack who were holding hands, and Sam, who got up to hug Jess as we arrived.

"The whole gang's back together," said Alex happily, trying to meet my gaze. I couldn't bring myself to smile again, so kept my eyes down resolutely as I sat. I tried not to remember the frayed black mass of thread hanging on the community centre wall.

"That's what I just said," said Jess.

"Hey, I was wondering if I could have a word?" asked Jack, getting up from the table before I sat down. He looked pale and thinner than usual, like his eyes were sinking in, or bulging or something. They had big bags under them anyway.

"Good luck. I've not got a thing out of him yet," said

Jess as I let Jack lead me to the vending machines, a little away from the group. Fewer people felt better.

"Don't do anything I wouldn't do!" called Alex.

"That leaves plenty of leeway for them!" I heard Sam joke as we walked away.

"Hey, so you know the dreams I'd been having?" said Jack, in a gentler tone than I was used to from him. He started fiddling with the machine. Neither of us made any attempt at eye contact. I nodded but didn't respond. "Well, I've been speaking to someone about them and I'm starting to think my disappearance had something to do with Adrian." My body clenched at the mention of his name, but if Jack noticed anything, he didn't let on. "I know you two got really close, really fast, but I'm starting to wonder how much we know about him, like where did he come from? Have any of us met his parents? Haven't you noticed things started to get weird after he arrived? Like the kidnappings and the school flooding and you're constantly calling in sick to school now. And I'm dreaming about people that look like him and—"

"Who did you speak to about the dreams?" I asked, cutting him off before he said something I'd have to punch him for.

"Okay, it's gonna sound a little weird, but he knows about this stuff. He's into witchy stuff and the occult and all of that. He's been helping me decipher my dreams," said Jack. My knuckles cracked as I clenched my fists involuntarily. "I've been speaking to that new kid Jude and—"

The bang echoed throughout the canteen as I slammed my fist towards the chocolate bars and crisps. Cracks ran the length and breadth of the vending machine glass, and my knuckles were bleeding.

"What the hell, Michael? Are you okay?" asked Jack, who'd jumped back as I punched the machine.

I flexed my hand, inspecting the blood trickling between my fingers. I knew it hurt, but it was numb, like I couldn't really process the feeling.

"Don't speak to Jude about Adrian." I spoke, but the voice wasn't mine. It echoed through the canteen, reverberating unnaturally.

"What? Why? What's wrong with Jude?" Jack asked, looking confused. Jess, Sam and Alex had gotten up from their seats now and were crowding around me. In fact, it felt like the whole canteen was staring.

"What happened? Did you slip or something?" asked Jess.

"He didn't slip, he punched it. Look at his knuckles," said Sam, pointing to my fist.

"How did you even punch that hard?" Jack asked, turning back to the shattered vending machine glass.

"That doesn't matter. If anyone asks, he slipped, and we all saw it. What's going on?" said Alex, who could always be relied upon to lie quickly and committedly to any authority figure.

"I mentioned Jude, and he just freaked out," said Jack, a note of accusation in his tone.

"Did someone say my name?"

My head shot up. I knew the voice from the phone calls from that day. There he was, a few feet back, with his stupid floppy black hair. Our eyes met and electricity ran through me.

He flinched. His were eyes a dull grey and staring widely as he took a step back. I could hardly believe it, but it looked as though his cheeks had flushed pink at the sight of me. I took a step forward and Jack stepped between us.

"MOVE, JACK." I hadn't meant to use the voice. My words shook the windows of the canteen, but I didn't care. I didn't care that the whole sixth form was staring at me. It didn't matter.

"Michael, don't be stupid. You're not this person. You're not gonna hurt Jude just because he was talking to me about dreams and maybe your boyfriend came up," said Jack quickly, certainty slipping into fear.

"No, I'm not," I said coolly, watching Jude unblinkingly.

"Good," said Jack, letting out a sigh of relief.

"Do you know why I am going to hurt Jude? Do you know what he's done? Do you have any idea what that little shit did to Adrian before he started whispering poisonous nasty thoughts to you about him?" I asked, spit flying from my lips. I pressed my face towards Jack until there was only an inch between us. Jack took a step back, shaking his head, anger and disgust and fear flickering across his face.

Mothers, Witches and Queens

"You stalked him, didn't you?" I said, looking past Jack to Jude, who was taking nervous steps back from the group.

"No, I didn't you don't—" said Jude.

"You stalked him, and you made him feel small, and then when he was good and scared you followed him to work and you attacked him, didn't you Jude?" My whole body was shaking, tight, like I could explode out the stocks at any moment. Jude shook his head, tears tumbling down his cheeks as he turned and sprinted out of the school.

"Get out of the way, Jack," I commanded, taking another step towards my dumbstruck wall of friends, each with their mouths hanging open in shock. "I said move." As I spoke, I grabbed Jack by the shirt and threw him into Alex before I started to sprint in Jude's direction. It felt good, to use my body, to move, not to be stuck pretending everything was fine, and that exams mattered. None of it mattered. It was all nonsense and distractions and I couldn't pretend to care about any of it anymore. I got to the front door just in time to see Jude disappearing down the road on a bicycle, his school jacket flapping behind him.

"If I ever see you near Adrian again, I'll fucking kill you!" My voice boomed out of me and sent a flock of birds squawking from a nearby tree. I also elicited a gasp and a horrified look from the receptionist at the front desk.

6

The sound of a key turning in the lock clicked through the silent house, and my eyes darted to the door. I'd been sitting opposite it all morning, wrapped in Michael's duvet on the floor just outside the entrance hall, staring at Gwen's cards and drifting in and out of some profoundly useless fugue state. The witches of Starkton group chat had offered their own suggestions after Terrance added me, but we'd all mostly drawn a blank so far. My breath caught in my chest as the latch clicked on the yale lock. I started scrabbling back, my heart racing, my eyes wide, my breath short as I moved so fast, I hit the wall behind me with a thud. The door started to open and stopped with a jerk. Caught on the chain, I held my breath, waiting for it to be burst off its hinges.

"Adrian, I'm home!" Michael's voice echoed through the house, and I almost melted with the relief.

"Coming," I squeaked, pulling myself to my feet by the kitchen counter and hurrying to the door, releasing the chain, and letting Michael in. The second he was over the threshold, his arms were around me, lifting me into the air, spinning me round as he peppered my face with kisses. Relief and joy rushed through me in equal measure. Suddenly I was as light as a feather and I could breathe again and I burst into laughter as Michael carried me, twirling through the house. Falling back into the squashy armchair once we got to the living room.

"You're home early," I said when I finally managed to catch my breath and contain the laughter.

"I know, isn't it great," said Michael, planting another kiss on my cheek as he squeezed me tight to him. Part of me knew something was wrong, that he was going to get himself in trouble, that I should say something, but all I wanted to do was be with him. To feel safe and warm and not afraid every time the door creaked.

"What should we do with the day?" I asked, deciding to enjoy the moment.

"I wanna go swimming with my boyfriend," said Michael.

"Me too," I said.

"We have so much in common," said Michael, chuckling. I laughed, and I could feel it happening, my chest opening up, my shoulders loosening, my cheeks aching from smiling. We got changed quickly into our swim shorts and a T-shirt for me, and a vest for Michael and set off, with Michael carrying me on his back, my arms looped around his chest, my head peeking over his shoulder.

"What were Gwen's cards and my duvet doing on the kitchen floor, out of interest?" asked Michael as we plodded down the lane. Michael cut through into the forest the first chance he got.

"Well, the cards were winning a staring contest with me, and the duvet was my shield against the cold alien horrors of the world," I said.

"Oh, so just the essentials then," said Michael, chuckling.

"Yep," I replied. A comfortable silence fell as Michael hiked through the forest until we came to the archway of trees, the tunnel that led to our lake.

"Does it look a bit murky, to you?" Michael asked as we approached. It had grown slightly duller and greener over time, in a way things in the fay forest didn't.

"Don't worry about that," I said, slipping off Michael's back as I approached the water, dipped a hand, and let myself feel it all. The whole body of the lake, formless and full. It became like an extension of me. I could feel the warmth of the sun bouncing off my cool mirrored surface, every blade of grass piercing me, every root drinking from me, breathing into me. As I became it, I let it out. Whatever that part of me is, that's fay, pouring life into the water. I sat back and looked at what I'd done.

"What was that?" Michael asked, kneeling next to me in

the grass, looking out over the crystal-clear blue waters, as a faint glow subsided.

"An old water nymph trick, kind of like connecting with the water. Legends says that the first Nimueh, who the lake was named for, could connect with the whole of lake Nimueh at once," I said, steadying myself against Michael as I let a spell of light-headedness subside.

"Do you think it's true?" Michael asked, stroking my hair as I rested against him.

"Dunno, but I know it annoys the current Nimueh that she can't do it," I said, chuckling and slowly blinking my eyes.

"You okay?" asked Michael, catching my eyes in his warm amber globes, a flicker of gold glinting in the daylight. My cheeks ached as a smile burst across my face and I nodded, nuzzling into his neck.

"Never better," I said, planting a kiss before I slipped my T-shirt off and let myself fall sideways into the water. I felt it run over me, setting my skin alight like electricity, breathing life into me from my scalp to the tips of my toes.

"Wait for me," Michael said, almost ripping his vest in his haste to get it off before diving headfirst into the water. I watched, admiring his athletic body twist through the depths before he surfaced next to me grinning and threw his arms around me.

"Let's always wait for each other," I said softly before kissing him tenderly, my fingers finding his shoulders, holding me close to him. He swam with me to the side of

Mothers, Witches and Queens

the lake, bracing me against the bank, one thick muscular arm on either side of me, and broke the kiss. He just looked at me. My stomach fluttered, and my skin prickled, and my cheeks burned under his gaze. Then my eye caught it, the trickle of red from his knuckle.

"What happened to your hand?" I asked, taking it in mine, inspecting it. Lots of little lacerations, trickling thin streams of red between his fingers.

"Oh, I had an accident at school. Don't worry about it." Michael's eyes flicked down as he spoke and made my stomach squirm nervously.

"I can heal it," I offered, placing my palm over his knuckle.

"No, wait, don't, it's fine, it doesn't bother me, I don't want you to wear yourself out over it," he said, slipping his hand from my grip and taking my chin, pulling me close to kiss me.

"But I like to heal you," I whispered, running a streak of kisses down his neck, eliciting a small shudder.

"Will you sing for me instead?" asked Michael, looking at me hopefully.

"I don't know any of your songs," I said softly. I'd not really got the hang of learning words to songs, and if I did know any, I was too flustered to remember them now.

"No, a fay song, from the forest," said Michael, gently lifting my chin, forcing our eyes to meet. I couldn't say no to those eyes. So, I took a deep breath and cast my mind back into the forest and I sang the song of new life. Our happiest song. It is said to call back to the spirits of the ancestors of the fay, summoning them to visit their new descendants.

My voice echoed through the forest, riding on the breeze and Michael's mouth fell open, the surrounding water rippled. Entirely without my meaning for it to, droplets drifted out of the lake, suspended in the air. Light shone through the countless floating orbs, casting rainbows all about us, and tears shone in Michael's eyes, dropping into the lake. Slowly, I let my voice shrink, the song fading until it was just a memory.

"I love you so much," Michael said, choking on his words. Then he froze as a clap rang out behind us. My eyes flicked up to see Olivier lowering her feet into the lake.

"Now, why didn't you ever sing that beautifully back in the forest?" she asked.

"I must have been lacking inspiration," I said, giving Michael a wink as Olivier lowered herself into the water. Her green gnomish robes drifted behind her like tentacles of seaweed as she floated towards us.

"To what do we owe the pleasure?" asked Michael, looping an arm around my waist.

"And how did you know we'd be here?" I asked.

"You weren't at Linda's, so I had Mu-Terra look through the trees and see if he could spot you. And you owe the pleasure to chaos, I'm afraid," she said gravely, whilst lifting her arm up into the air and watching a vein of water trickle down it.

Mothers, Witches and Queens

"What kind of chaos?" asked Michael.

"Goblins have been running into fay territory," said Olivier.

"Like another invasion?" I asked, but Olivier shook her head.

"It's more like they're running away from something. We keep finding them, hiding in caves and such. We hadn't heard a peep from them since they took back The Hut, but now, suddenly, something's happening in their lands. Regardless, there's a chance they might start coming through to town again, so I thought you'd like a warning," Olivier explained.

"Any ideas what they're running from?" I asked.

"Some theories. I tried talking to some of them but couldn't make much sense of what they were saying, something about voices in trees." Olivier gave a resigned shrug.

"Well, we made a discovery," said Michael, giving me a nod of encouragement.

"We went through Gwen's stuff, that is… the woman who erm … who took … anyway, the one that Michael said had a weird ghost lady attached to her. We found a deck of tarot cards that her friends didn't recognise, they looked handmade. There were these little illustrations. One looked like me, one looked like Nimueh and one of them looked like the shade Michael had seen," I said.

"It was titled The Hidden Queen," said Michael. Oliver's brows furrowed at the mention of the name. "Mean anything to you? Adrian said she looked a bit like

Morgana." Olivier nodded, her eyes closing in concentration, as if she was trying to work out a complex bit of maths.

"It's an old legend, about a powerful enchanter who opposed Merlin, but was defeated. In some versions of the story she died, others said that she was imprisoned. Merlin was very tight-lipped about it, and no one else had been around long enough to remember." Olivier spoke with her eyes closed, like she was reading the story off her eyelids.

"Well, could she be something to do with the shade?" asked Michael.

Olivier shrugged. "It's possible, I suppose. She was an enchanter. If she really was imprisoned, she might still be around, but why would she wait till now to do something and what would she be up to and where would she be?" Olivier wasn't talking to us anymore. She was thinking aloud, posing questions to herself. I'd seen her do it before.

"Something to think about," I said, watching her climb out of the pool and start towards a particularly thick tree.

"I'll do some research," said Olivier, not turning back to wave as she stepped out of Starkton woods and into the fay forest.

"Well, that certainly captured her imagination," I said with a chuckle.

"And it was you who found the clue," said Michael, scooping me up in his arms, his heat rushing into my skin as he held me against him and kissed me deeply.

7

"You got suspended!" Mum yelled from the entrance hall as the bang of the door slamming open echoed through the house. Not even waiting to see if I was actually home before she started shouting at me.

"You got suspended?" Adrian whispered with a worried look on his face as he put down the Xbox remote. I'd been taking another crack at showing him video games. He hadn't really got the hang of it yet. He kept making his character look at the sky when he tried to walk forward, and constantly gave the remote to me anytime anything happened. It was adorable.

"Don't worry about it," I said, planting a kiss on his cheek just as Mum burst into the room, red faced and flustered. Somehow, she was so angry it'd made her hair messy. I knew it wasn't the right thing to do, but it was almost making me laugh.

"What are you smiling at? This isn't funny, Michael, this is serious, this could go on your permanent record," said Mum.

"I think those might be a myth, Mum." As soon as I said it, I knew this was not the right thing to say.

"Don't you get smart with me young man. This isn't funny and what's more, it's not like you... fighting people?" Mum's anger was boiling down into worry and disappointment, which was much worse.

"I didn't fight anyone," I corrected her, running my thumb over my cut-up knuckle without thinking.

"But they said you chased a boy out of school grounds, shouting at him," said Mum, perching on the arm of the sofa, studying me, searching for understanding.

"Yes, after I punched a vending machine, but I never laid a hand on him," I said. Not that I wouldn't have if I'd been given the chance, but that wasn't really the point.

"But why, Michael? What could he have possibly done? This isn't you, you're not a bully, you're a sweet boy," said Mum.

"Can I explain later?" I asked, aware of Adrian's big blue eyes on me, full of worry. If he knew what had happened, he'd blame himself. That's what he always did, take the blame, accept the fault.

"No, Michael, this is serious, we need to talk about this," said Mum, fanning herself. In her fluster, she'd forgotten to take off her coat and now she'd worked herself

Mothers, Witches and Queens

up into a sweat. Why she insisted on wearing a coat in summer, I don't know.

"I don't want to talk about it right now," I said. I couldn't think of a good lie, so I defaulted to good old obstinance.

"Michael, this isn't like you. You don't just not talk to me, you know this, you can talk to me about anything." Mum knelt down in front of me and took my hands in hers. It was like she was begging and the guilt of it made me feel like I might throw up.

"I'll get us some tea," said Adrian, suddenly bolting out of the room. I watched him go and seized my chance.

"It was Jude, Mum," I whispered into her ear.

"Who?" she hissed back.

"The boy, the one who was there when Adrian got kidnapped," I said.

"Oh, he goes to your school?" asked Mum, sitting back a bit, transformed from a concerned parent into the office gossip at the drop of a hat.

"Yes, he's new, and he's saying shitty things about Adrian to my friends and…" I let my voice tail off as I could hear Adrian's footsteps coming back. Mum got back on her feet and let her face fall into a frown as she dropped back into the character of an angry mother. I don't know if she got exactly why I didn't want Adrian to know the details, but she certainly played along well.

"Here you go, Linda," Adrian said, offering Mum a

glass of water, which she drank as though she'd just escaped the Sahara.

"Michael, whatever the reason is, getting suspended is still not acceptable. It could affect your grades and could hurt your chances of getting into uni," she said. I took a deep breath.

"I've been thinking about that as well, that is, I'm not sure if going to uni is really what I want anymore," I said. Mum's body language shifted, and I realised quickly that this probably wasn't the time to bring this up.

"What do you mean, you don't want to go to uni?" A flash of genuine anger coloured her tone.

"I mean, it's not what I'm interested in anymore. I think I was only ever thinking about going because I didn't have any better ideas," I said. The words were pouring out of me, like once I'd started the boulder rolling down the hill, I couldn't stop it and it was threatening to crush us.

"You want to be a physiotherapist or a sports scientist, you've always said that," said Mum.

"Or personal trainer or a P.E teacher. I used to say a lot of things, Mum, because I didn't know better. I didn't know what was out there, and I was physical, and I was good at sports, and it just made sense, but it doesn't anymore. It doesn't make sense, and I can't pretend to care about that stuff anymore," I said.

"Because of magic!" Mum's eyes flicked to Adrian and exasperation rang in her voice. I could feel him recoiling behind me. My chest was tight and I felt hot. My breath caught and I almost felt giddy.

"Don't look at him like that. It's not his fault, so what if it's because of magic? I get shown a whole new world and I'm supposed to pretend it's not there, pretend to care about some footballers' Achilles tendon? Go to school for years to learn how to treat an injury Adrian could fix in five seconds flat, it's ridiculous," I said, my voice big and loud.

"And how are you going to live when you throw away every opportunity? What happens then? When you need a house or a car or food?" We were yelling, we were standing and yelling and pointing and spit was flying.

"Maybe I won't live here anymore. Maybe I don't want to be a part of it all. Maybe, maybe I want to be a part of Adrian's world with Adrian," I retorted. The anger across Mum's face vanished, shifting into what looked like fear and again I felt like I might be sick from the guilt.

"Michael what are you saying?" Mum's voice cracked as she spoke.

"I'm going to my room," I said, grabbing Adrian by the wrist and dragging him out of the room, before I said something else, another thing to regret. I slammed my door behind me and sunk to my knees, panting.

"Are you okay?" Adrian asked, sat opposite me, his knees pulled up to his chest. He wasn't, I could see that much. I scanned his worried face, his watery eyes, his flushed cheeks, his freshly bruising wrist.

"What happened to your wrist?" I asked, taking it gently in my hand and inspecting it, noticing the finger marks slowly fading.

"Nothing," he whispered, his eyes flicking down to the floor.

"Was it me?" I asked, swallowing hard as my mouth dried.

"It doesn't hurt, don't worry," said Adrian, flashing me a smile as he closed towards me, laying back into my lap.

"I didn't mean to," I said softly, blinking my stinging eyes.

"I know, you're a prince," he said, as if that excused something. It didn't.

"That doesn't mean I get to hurt you, Adrian," I replied.

"It means you're stronger than you realise," he said, smiling up at me from my lap. I knew what he meant, but it still didn't feel right. Nothing I did felt right recently.

"You didn't really fight someone, did you?" Adrian asked.

"Nope, and a good job too apparently, what with my super strength." I attempted a smile and one broke out across Adrian's face in turn, which made mine feel more real.

"So, what did happen?" he asked.

"I punched a vending machine because someone made me mad, that's all," I said. I couldn't tell him what had happened now. He'd just started smiling, and he didn't smile enough these days.

Mothers, Witches and Queens

"What did they say?" said Adrian.

"Just some homophobic stuff. They didn't even say it to me, just Alex and Jack," I lied. I didn't like to lie to Adrian, but I disliked him blaming himself even more.

8

Linda had been diligently delivering Michael's school work, each evening on her way home from work. The idea was that he wouldn't let himself fall behind on it, but so far, all it was doing was forming a tower. Before long, it would be load bearing. Michael kept saying we could use it to play Jenga, but I didn't know what that was. It was a Thursday lunchtime when Michael and I heard the key turn in the front door lock, followed by the sound of door catching on the chain.

"Can someone let me in?" came an unfamiliar voice from the entrance hall.

"Dan?" Michael asked the empty space in the hallway.

"Yes, it's me. Since when did we get a chain put on the door?" Michael unlatched the door and Daniel stepped in. The resemblance between Michael and his brother was obvious. They shared the same dark floppy hair, amber eyes, and I suspect they'd share the same jaw if it weren't for Daniel's chubby cheeks. Although the younger of the two, Michael was taller and broader than his brother, with a more athletic frame.

"It's a recent thing," said Michael as Daniel stepped into the house and immediately pulled him into a tight hug.

"Bloody hell, Mikey, you've grown, did you get a gym membership or something?" said Daniel.

"Must be something in the water," Michael said with a laugh. It would probably be more trouble than it's worth to try and explain the effects being a fay champion had on the body.

"And you must be Adrian? Mum's told me all about you," said Daniel, letting Michael go and crossing the entrance hall to offer me a handshake. His grip was firmer than I expected, and his eyes were intense. I got the sense I was being appraised.

"I am, and you're Daniel. It's nice to meet you," I said, wondering if Linda had mentioned that I was a magical fay being when she'd been telling Daniel all about me.

"I thought you weren't coming home till the summer holidays," said Michael as we headed into the living room.

"I got some time off, and I thought I'd pop down to see everyone, meet the mysterious new boyfriend that's stolen my baby brethren's heart," said Daniel.

"Ugh, you're as bad as Mum," said Michael, turning a deep shade of red before flopping face first onto the sofa, which I perched myself on the arm of.

Mothers, Witches and Queens

"Am I mysterious?" I asked, watching him carefully, as if I'd somehow be able to tell from a twitch of the eye what he knew about me.

"Well, you and Michael managed to convince Mum to let you move into Michael's room. She'd never let me have a girlfriend overnight, let alone move in," said Daniel.

"You never had a girlfriend!" Michael shouted, his voice muffled by the sofa.

"No need to rip me to shreds like that Mikey, just because you're the Romeo of the family," said Daniel.

"Ugh…" Michael groaned from the sofa and smashed a pillow down on top of his head making a Michael sandwich.

"Why aren't you two in school anyway?" Daniel asked.

"As if Mum hadn't already told you, I got suspended," yelled Michael into the sofa.

"I was going to let you tell it to me from your side of the story, if you'd ever get up from hiding inside the sofa," said Daniel.

"It's complicated," said Michael, rolling onto his back.

"How complicated can it be? It's only high school," said Daniel.

"Someone attacked Adrian and then started spreading nasty rumours around school about him. So, I might have … threatened to kill them," said Michael.

"When you say attacked, how dramatic are you being?" asked Daniel in a slightly teasing tone.

"Is it dramatic to call it an attack when someone smacks you around the back of the head with a blunt object?"

Michael asked in such a pointed tone that it didn't feel like a question at all. Daniel's eyes bulged slightly unsettlingly in shock, which is something I'd never seen Michael's do.

"So, you got properly attacked then? And the kid that did it is still in school? You'd think they'd have kicked him out," said Daniel.

"I was at work," I said, hoping the next question wasn't why he attacked me, because that one would be hard to explain.

"Are you okay now though?" he asked, looking genuinely concerned, which made me feel a bit guilty for being so wary of him.

"I'm fine now," I said.

"Why did they attack you anyway?" Daniel asked. There it was.

"Erm, homophobia I think," I lied.

"Okay well, maybe you were justified in threatening to kill them. Still stupid to do it in front of school staff though," said Daniel.

"To be honest, I don't really care about school anymore," said Michael.

"What about uni?" Daniel asked. Michael shrugged and scootched along the sofa, pulling me off the arm and into his lap, as his arms wrapped tightly around me. I took a deep breath. I hadn't realised how tight my chest had been. "Since when don't you care about uni?" Daniel's expression shifted to annoyance for a moment as his eyes flickered

Mothers, Witches and Queens

over me. Leaving me with the unmistakable feeling that I was being blamed for something.

"I've got different priorities now," said Michael.

"Please don't tell me you're giving up on school and uni for a boy. No offence Adrian." Daniel's tone was quickly becoming more and more scathing.

"You've got no idea what you're talking about," Michael bristled, his grip on my waist tightening slightly.

"And you've got no idea about the real world, what happens when you need money and you want to get a job, are you going to put 'in love' on your CV?" For some reason, as he was speaking Daniel made little quotation mark signs with his fingers which seemed infuriating, even to me.

"And I suppose you know all about the real world, going to uni and doing about 3 hours a week in a coffee shop," said Michael, the volume of his voice steadily rising.

"It's sixteen actually!" Daniel shouted.

"Oh, my mistake, in that case you really do know all about the real world," said Michael, now with air quotes of his own.

"Fine, whatever, of course you know best and everyone else is just out to get you, I'm sure. Just you and Adrian against the world." Daniel had gotten up from his seat now and was doing a startling impression of Linda from the other night. I physically felt myself wince when he dropped my name, confirming what I'd been afraid of. I was coming between Michael and his family. Just like I'd come between him and his friends the other day at school.

"I don't understand why everyone else is taking it as some sort of personal affront that I don't want to go to uni to study something I'm not even interested in anymore," said Michael.

"Because we care about you and we don't want to see you— are you seriously checking your phone right now?" said Daniel. I'd almost jumped out of Michael's lap when his phone buzzed in his pocket.

"Yes, it's Alex," said Michael, his brows furrowing as he scanned what looked like a fairly long text. Alex did tend to be a bit verbose. Hopefully, he was looking to make amends. The thought of Michael falling out with Alex and Jack had been weighing on me.

"We are in the middle of a conversation, Michael," said Daniel. The resemblance to Linda was even more striking when Daniel used Michael's full name.

"Yes, and I can't wait for that to be over. Come on Adrian, let's go for a walk," I didn't have to be asked twice and slipped off Michael's lap, scurrying past Daniel to the door.

"Are you seriously walking out in the middle of this discussion?" Daniel asked, following us to the door, growing redder in the face by the second.

"I seriously am!" said Michael, holding the door open for me and then slamming it behind us with such force I thought it might pop its hinges, the bang echoing down the street.

9

"I'm sorry you had to see all that. We're not normally like that," I said as Adrian and I walked hand in hand down the street. My jaw still set tight from the argument with Daniel. It was bad enough with Mum constantly going on at me about uni. I didn't need Daniel doing it too.

"Don't worry, I'm sorry if I've been causing some friction between you and your family and friends." There it was, Adrian blaming himself again. This was exactly what I was worried would happen.

"Adrian, look me at," I said. We'd stopped walking, Adrian was looking out into the road. I think he was trying not to cry.

"Okay," he said. His voice was small, and even when he turned his head, his eyes were downcast. I stooped a little to meet them, his big blue eyes.

"None of this is your fault. Uni was never this big

thing for me, it's just what I was gonna do because I didn't know what to do. Now I know there's more out there for me and you didn't make me a champion, you just showed me a world I could be a part of. That's what I want. I want to be with you in your world, not just going through the motions doing a degree, because it's what people do. Mum and Daniel are just scared because it's different from what they know," I said. Adrian sniffled and a little smile peeked through, like a ray of sunshine on a cloudy day.

"I just feel like you keep having to choose me over everyone else in your life," he said. His voice cracked as he spoke and next thing I knew I'd picked him up and was hugging him tight, his feet dangling a few inches off the floor.

"Don't worry, Adrian, we're family, we fight, and we'll make up. It'll be fine. And anyway, they're the ones making me pick a side, not you. All you ever try to do is make peace. In fact, that's what we're doing right now," I said.

"We are?" Adrian asked.

"Yep, Alex and Jack are on a long lunch. They've got a free period. We're meeting them at Alex's," I said.

"I've never been to Alex's," said Adrian, perking up slightly.

"It's nice," I said. I set Adrian down and took his little hand in mine as we set off down the street, breathing what felt like the first proper deep breath I'd taken all day.

"What is sports science?" Adrian asked as we turned

Mothers, Witches and Queens

down into the nicer bit of town, where the greasy spoons turned into cafes all of a sudden.

"Why d'you ask?" I said.

"Your mum and brother both seem very committed to you studying it," said Adrian, looking up at me, his twinkling blue eyes peeking out from behind his shiny blonde hair. When the light caught him, it was almost impossible not to stare. Sometimes I'd find myself just looking at him, sitting in the garden or at the window. God knows how long for, I could completely lose myself in his face, in the curves of his cheeks, his soft lips, his dimples, his perfect smile. I think this must be what it's like for people who actually get art. "Michael?" Adrian said.

"What, sorry? I forgot what we were talking about," I said. My cheeks were burning up. Adrian looked at me quizzically for a second and a little laugh escaped him. It was like music.

"It doesn't matter. What were you thinking about?" he asked.

"Art," I said.

"I didn't know you liked art," said Adrian.

"I think I'm starting to see the appeal of it," I said with a chuckle as we turned onto Alex's street.

"This is a bit different," said Adrian, looking up the street. Unlike most of the residents of Starkton, Alex didn't live in a row of terraces. His street was built ages ago, and all the houses looked appropriately old and posh, and all had their own massive trees in their massive gardens. I'd always thought it was very impressive. Alex insisted all it really meant was that the phone signal was bad, and the houses were impossible to heat. He sounded like a character from Downton Abby.

"I thought you'd like it," I said. Adrian had made his way over to one of the massive trees. They were nothing to the fay forest, but by Starkton standards, they were monsters.

"Which one is Alex's?" Adrian asked, as he literally hugged a tree so wide around that he would need another set of arms to wrap all the way around it.

"This one," I said, taking him by the hand and leading him around the side of the house, past a wall overgrown with wildflowers to Alex's back garden where Alex and Jack were sitting out, sipping what looked like iced lemonade. Alex liked ice with almost everything. Jack got up from his seat when we rounded the corner and crossed to meet us. He looked like he was going for a handshake and then aborted to a hug and but by that point I'd gone for a handshake, so he ended up walking into my fist.

"Well, that was awkward," said Alex with a chuckle.

"Good start," I said, laughing nervously and scratching the back of my head, doubtless flashing a pit stain.

Alex poured us drinks, perhaps to evade the inevitable awkward conversation we had to have.

"Listen, okay, ugh I hate this, Adrian. Did Jude attack you at work?" Jack seemed to almost combust with nerves.

Mothers, Witches and Queens

"Yeah," said Adrian, from one of Alex's sun chairs. He was picking at his fingers anxiously.

"Okay, well then, fair enough, he's a dick and I'm sorry for listening to him. Let's never talk about it again." Jack spoke so quickly it seemed as if he was trying to beat a deadline. The bags under his eyes were bigger than ever. Adrian drained half his lemonade in a single gulp.

"Don't you get brain freeze?" Alex asked.

"What's that?" asked Adrian.

"Is he joking?" asked Alex, handing me my drink before he took his seat back at the table.

"Nope," I said, taking a seat next to Adrian.

"So, can we talk about the dreams?" Alex asked, looking at me as though he expected me to know what he was talking about. Obviously, from the blank expression on my face, he quickly realised that I didn't.

"It's awkward. Can we drop it?" said Jack, avoiding eye contact with all of us as he spoke.

"You're barely sleeping and when you do sleep you wake up screaming, so no, we can't," said Alex in an unusually firm tone. Jack was almost squirming in his seat now.

"Jack, just ask it, I won't get mad," I said, pangs of guilt washing over me again. Jack hadn't done anything to Adrian, he was a victim too, and we were lying to him. I didn't really have any right to be mad at him.

"It's just, I'm having these dreams, been having them for a while now and they are getting worse, and this woman is always in them, and she looks just like Adrian. No offence Adrian, I'm not blaming you, it's just Ju..." Jack paused, the name hanging, unfinished, in the air.

"He wakes up screaming for help and sometimes he says Adrian's name in his sleep," said Alex, saving Jack from the end of his sentence. Any façade had dropped now. Jack was exhausted, and Alex was worried.

"I get it, but I don't know what we can do..." I said.

"They're not dreams," said Adrian, catching me in the middle of struggling for excuses. Alex and Jack both turned so quickly they almost fell out of their garden furniture.

"What?" asked Jack, suddenly full of desperation.

"Adrian, you don't have to," I said, slipping my hand into his under the table. He squeezed it tight and took a deep breath.

"They're memories. The person you're dreaming about is my mother. She was involved with the people that kidnapped you," said Adrian.

"W-what are you saying? That doesn't... Adrian, he dreams about little green men with razor-sharp teeth and being trapped in a cage being dragged through a black forest by giant spiders. They can't be memories, they're not real." Alex was talking a mile a minute, whilst Jack had gone completely mute, staring at Adrian wide eyed.

"They are real. I'm so sorry for what happened to you, Jack." Adrian's face was stiff, stoic almost, but a tear was sliding down his unflinching cheek. Alex fell quiet. I could see it on his face. He'd been searching Adrian for a clue that he was lying, but there wasn't one, because he wasn't. Silence hung in the air.

"Was it you? Did you do it to me?" asked Jack, his legs trembling. He got up from his seat, backing away from Adrian. Adrian shook his head, opened his mouth and mouthed the word 'no', but he couldn't seem to make a sound.

"Jude said it must have been to do with you. I knew it was real. I knew—"

"Jude doesn't know what the fuck he is talking about. Can we not listen to Jude?" I barked more loudly than I meant to. Alex even jumped a bit.

"Wait a second, pause, pause," Alex was on his feet, hands in the air like he was surrendering to some invisible highway man.

"If you didn't have anything to do with it, why was your mother involved?" Jack asked, his tone unmistakably accusatory. Adrian was shaking, sitting ridged, his mouth opening and closing like a fish out of water. It was happening again. He was being blamed again, blaming himself again. I was so tense I felt like I could punch clean through a brick wall.

"Cause his mother is an evil piece of work. She tried to convince me to leave Adrian to die the second time I met her," I said, speaking for Adrian.

"What? Leave him to die? Can someone start making sense please? Context. Full sentences," said Alex. Jack had fallen silent again, his eyes glued to Adrian.

"Stop looking at him like that Jack, he didn't have anything to do with you going missing. He did save you though. You owe Adrian your life, I owe Adrian my life, so does my mum and all the other kids that went missing too. Adrian saved everyone, so will you stop looking at him like he's some kind of monster?" I was standing now. I don't remember getting up, but I was up, planting myself between Adrian and Jack. It felt urgent, it was urgent. Adrian couldn't take anymore blame, anymore of people looking at him like that.

"Okay... well... we've all gone mad, so that's something," said Alex, flopping back into his chair exhaustedly. He was shaking too now, splashing lemonade down his shirt as he struggled to take a sip. Jack was still standing and staring, but his face was shifting, accusation was gone.

"Where was I?" he asked, after what felt like an age.

"Crazy town, population us," quipped Alex unhelpfully.

"The fay forest," said Adrian, from behind me, finally his voice was back. I knelt beside him, taking his trembling hand in mine.

"Same difference," said Alex, earning a glare from Jack.

"Where is that?" Jack asked.

"It's hard to explain. It's sort of... parallel." Adrian was struggling.

"If anyone could start making sense, anytime now," said Alex, ignoring Jack's glare as he tapped an imaginary watch on his wrist impatiently.

"The only way to describe it is..." I paused. I knew the

Mothers, Witches and Queens

next word out of my mouth was not going to help the situation.

"Magic." Adrian finished my sentence for me. Jack did not look impressed.

"If you came here to make me feel stupid, it's working, job done, you can fuck off now," he said, a wall going up around him in real time as he started to shut himself off.

"Can't you just trust us?" I asked pathetically, already knowing the answer.

"Trust that Adrian's mum kidnapped me and took me to a magical world but that it's all fine now and none of us are going literally insane? No, funnily enough, I can't." Jack spat the words.

"Fine. I'll show you," I said, crossing to the large tree at the bottom of Alex's garden. Its roots were doing a good job of pushing their back wall over. I took my shard of Excalibur and ran it along the bark of the tree and stepped through. For a second, I was in the fay forest. eternally green, eternally wild. I took one deep breath, breathing it in, and stepped back into Starkton, returning to the amazed faces of Alex and Jack.

"How did you just… is my tree magic?" Alex asked, crossing the garden to run his hand along the bark of the tree.

"No, this is," I said, showing him the small jagged black-green rock dangling around my neck.

"Why did I get taken?" asked Jack, still staring, unblinking.

"Completely random, the mirelings, that is, those creatures that took you. They were just looking for anyone who could use one of these," I said, pointing again at the stone.

"And you brought me back?" asked Jack, his eyes falling to Adrian.

"It was Michael mos—"

"Adrian sacrificed his own body to find you and my mother, snuck us to where you were being held prisoner, offered his life as collateral in trade for yours and then overthrew a dictator to get you back and never asked for thanks once." I cut Adrian off, which I didn't like to do, but he was about to give me all the credit again and right now I really needed him to take it.

"Well, Adrian's definitely going on the Christmas card list," said Alex, and in spite of myself, a bark of laughter burst out of me. I watched as Jack lurched forwards, almost staggering. My chest tightened. I took a deep breath, fighting the urge to make him back off. Then he dropped to his knees in front of Adrian, looking more exhausted than ever.

"Thank you," he said softly as tears spilled down his cheeks. "Thank you for telling me and thank you for saving me." Adrian all but fell off his chair into a teary hug.

10

As nice as it was to know that there were no secrets between Michael, Alex, and Jack anymore, the atmosphere in Michael's home was getting colder by the day. Michael and Daniel had become monosyllabic, and Linda hadn't seemed herself for a while, turning quiet, shy and deferential. As much as Michael told me it wasn't my fault, I couldn't help thinking that it was, at least in part. It was obviously bothering Michael too, but he didn't seem to know how to thaw the ice and neither did I, so we'd taken to being out of the house as much as possible. Today we'd decided to visit the witches at the community centre. Apparently, Enid was going to be there, and I'd not met her yet.

"Off out?" asked Daniel from the kitchen as we headed for the door. Michael was in cargo shorts and a vest, which was all he had left as I'd taken to wearing all of his hoodies and sweaters. I'd given up almost entirely on wearing clothes that fitted me, aside from trousers, of course. Today I was wearing a nice pair of pink slacks Alex had lent me to go with Michael's cream sweater. Apparently, once upon a time, it had been white, until it was washed with an orange sock.

"Yep," said Michael as the door clattered shut behind us.

"Aren't you warm?" he asked as we walked down the street to Alex's hand in hand. Jack had agreed to give us a lift the rest of the way. He'd passed his driving test impressively quickly. Whatever that meant.

"A little," I said, rolling up my far too long sleeves, which immediately rolled down again. The summer sun was having another pass at cooking the Starkton tarmac. I didn't sweat nearly as much as Michael seemed to, but it could be a bit uncomfortable all the same.

"We could go shopping if you like, for more clothes in your size," he said.

"Do you want me to stop wearing yours?" I asked, doing my best to hide how disappointed I'd be if the answer was yes. I couldn't put a finger on why exactly, but I just felt safe in Michael's clothes. Perhaps it was because they were big enough for me to hide in, that or the smell.

"Not if you don't want to, whatever you want I don't mind," Michael smiled and deep in the pit of my stomach I felt warmth rising up into my chest, filling me up until I was at risk of bursting.

"I love you!" I said, flinging myself at Michael, wrapping my arms around his neck as his hands slid beneath me and he carried on down the road with me in his arms.

"I take it you're sticking to my clothes then," he said.

"Maybe I just like your style," I said, resting my head on Michael's shoulder.

"I don't think anyone's ever accused Michael of having style before," came Alex's voice from behind me.

"Hey, I went shopping with you that one time," said Michael in a mock offended voice, plopping me down next to Jack's car. Jack was already inside, fiddling with all the buttons and dials.

"So, why are we dropping you off at the old community centre?" asked Alex, climbing into the front passenger seat.

"We're going to visit our witch friends," said Michael.

"Naturally," said Jack, chuckling.

"Did I ever mention that I love knowing that you're a fay?" Alex asked, beaming back at me as he twisted round in his seat.

"Once or twice," I said. I couldn't help but smile. Alex had an innate enthusiasm about him.

"Do you want to come in and meet them?" Michael offered.

"Would love to, but we can't. We're going on the train to Manchester for a shopping day. You'll be alright finding your way back, right?" asked Alex.

"We'll be fine, don't worry," said Michael. The drive was smooth, except for the moments where Alex, apparently unnecessarily, would alarmingly blurt out warnings and expletives. Jack accused him several times of being a terrible passenger.

"Thank you for the lift," I said as I climbed out of the car.

"Thank you for saving me from a lifetime of imprisonment in a forest of nightmares," called Jack as they drove away.

"Well, that's certainly one way to get free lifts out of someone for life." Michael chuckled as we headed into the building.

A voice carried through the slightly open door to the coven meeting room. "Don't panic, just let me do the talking, okay?" It was Penny.

"You two should have told them, before they got here, they won't appreciate being ambushed," came a second, sterner voice.

"Well, consider my interest piqued," said Michael, with a cheeky smile that immediately dropped into a stern glare as he pushed the door open and saw who Penny had been talking to. Standing with her was an older woman in brownish green overalls and white hair, who I guessed was Enid, and Jude.

A shiver ran down my back and a painful pulse radiated through my body, originating at the back of my head at the sight of him. My breath caught in my chest and I couldn't seem to take in a lungful of air. I grasped desperately for Michael's hand, who'd frozen still in the doorway.

"What is he doing here?" Michael's voice was low and

Mothers, Witches and Queens

rigid, like he was struggling to open his mouth wide enough to speak past his clenched jaw. Jude didn't say a word, but his eyes were fixed on Michael.

"He thought… well, we thought… I thought—" Penny stumbled over her words.

"For heaven's sake, Penny, spit it out," Enid snapped, barely watching the scene as she fiddled with what looked like a fishing hook.

"Jude wanted to apologise. He wasn't himself, neither he nor Gwen were," said Penny, fidgeting awkwardly from one foot to the other.

"And what about after, when he was whispering nasty little ideas about Adrian into Jack's ear?" Michael's words dripped with anger. I couldn't blame Penny for being nervous.

"Jude?" Penny already sounded half defeated and desperate as she turned to Jude. Apparently, she had no explanation for his behaviour, which I'd guess she'd not known about it.

"I'm sorry," said Jude, barely taking his eyes off Michael for a second to direct them at me. They were glassy, almost vacant.

"Is that the best you can do? For attacking him, for terrifying him? He still has nightmares you know!" said Michael. He shifted, putting himself between Jude and myself. Jude was completely different when he was looking at Michael. His eyes came alive and his expressions would flicker and shift. When he was looking at me, he almost seemed numb somehow.

"I have these dreams—"

"We've heard all about the dreams," Michael barked, cutting him off.

"Jude's aren't like the rest of our dreams," said Penny.

"What are they like?" I asked, peeking around Michael. Part of me wanted to run away, but another part of me, a smaller, quieter part perhaps, wanted to know why. Why someone so seemingly harmless would be driven to hurt me, when the rest of the witches had only wanted to help?

"The others dream about stuff happening to you and Michael, stuff that's already happened or was happening usually. I have those dreams sometimes, but most of my dreams were about me and Michael." Jude's eyes lit up as he spoke. I recognised what he was feeling.

"Doing what?" Michael asked, no less stiff than before.

"All sorts of things," said Jude. "Going to school together, going to the cinema, swimming."

"Those are all things me and Adrian do together," said Michael, a little confusion mingling into his tone.

"I think he fell in love with you, in his dreams," I whispered to Michael's back.

"Gwen convinced me that if we could just get hold of Adrian, and get to the fay forest, all of my dreams would start to come true. She said we'd be more powerful in the fay forest, that we could make our dreams real. I let myself get carried away by her plans. I didn't realise she wasn't herself. I'm sorry." Again, he looked at me, and all that expression and hope and dreaminess dropped into a dull numbness. It was almost chilling.

"Well, I think I can understand falling in love with Michael," I said, watching with increasing fascination as Jude's light seemed to flicker on and off when he was or wasn't looking at Michael.

"Adrian, you don't have to accept any of this," said Michael, who either wouldn't or couldn't stop himself hating Jude.

"Michael is right. You don't have to forgive me or make excuses for me, but I was hoping I could maybe try to earn your forgiveness," said Jude. His words sounded sincere, but as he walked towards me, there wasn't even the slightest hint of life in him.

"That sounds fair," I said, resisting the urge to back away from him.

"Could we start with a hug, to seal the apology?" he asked vacantly.

"I-I'd rather not." I stuttered over the words, swallowing my guilt as my body involuntarily stiffened, although Jude didn't seem to care, his expression was detached and absent.

"Michael?" Jude turned, arms outstretched, almost draping himself across Michael as he went.

"No, you can't hug me," Michael said, taking me by the wrist as he backed away from Jude. Jude stumbled forward and then came to a complete stop for a second. Suddenly awkward with his arms outstretched, he stuffed his hands stuffed into his pockets.

"I should go. Thank you for hearing me out," said Jude flatly, and turned to leave. It was five seconds before a tingling sensation ran up my spine and as I span on the spot, I found myself face-to-face with Jude, only I knew it wasn't him. His hands outstretched like claws reached for the back of Michael's neck, his eyes blazed red. Without thinking, I thrust my palm forward, channelling water into his chest and slamming him off balance, sending him stumbling into the door which he fell through.

"What the fuck?" Michael growled, already having wheeled around, his shard of Excalibur forming a silver hammer in his hand.

"Wait," Penny yelled, pausing Michael's advance just long enough for me to slump into him as a sudden wave of fatigue washed over me. Michael's arm wrapped around me and held me up, giving Jude, no longer red eyed, but confused and pale looking, just enough time to disappear out of the doorway.

"What the hell was that?" I mumbled breathlessly.

"Not Jude," muttered Enid.

"He had the shade above him," said Michael, taking a step towards the door before pausing. I could feel the strain in his body, the competing urges to chase Jude and hold me.

"Like the one controlling Gwen?" Penny asked?

"Yes," he said gravely as both arms wrapped around me, pulling me to his side. There was a pause and silence fell, as

Mothers, Witches and Queens

we all waited for one of us to speak first, to know what to say. Already I was racing through thoughts. Jude, or rather the shade, had been reaching for Michael's neck. I could only think they were after his shard, a way into the fay forest. Just the same as when they'd kidnapped me.

"Nice hammer," said Enid, eventually breaking the silence as she hobbled over. "I favour a filleting knife myself," she said, flashing the nasty-looking blade she kept at her waistband.

"You weren't really going to use it on Jude were you?" asked Penny, her voice wobbling.

"My knife?" asked Enid.

"No, the hammer," said Penny, scowling at Enid.

"I was actually," said Michael, an air of defiance in his voice.

"But it's not his fault, is it? If something is possessing him like it did Gwen," said Penny defensively.

"No, but he did kidnap the lad's beau Penny, and was grabbing for his neck. Can't exactly blame him," said Enid who was in the process of lowering herself, quite awkwardly, onto one of Liz's various cushions that were scattered around.

"Luckily, there wasn't any need," I chipped in, wary that tensions were building.

"Yes, that was quite something. I bet you'd make a good fisherman," said Enid, flicking some grime out from beneath her thumbnail with her knife.

"But did you have to hit him quite so hard? You sent him flying," said Penny.

"Are you seriously blaming Adrian right now?" Michael bristled.

"He's Penny's current project," said Enid.

"That's not very nice, Enid. He's just not had a very good go of it lately. His parents aren't very nice about him being gay. And to be honest, they weren't much good before they knew either. He's just moved house, and unlike the rest of us, when our crafts started to get more potent, he just got those romantic dreams," said Penny.

"Perhaps that is because he never sticks at a craft for more than seventy-two hours," huffed Enid.

"He's a member of our coven just like you and he deserves respect, just like you. Just look at his succulent. Does that look healthy to you?" asked Penny, gesturing to Terrance's window succulents. The worst by far was Gwen's, which was now an almost entirely black and was sagging and cracking along the edges where it had dried out. Besides, it sat Jude's, which didn't look much better. It was turning a reddish-purple hue and seemed to have withered slightly.

"Hang on, those are new," said Michael, pointing to some smaller succulents on the far-right side of the shelf.

"Terrance just added those. They're for you two and your mother Linda. He said you made a wonderful impression, although he's not got your name tags made up yet," explained Penny.

Mothers, Witches and Queens

"Psychic vegetables aside, I believe we just witnessed a member of our coven possessed. I can't help feeling we should probably do something," said Enid, shifting the conversation.

"They're not vegetables," Penny muttered bitterly.

"Have either of you heard of The Hidden Queen?" I asked, trying to follow Enid's lead, who was already reminding me of Olivier.

"The who now?" said Enid, who seemed glad of the excuse to stop talking about Jude.

"It's just something that popped up in Gwen's things. We think it might be related to whatever was controlling her and Jude," I said, producing the tarot card and handing it around. Penny and Enid looked at it in turn.

"She doesn't look very nice, does she?" said Penny, which elicited an eye roll from Enid.

"Also, I was wondering where Gwen might be now. I mangled her hand pretty badly when I rescued Adrian," said Michael, taking the card to have another look at it.

"She's in the woods somewhere," said Enid, with a surprising amount of confidence.

"How do you know?" I asked.

"Saw it in the entrails. She's definitely in the woods. Couldn't tell ya where exactly or why, but that's where she is," said Enid.

"I suppose whatever that shade is, it must still be in control of her or she'd have come out of hiding," said Michael, passing the card back to me.

"She must be waiting for something," I said, thinking aloud as much as anything.

"What makes you say that?" asked Michael.

"Well, whatever it was or is, or whatever, it was pretty proactive before. Stalking me, kidnapping me, trying to take what it wanted. If it's content to hide out in the woods, it must think it's going to get what it wants some other way," I said.

"Or that Jude is going to get it instead," said Enid ominously.

11

"Michael, could you get the door please? I'm on the phone," Mum shouted up the stairs from the kitchen. Right when I was in the middle of my last set of press ups.

"I'll get it," said Adrian, climbing off my back, which made the whole thing altogether too easy. Adrian said it was because I was a champion that I was getting so strong. Whatever the case may be, it meant the home weights kit mum got me for my sixteenth birthday was totally useless now. I finished the set anyway and pulled on some shorts and a vest. Answering the door in just a pair of boxers didn't feel very polite, even if we were in a heat wave.

"Who is it?" I called, jogging down the stairs.

"Dunno," came Daniel's voice from the living room.

"Wasn't asking you," I replied. I hesitated when I got to the entrance hall. Whoever was at the door, Adrian hadn't let them in. In fact, he'd followed them out and closed the door behind him. Muffled sounds of speech were just about carrying into the entrance hall.

"Adrian, is everything okay?" I asked, pulling the door open. I found myself staring at the perfect, piercing blue eyes of Nimueh. She wasn't wearing a long flowing dress anymore though, more of a utilitarian leather tunic, similar to what she'd given me to wear when I was to become her champion. Her hair was now in a long tight ponytail and she looked all together more formidable.

"Hello, Michael," Nimueh's voice rumbled huskily as she locked eyes with me. She'd lost none of her arrogance, even if her clothes were fraying at the edges.

"What do you want?" I asked, stepping between her and Adrian as he shut the door behind me.

"I've come to make a trade," she said coyly, not breaking eye contact for a second. I imagine this is what it must feel like to lock eyes with a snake. Like if you look away for even a second, it might strike.

"What do you want?" I repeated.

"I want Adrian to grant me access to my lake," she said, with particular emphasis on the 'my'. Adrian and Olivier had worked together to make sure she couldn't get back in, after the mirelings finally vacated Lake Nimueh's shores.

"You could always ask Olivier about that. There was no need to come all the way out here," said Adrian, slipping his hand into mine behind my back.

"She has no business granting me permission to enter

Mothers, Witches and Queens

my home, it's bad enough having to ask you," said Nimueh, a snarl creeping into her voice.

"Don't speak to him in that tone," I barked.

Nimueh's nostrils flared, and for a second, I thought she'd jump for me, but she took a deep breath and stepped back.

"I don't come here empty-handed, like I said. I want to trade," said Nimueh. As she spoke, her shoulders rolled back, her tone softened, her eyes seemed to sparkle and flood with kindness. Suddenly the resemblance to Adrian was unmissable, the haunting eyes, the perfect alabaster skin, the shiny hair. It was like watching something shed its skin and transform.

"What is it you're offering?" asked Adrian.

"I know about The Hidden Queen," she said. A cruel smile curled her lips.

"How do you know that we're looking into that? Have you been spying on us?" I almost yelled and strangled my voice just in time. The last thing we needed was Daniel coming to the door. Although the cackle Nimueh loosed made the whole exercise seem pointless, anyway.

"Not you two. As much as it might surprise you to hear, I'm not particularly interested in the ill-fated romance of my disappointing son and his wasted champion," said Nimueh.

"Don't talk about him that way," I snarled, and her grin widened.

"Olivier has been making such a fuss trying to find what she could about it all. Inevitably word would reach me eventually. I may not hold my position any longer, but some still respect the old ways." She spoke with all the wasted grandeur of a deposed monarch, which I suppose is sort of what she was.

"What is it you think you know?" asked Adrian, a note of steel making its way into his voice now too.

"I know it's to do with The Hut. It's part of why Merlin was precious over that gnarled old trunk," she said.

"How do you know that?" Adrian asked, taking a step towards her. Her bait had worked.

"There was a time where Merlin and I would keep confidence. I spent many a night in his personal libraries," said Nimueh. Her cruel grin shrank to a coy smile and my stomach lurched. A small dark thought popping into my head of Adrian's mother and Merlin together.

"Is that all?" Adrian asked, either the same thought hadn't occurred to him, or he was ignoring it.

"Well, there is that, and the mirelings fleeing their own land. They seem to be evacuating The Hut in particular, gibbering about voices and whispering from the trees," she continued.

"Olivier did mention that mirelings had been behaving oddly," said Adrian, turning to me.

"Because something is happening inside The Hut, and if you want to get to the bottom of it, there's only one person who can help you: Merlin," said Nimueh.

"Merlin is a prisoner in mireling territory. He can't help anyone," I said.

Mothers, Witches and Queens

"So, break him out. You were the ones that put him there in the first place. Wouldn't you say you owed him that much?" Nimueh's voice was rumbling again, like the self-satisfied purr of a smug cat.

"You know that he literally tortured your son, not to mention the fact you were scheming to depose him yourself. Adrian's plan to get him imprisoned was just an improved version of your own selfish plans." The words poured out of me before I could stop them. I was sick of her and her nasty little jabs at Adrian. It was like she wanted to watch him squirm.

"You can fight it all you want. He's the only person that can help you get what you want and now you need to give me what I want," said Nimueh, talking past me to Adrian.

"I'm not going to give you access to the lake. Talk to Olivier, she's on the council of the fay. I'm not in charge of anything anymore, just like you," said Adrian bluntly.

"I'm not begging a half breed for access to my own home," Nimueh snarled, jerking forward as she spoke, leaving only inches between herself and Adrian, saliva flying from her mouth as she spat the words. Adrian flinched and cowered away from her, his grip on my hand tightening.

"Don't speak to him like that!" The command reverberated out of me as though it was already an echo, as if I was in a cave it had been bouncing around inside. Nimueh's eyes glazed over and she fell mute.

"You voiced her," said Adrian.

"Leave," I said, this time on purpose. In an instant she turned on her heel, disappearing down the path.

"That would have come in handy a few years ago," Adrian said.

"I'm sorry, I wouldn't usually use my powers like that but... I was just sick of her speaking to you like that and she wasn't any help, anyway. She was just messing with us," I said.

"Actually, she did give me one idea," said Adrian, a mischievous smile was creeping across his face.

"We're not breaking Merlin out, right?" I asked.

"No, but we could pay those libraries she was so proud of lounging around in, a visit," said Adrian, giving a wink.

"Mum, we're going out!" I shouted back into the still half-open door and then slammed it closed and Adrian and I hurried across the road to Mr Davies' oak tree.

12

Olivier met us as we entered the forest and walked us to Merlin's old residence. We'd have gotten lost on the way without her. Since he'd been overthrown, permission to reach his old home had been revoked for almost everyone, for security reasons. Besides the odd elf and gnome milling about tending to the roots along the yellow brick path, it was a relatively uninterrupted walk. Although I could still feel eyes on me, apparently it didn't matter that the courts didn't rule anymore. Even an ex-fay lord was worthy of a good ogling. Then again, I was also standing next to a prince champion, so maybe it was that. I distracted myself by filling Olivier in on Nimueh's visit as we walked.

"Well, that doesn't surprise me. She wasn't a very good mother, or leader, or person really," said Olivier as we rounded the corner of Merlin's hillock, now overgrown with thorns and nettles. His small doorway was guarded on either side by particularly tall sylphs, whose hands grazed the floor as they stooped slightly as most full-grown sylph do.

"Councillor Olivier," said the guards, both giving a quick deferential bow before letting us pass into Merlin's former home. The small entrance hall remained largely unchanged. We descended the staircase into the first major room. Scrolls and shattered glass vials littered the floor of the laboratory, just as they had the last time we were here. Unlike when Merlin lived here, the torches weren't lit, instead the darkness was overcome by gently glowing phosphorescent fungus. My stomach squirmed as memories of this place threatened to fill my mind and my eyes darted around the room instinctively, scanning for any sign of the old enchanter. Even though the logical part of me knew he wouldn't be there. I couldn't quite talk myself out of my breath quickening and my chest tightening as I attached myself to Michael's arm.

"Are you okay?" he asked, wrapping his other arm around me protectively.

"It's just a bit … unsettling, being back here, it brings back memories." I said, trying to ignore the image of Merlin's silvery cauldron forcing its way into my mind. Of him breathing black smoke into my lungs, of his voice bouncing around my head, rocking me with so much pain I thought I would surely die. In spite of myself, my chest was tightening, my hands were clammy, darkness was encroaching on the corners of my vision.

Mothers, Witches and Queens

"Adrian? Adrian, are you okay?" Michael asked again.

"C-can't catch my breath," I wheezed, slumping against Michael as my legs went numb. He dropped to his knees, holding me in his lap.

"Breathe Adrian, just breathe, just breathe, love," said Michael. He was trying to sound calm, but I could hear the quaver in his voice. I felt his hand gripping mine tightly. I focused on that, on my hands, on the tightness, squeezing his back as hard as I could. Just the squeezing and squeezing and tightness and little by little my chest started to loosen. I realised as my breath started to return to me that I'd shut my eyes tight.

"Is he okay?" Olivier's voice sounded unusually panicked.

"I'm okay now," I said. I opened my eyes, and there they were, Olivier and Michael both kneeling, looking down at me, with faces full of relief.

"I'm so sorry I brought you here, Adrian, I didn't think," said Michael, as he ever so gently pushed my hair out of my eyes.

"Don't be sorry, it was my idea to come here, not yours," I said softly, struggling to sit up.

"Why don't you two wait upstairs with the guards, and I'll have a look around," said Olivier, standing and offering me a hand up.

"I think that's for the best," said Michael, placing a supporting hand at the small of my back as he guided me back up the stairs. Scarcely could I remember a time when I felt more relieved to get out into the loamy air of the fay forest. I looked around the emerald world, filling my lungs as my chest finally loosened.

"Better?" asked Michael, smiling down at me.

"Much, and now I think you should go back down and help Olivier," I said, giving his hand a squeeze.

"I'm sure she won't mind me staying up here," said Michael.

"She won't, but it was our idea to come here and now we've left her down there alone and two heads are better than one. Not to mention you're the only one of us who's actually seen the shade, not just a sketch of it. You might see something the rest of us would miss," I said, reaching up on my tiptoes to plant a kiss on his cheek.

"Are you sure?" he asked before lifting me from my lower back with one arm, pressing our lips together as his other hand cupped the back of my head. A shiver ran through my whole body, prickling my skin as I resisted the urge to slip my hands under his shirt in front of the sylph guards.

"I'm sure," I breathed huskily, gazing up into his warm eyes as the kiss separated and he held me an inch from his face. He smiled, his cheeks turning crimson, planted one more kiss and gently set me down.

"Okay, I'll be as quick as I can," he said. Michael disappeared into Merlin's labyrinthine home and I smiled as I watched him go, only slowly becoming aware of two pairs of sylphan eyes on me. I tipped my head towards the staring guards and they snapped back to attention, as if they'd never been looking.

"That was hot," the taller one whispered to me.

"I know, right?" I said, as a peel of laughter rolled out of me.

* * *

I didn't like leaving Adrian, especially not after a kiss like that. I'd much rather find a private spot in the forest and have my way with him. Unfortunately, he was right, as he usually was, and the quicker we found what we were looking for, the quicker I could get him back home safe and sound. Not to mention, it would be good not to be living in fear of a possessed Gwen turning up at our door with a blood monster in her wake.

"Is he okay?" Olivier asked, whilst inspecting a pile of scrolls, tossing each one over her shoulder once she was finished with it. I got the sense she was quite enjoying chucking Merlin's things about.

"I think so. It's not the first time something like that's happened," I said as I looked around the room somewhat aimlessly, hoping something Hidden Queenish or shade-like might catch my eye. Perhaps I'd know it when I saw it. I didn't really know what I was doing. I'd never been much of a researcher.

"I didn't think it was. Let's check his war room," said Olivier, crossing to a torch mount on the far wall. She pulled it down and a creaking, groaning sound filled the room. The ground shuddered momentarily and then all at once, a patch of stone floor began to fold away. A descending entrance to a spiralling staircase emerged in the middle of the room.

"Did he have any rooms he didn't hide behind a pulley or a lever?" I asked, following Olivier as she descended the staircase.

"Not from his main quarters, although a lot of stuff leads off from down here. It's a bit like a rabbit warren. You've just got to know the right lever to pull to get into it, that's all," she said. As we reached the bottom of the staircase, torches burst into flame along the walls of what turned out to be a large, circular room. Five arched doorways surrounded us. In the centre stood a vast table, the length and width of roughly two snooker tables, which I'd always thought were overly large anyway. Upon it were little figurines and raised sections, like a topographical map, the largest of which was Grandfather Tree, which ascended about twice as high off the map as anything else. Followed by The Hut, which was about half the height, but sprawled out much wider. It sat right on the border of the area marked 'mireling swamps', which was a much murkier, darker green than the area marked 'fay forest', which took up most of the table.

"This has got to be the biggest table I've ever seen," I said.

Mothers, Witches and Queens

"You should see Muterra's dining table. It could double as longboat," said Olivier with a chuckle, as she crossed to some discarded papers to flick through.

"Where do these arches lead?" I asked.

"Oh, right, his library, his main lab, the one upstairs is just a front, his bedroom, his baths, and his personal museum." Olivier pointed to each arch as she named them.

"I'm not sure which is more ridiculous, that he has his own baths or his own personal museum," I said.

"The latter, if you ask me," said Olivier, who'd set off walking towards said museum.

"We're not gonna try the library first?" I asked.

"I've spent hundreds of hours in that library and never seen any mention of The Hidden Queen. I've spent considerably less time in the museum," said Olivier.

"I can guess why," I said, as we made out down the corridor. Flickering torch light illuminated the yellowing brick work, until the pathway opened out into a domed room. Rows of glass display cases lined the room, whilst various paintings hung on the walls.

"You start bottom right, I'll start top left," said Olivier, splitting off from me to go and glare at various displays in the far corner of the room. The first case I came to was in the far right corner and contained an unfurled scroll of parchment. It took a moment to realise what I was reading.

Announcing the birth of the 21st generation in the line of Nimueh

Adrian Lake

Beneath the announcement was a picture, a pencil and water-colour sketch of a baby, with a shock of blonde hair and piercing blue eyes.

"Olivier, why does Merlin have documents announcing the birth of Adrian in this cabinet?" I asked, unable to peel my eyes away from the picture. I knew it was Adrian. Even as a baby I could recognise his perfect little features. Naturally, Mum had bombarded Adrian with so many of my baby pictures that I'd gone numb to the embarrassment by now, but I'd never seen one of Adrian. Nimueh wasn't exactly the baby book type.

"Oh, I forgot that was there," said Olivier, crossing the room.

"Why is it there, is what I'm asking," I said. It was making me uneasy, to think of Merlin treasuring something like this, something to do with Adrian. I didn't want to think of him possessing any part of Adrian.

"This is a museum and his birth was quite historic," explained Olivier in a tone that implied I probably shouldn't have needed that explaining.

"Because he was a fay lord?" I asked.

"Because he was the first male to be born to the line of Nimueh in twenty-one generations, it was quite a scandal. Was the talk of the forest for years," she said.

"He never told me that," I said, turning to face Olivier.

"Does that surprise you? He grew up with everyone he ever met knowing who he was, what an upset his birth had been. Why, when he met someone who didn't know, would he tell them?" she said.

"Why was it an upset?" I asked, around the lump forming in my throat.

"The fay have long memories, are fond of tradition and the line of Nimueh is passed down through mothers. The dryads were the de facto leaders of the courts because of their connection to the forest itself. But no one family line is more illustrious than Adrian's. People didn't like to see it disrupted." A forlorn look had fallen across Olivier's face.

"So… people had a problem with Adrian?" I asked, as awful images of little Adrian growing up hated flickered through my mind.

"Not quite… he was still a high fay lord-in-waiting. It's more like there was an atmosphere, something unspoken. It didn't help that Nimueh treated it as a personal failure that she'd had a son. Adrian was sensitive, even as a child. He knew people treated him strangely, even before he knew why," said Olivier.

"Was it like that when you were born too? You're from the same family, right?" I asked.

"Oh no, I'm descended from the same man as Nimueh. We don't share the same mother. I wasn't really considered connected to the Nimueh line. Not to mention, Mum was a gnome, so I was much more in the background, not like Adrian," Olivier said.

"Is this why Nimueh is so awful to him?" I asked.

"Well, she was never exactly a treat, but she was worse to him. She definitely held that against him," she said.

"He never talks about this stuff. Should I talk to him about this stuff?" I asked. Olivier shrugged and her eyebrows furrowed for a moment before she spoke again.

"Adrian was scared to become an agent of the Excalibur system, you know. He saw it as a responsibility, something he might fail at. A chance to let everyone down, let everyone down again, is probably what he'd have said. He didn't see the upside, but I did. I pushed for him to become an agent, because in the still world, nobody would know him, nobody would know about his birth, nobody would think he was a let-down. It was a chance for him to just be him, outside the fay forest, then he met you and he got exactly that. It's no wonder he never wanted to come back." Her eyes were sparkling. She gave a little sniffle and turned away from me, wiping her nose with her sleeve.

I remembered the first day I met Adrian, the light, breezy boy that literally fell into my life. I was under his spell from the first moment. I'd never have guessed he was running away from so much. My eye wandered across the exhibition, seeking a distraction, and I found myself drawn to a painting in the far corner of the room. It was split down the middle. On one side was a picture of a man with flowing grey hair and wise eyes, floating above a silvery cauldron. The backdrop was a dark and cloudy night with a crescent moon peeking out. On the other a woman, surrounded by orange autumn leaves and trees, bathed in sunlight, with

Mothers, Witches and Queens

wild red hair painted almost like fire, floating above a tree stump.

"Who's that?" I asked, pointing to the painting.

"It's Merlin and Morgana. It's very, very old. This must have been done before the civil war," said Olivier, sending a jolt of excitement through me, as she studied the picture. Adrian had mentioned that name before when he'd been studying Gwen's cards.

Goosebumps tracked across my spine. The memory of the shade burned in my mind, settling like a mould over the image before me. They had the same hair, same face shape, but what I couldn't tear my gaze away from was the eyes. Bright red, almost glowing. Adrian was right, they did look similar. I noticed as I stared that Morgana's eyes looked directly out of the painting, whilst Merlin's were cast sideways, as if he was stealing a glance at Morgana.

"Could it be her?" I asked.

Olivier frowned. "Well, the prevailing story suggests Merlin killed her, but some versions speak of her being imprisoned," she said.

"Were they lovers?" I asked, my mind flickering back to all the times Adrian and I would meet people and I'd catch myself staring at Adrian, rather than the person we were talking to.

"Why d'you ask?" Olivier asked.

"Look at the way he's looking at her," I said.

"According to the stories she was his apprentice, but it was so long ago, and the only person there at the time refused to elaborate. Merlin was very tight-lipped about his past," she said.

"But did he ever have any lovers?" I asked, a little impatiently.

"None that weren't kept a secret," said Olivier, watching me as I traced a line from Merlin's eyes to Morgana with my finger.

"I have a hunch," I said and set off back down the tunnel out of the museum. "Merlin was a man who kept secrets and didn't like to show weakness, right?"

"Correct," said Olivier.

"If she was his lover, then perhaps he couldn't bring himself to kill her and that's why the imprisonment story exists. But that would be a weakness, so perhaps he tried to steer the story towards the idea he killed her. And invented the idea of her as his apprentice, rather than his lover," I said.

"Following so far," said Olivier.

"Okay, assuming all that is true, he wouldn't keep information about his lover in a museum. He'd keep it in his bedroom," I said, turning down the arched corridor Olivier had pointed out earlier.

"You're making a lot of assumptions right now, Michael," Olivier warned.

"I've got what Mum calls a piggy feeling, just go with it," I said as we stepped out into a rather lavish bed chamber. As in the war room, torches flickered into light upon our entrance. The walls were decorated with more paintings.

A bookshelf rested against the far wall, next to a fireplace and an armchair. In the centre lay an enormous fourposter bed, with green curtains draped across each side.

"You check the bookshelf," I said as I started taking a lap of the room, scanning each picture in turn. They were somewhat chaotically dotted across the walls in various frames, from large ovals to small squares at seemingly random heights. There were all sorts, ranging from lakes to impressions of Excalibur, to forest vistas, even the odd portrait of Merlin himself, but no sign of Morgana. I sighed and sat down on the corner of the bed, pushing the velvet curtain back slightly, when a glint of red caught my eye.

I'd expected darkness behind the curtains, a secluded undisturbed place to sleep, but in fact it was cast in a faint red glow. I looked up and froze. For a moment I was looking into two piercing red eyes, but as my eyes adjusted to the light, I realised they were rubies. Glowing rubies set into a wooden carving in the ceiling of the bed frame.

"I think I'm knowing it when I see it," I said with a slight grin, curling my lips, thinking of how frustrating Adrian had found that instruction.

"What've you found?" asked Olivier, pulling back the curtain properly, to look into the ruby eyes. Firelight flooded into the curtained chamber of the bed, revealing the full wood carving. Above Merlin's bed, where he slept each night, there was a beautiful woman with flowing hair and piercing glowing eyes surrounded on all sides by craning forest branches.

"Okay, I'm coming round to the lover's theory," said Oliver, reaching up to run her fingers over the woodwork. Both of us flinching slightly as upon brushing her finger over one of the rubies, it clicked back into its setting for a moment.

"What was that?" I asked.

"Well, he did love a secret mechanism," said Olivier. Reaching the other hand up, she pressed both eyes at once. There was a clicking, whirring sound as they ascended into the carving, and at the same time a hatch popped open at the carving's feet. Releasing a small shelf, upon which lay a book.

"He had a flare for the dramatic. I'll give him that," I said, reaching up to grab the book. It was a notebook with a handwritten title.

Solving Morgana

"Give it here," said Oliver, adjusting her glasses as she took the book from me and began to skim read it voraciously. I'd have protested were it not for that fact I'm not particularly good at reading squiggly joined up writing.

"What's it say?" I asked, in response to which Olivier held up a finger as if to shush me.

"She was his apprentice, showed great promise blah blah blah, he thought she might prove even more skilled than him, blah blah blah," Olivier said, flicking through the pages, her eyes wild, overtaken with urgency. "I think he was halfway between scared of her and attracted to her. He mentions her appearing in his dreams, dreaming of her taking a throne, to rule over fay and mirelings alike. He suspected it wasn't him dreaming of her, feared she might be trying to exert her will." At this, Olivier and I locked eyes.

"That must be what she did to Gwen," I said.

"But why would she not have done it before now?" asked Olivier.

"Maybe Gwen reached her somehow, when the coven started to have their psychic dreams," I said, speculating.

"But then, where is she?" asked Olivier.

"Keep reading," I said. Olivier nodded, her eyes returning to the book as she carried on skimming.

"He was falling for her, but part of him knew she was manipulating him. He chose himself over her, but he couldn't bring himself to kill her so he…" Once again Olivier looked up from the notebook, her eyes wide, the effect only enhanced by her glasses.

"What?" I asked, developing the same feeling of urgency.

"He sealed her inside The Hut, physically in the wood of the thing. She's still in there now, trapped in a dream inside a tree," said Olivier, dropping the book.

"Hidden away," I breathed, goose bumps prickling my skin.

"A Hidden Queen," said Olivier, as a shiver ran down my back.

"Nimueh mentioned something about mirelings turning

up scared, complaining of whispers from within the trees," I said, climbing off the bed.

"Whatever woke up the coven in the still world to their dreams, it must have reached Morgana too," said Olivier, following me as we raced out of the Merlin's room, through the war room, up the spiral staircase and out of the entrance into the green half-light of the forest, barely even noticing we were panting as adrenaline coursed through.

"What got you two all sweaty?" Adrian asked, perched on a tree stump opposite the door. He was halfway through making a daisy chain.

"We've found her!" I all but shouted, both sylphs jumping from the sudden volume.

"Shhh… not here," said Olivier, taking me in one hand and fetching Adrian before stepping onto the winding path of the forest.

"She was in there?" Adrian whispered, looking up bewildered.

"No, this was," said Olivier, slipping the notebook into Adrian's hands. As we walked, he started to skim read, and I watched as his eyes peeled wide.

"Well now I know why Gwen wanted to get into the forest so badly," said Adrian, now safely ensconced in Olivier cottage.

"She wants to break herself out. She might even know Merlin is out of her way too," said Olivier, chewing nervously on a pencil.

Mothers, Witches and Queens

"This explains Jude's dreams about you too," said Adrian, looking up at me.

"We need to warn the coven. She might try to control someone else. They've all had weird dreams," I said, standing suddenly.

"And what do we do about her? If she's making mirelings go mad, it might only be a matter of time before she starts taking control of them too," said Adrian, looking worried.

"Clearly, she needs something mirelings don't have, or she'd surely be out already. She'd just have to twist the mind of one goblin. Anyway, you leave this side of things to me. All you two have to do is make sure Gwen, or Morgana, I suppose I should say, doesn't find a way into the fay forest," said Olivier, who was already in the process of changing into more formal robes, she must have been planning a council meeting.

"Let's get back then, before Daniel and Mum start looking for us," I said, taking Adrian's hand.

"Do you think we'll be able to get Gwen back?" Adrian asked as we approached the grove.

"I hadn't really thought about it," I said. I must admit, although I knew it wasn't her fault, I still found it hard to forgive the woman who had smashed Adrian over the back of the head.

"I hope we can. All she wanted was to be a witch after all," said Adrian, as he took my hand and we slipped through the tree, back into the world of Starkton and grey skies and—

"What the hell—" Adrian and I froze as sitting at the bottom of Mr Davies' driveway, watching us step out of his old oak tree, was Daniel, eyes wide, mouth agape.

"Daniel, we can explain," I said, watching him get to his feet, but he wasn't looking at me. His eyes were fixed on Adrian.

"You'd better," he said.

PART III

CORONATION

1

Since the discovery in Merlin's bedroom, Adrian and I had been spending the last couple of days stalking Starkton woods on the lookout for Gwen, but to no avail. So, we decided to take a day off. Hopefully, with us gone she'd come out of hiding. That was the theory anyway.

"What are you up to Mr?" I asked from the armchair. Adrian was perched cross-legged under a blanket, glued to his phone, even though Charmed was on. Adrian didn't miss Charmed for anything, and I still wasn't entirely convinced he knew how to use that phone. There was a very real chance that whilst he thought he was texting someone, he may in fact just be writing notes to himself in the notes app. Whatever the case, he was fully absorbed.

"What? Sorry I'm not doing anything," said Adrian, quickly shoving his phone down under the blankets before turning to me with an innocent smile plastered across his face. His alabaster cheeks burnished pink, his sapphire eyes twinkling, his white blonde hair tumbling down like shafts of golden light peeking through the clouds, shining across the ocean.

My mouth was very dry. I'm not sure how long I spent open mouthed staring at him, long enough for my mouth to get very dry.

"You're up to something, but don't worry, I'll get to the bottom of it, you'll see," I said, climbing out of my chair.

"Where are you off to?" asked Adrian, who now seemed to be messing with his phone under the blankets.

"Cup of tea?" I asked.

"Oo yes please!" said Adrian. His eyes lit up more than they already were if that was at all possible. I'd been out of the room for two minutes at most when I heard what could only be described as a whoop of delight from the living room.

"If I didn't know better, I'd think you had a fancy man on the side," I said, poking my head round the corner, kettle in hand.

"Like a guy in a suit with a twiddly moustache? Why would I keep one of those on the side?" asked Adrian, looking genuinely puzzled. My cheeks ached, and I realised I was grinning like a goon, overwhelmed by the urge to hug Adrian and kiss Adrian and squeeze Adrian. I guess this is what people mean when they say that cuteness causes an aggression response.

Mothers, Witches and Queens

"You okay, Michael?" he asked. I must have been staring at him again.

"Listen, okay, this isn't fair. I keep trying to confront you, but you're being mindbogglingly beautiful and it is making it very difficult for me to think straight," I said, pouting as I dumped the kettle on the kitchen side and all but leaped onto the sofa next to Adrian.

"I'm not doing it on purpose, I promise," said Adrian, quickly shoving his phone under his bum as I landed with a thud on the sofa.

"Are you sure? It's very suspicious the way your eyes twinkle and your hair cascades and your lips be all... you know, soft and... nice you know... how they are..." My thoughts drifted off as I found myself hypnotised by his soft, thick, pink lips, his smile, perfect and sweet and innocent.

"Michael?" Adrian asked again, his eyes big and bright and distracting as usual.

"You're doing it again, you're distracting me, and I won't stand for it," I said, as I began tickling him along his ribs. Adrian squirmed, grabbing me by the wrists as peals of laughter erupted out of him. He was wiggling furiously, but he couldn't get away. For one thing, I'm much stronger than he is, and for another, he was sitting on his feet.

"Michael, ahh stop, hahaha, Michael I'm gonna peee!" Adrian squealed between panting and laughing as he fell over backwards lying across the sofa and I scrabbled on top of him, pinning him down.

"I can't let you go until I find out what you're up to!" I said, sticking my tongue out as him as he squealed and giggled and squirmed.

"It's a surprise!" he managed to shout between the laughing fits.

"For me?" I asked, pausing to let him catch his breath as he lay beneath me panting and giggling and being generally heart meltingly adorable.

"Of course, who else?" Adrian asked, as he sat up and hugged me around the waist.

"Have I spoiled it?" I asked, knitting my fingers into his hair as he hugged me.

"Do you know what it is?" Adrian asked in a muffled voice, speaking into my vest.

"Haven't the foggiest," I said.

"Well then it's not spoiled, now weren't you making us tea?" Adrian asked with a wink, as he relinquished the hug.

"On it, right away, you keep being surprising," I said as I climbed off him, heading back into the kitchen. The sound of Daniel's bedroom door clattering shut caught my ear as I clicked the kettle on. He'd barely left his room for the last couple of days. Adrian had suggested I speak to him, and part of me wanted to. Part of me wanted to apologise. I hadn't meant to hurt his feelings, but then I'd remember him yelling and jabbing his finger at Adrian. Trying to tell me how to live my life and then it'd all happen again. My jaw would get tight, and I'd get hot, and I'd want to yell.

"Tea's ready," I said, carrying in a tray with two mugs

Mothers, Witches and Queens

full of tea and a large teapot for refills. With Adrian it was always a good idea to have refills.

"Thank you," said Adrian, getting up from the sofa. As I laid the tray down on the table he leaned in and planted a kiss on my neck. A shiver ran along my skin, leaving a wave of goosebumps in its wake.

"Ready for a break?" I asked. My voice was low and rumbling, my hands already snaking around his body. One slipping under his shirt, taking a firm grip of his hip, eliciting a gasp, the other sliding to his thigh.

"Yea," Adrian breathed, almost soundlessly as our eyes locked, his half lidded and irresistible, a small smile curling at the edges. Without another word I lifted him off his feet, holding him against my body. Adrian wrapped his legs around my waist as I carried him up the stairs. One hand took my neck from behind, pulling me into a deep, hungry kiss, stealing my breath, the other glided under my shirt, prickling my skin as his fingers traced the ridges of my back. I'd noticed Adrian was particularly passionate about my back. I broke the kiss, and began attacking his neck, coaxing out his aching irresistible moans as his breath caught in his chest, his nails digging into my shoulders and neck as I kicked my bedroom door shut with such force it's a wonder it didn't burst its hinges.

Adrian and I spent the rest of the day wrapped up in each other's bodies in my bed, him occasionally demanding I shut my eyes so he could do something conspiratorial on his phone. I didn't mind. In fact, it was the best day I'd had in ages.

"Shower time, Mr," said Adrian, after an alarm rang on his phone.

"What's the alarm for?" I asked, not moving. To be fair, he hadn't either, and he was currently using my chest as a pillow.

"Cause you're stinky!" said Adrian, pointing to my armpit.

"You didn't seem to mind earlier," I said with a wink and watched his face flush pink, drawing me into a cheek aching grin.

"It's for the surprise," said Adrian as his cheeks darkened further whilst I not so subtly flexed my bicep at him, pretending to scratch my head.

"Are you okay Adrian? You're turning red. Maybe you've got a fever," I teased, barely managing to keep a straight face.

"Just get in the shower!" he said, doing his best to sound authoritative. It wasn't very convincing.

"Okay fine, but only because I'm worried you'll turn into a tomato if I stay here any longer," I said, kissing him on the nose as I slipped out of bed, heading for the shower. When I got back to my room Adrian was gone and an outfit was laid out for me. My favourite pair of baby blue linen shorts and a pink polo shirt Adrian had got me that wasn't really big enough for my arms. I'm pretty sure that is why he'd got it for me.

Mothers, Witches and Queens

"What is he up to?" I said to myself as I got dressed and headed downstairs, looking for my scheming boyfriend.

"Adrian?" I called as I got into the kitchen and found it completely empty, aside from the addition of a few corner shop plastic bags. I got no response, but there was a rustling sound coming from the living room.

"SURPRISE!" A wall of sound, jumping people and splayed arms hit me as I pushed open the door to the living room and I almost jumped out of my skin. It took me a moment to register who I was looking at. Jack and Alex and Jess and Sam and, of course, Adrian. They were lucky I didn't reach for my shard of Excalibur with the shock they gave me.

"What's all this for?" I asked as I struggled to catch my breath.

"It was all Adrian's idea. He's had us all in a group chat all day. Like a little general, he's been ordering us around," said Alex with a chuckle.

"We brought snacks," said Sam and Jess as each took a step apart, revealing the coffee table, waving their arms before it, as if they were presenting a prize on an old game show. It was laden down with crisps, spicy dips, gummy sweets and those ring biscuits everyone used to have at kids' parties.

"And we brought the drinks!" said Alex as Jack raised his arms, holding an intimidatingly large bottle of clear booze in each hand.

"You've got juice and stuff, right?" asked Jack.

"Mixers, he means mixers," said Alex.

"Whatever, yes, mixers," said Jack, rolling his eyes.

"I don't understand, why... why did you do all this?" I asked, turning to Adrian as a heady mix of confusion and excitement washed through my system.

"I just thought, what with you being suspended, you wouldn't be able to see your friends and it might be nice to see them right now, with everything that's been going on. I hope you don't mind," said Adrian, suddenly nervous.

"Mind? Of course, I don't mind, this is amazing!" I said as that cute aggression feeling kicked in again and I rushed him, scooping him up in my arms and spinning him round the room, peppering him with kisses.

"Right, now that that's settled, what do we do first?" I asked as I set Adrian down and he wobbled into me. Apparently, I'd made him a bit dizzy.

"Let's play a drinking game, I suggest, never have I ever," said Alex, with a big grin on his face.

"Alex, you get that if we call something you have done you have to drink?" said Jess.

"Yep," said Alex.

"And you have always done everything," said Sam.

Yep," said Alex, his grin broadening.

"Oh, he gets it," said Jack.

"So, Alex just wants to get drunk then?" asked Adrian, altogether too earnestly.

"Bingo!" declared Alex, as Sam and Jess fell about

laughing. Jack started pouring drinks into a stack of those red plastic cups you see in every American teen movie.

2

My mouth was dry, and my head was pounding. When I opened my eyes, my vision blurred at first, but slowly the room swam into view. I was in Michael's lap, in the armchair. Alex and Jack were next to each other on the floor with just cushions around them, whilst Sam and Jess spooned on the sofa. Open bottles and cups and crisp wrappers were scattered around the room. As I sat up, my head rocked like there was a boulder rolling around in there and I had to resist the urge to be sick. The room was cast in that strange blue half-light of the early morning. It must have been four, maybe five o'clock. I gently slipped off Michael's lap and tiptoed my way through the wreckage of last night towards the kitchen in search of relief. I had my head under the tap, letting the cool soothing water flow into me, drinking as much as I could, whilst any I spilled absorbed into my skin, when I heard Daniel's voice.

"You know we have cups for that right? Or do they not have those in whatever place you're from?" He was holding a nearly empty bottle. It looked like one Alex had brought. Apparently, the name meant water in another language, but it tasted nothing like water.

"Sorry, I was just in a rush I guess," I said, turning the tap off while I went to get a glass.

"You've got much bigger things to apologise for than that you know," said Daniel. He was swaying on his feet as he spoke, his words coming out a little slurred.

"I'm sorry we kept our secret from you, Daniel. Nobody meant to hurt your feelings," I said softly as I filled my glass.

"Not just that though, is it? You... well, maybe I shouldn't say," said Daniel. He swayed backwards onto his heels and closed his mouth tight, as if he was trying to stop something from getting out.

"Say what?" I asked, a little spark of panic lighting through me. Daniel had plenty of nasty things he had no problem saying to me. I dreaded to think what he was holding back.

"No, it's not for me to say," he said, shaking his head and upsetting his balance, sending him clattering into the kitchen counter.

"Maybe you should sit down," I said as I took his hand, hoping to steady him, but he snatched it back, knocking a red plastic cup flying across the room. I flinched away, my head pounding at all the movement.

"Don't touch me. You don't get to touch me," he said, steadying himself on the wall.

"I'm sorry. I was just trying to help," I said.

"Ha! That's a good one," he sneered, pulling himself up to his full height.

"What d'you mean?" I asked, my voice strangling slightly.

"Fine, I'll tell you, but don't say I didn't warn you." Daniel paused, steadying himself. "You're the opposite of helpful. You're ruining Michael's life, you know. Getting suspended from school, giving up on uni, falling out with his family. All so he can lark about in the woods with you. Do you really think you're worth all that?" Daniel lurched forward, jabbing his finger into my chest as he spoke, it stung, and his breath stunk of alcohol.

"M-Michael said he was choosing what he wanted for himself n-not for me." I stuttered pathetically over my words as I took a step back, willing myself not to cry. I'd asked for this. I couldn't go getting upset about getting what I'd asked for.

"And you believed him? No offence, Adrian, but I thought you were smart enough to have figured this out for yourself. He's only saying that shit for you. None of it's true," said Daniel.

"I th-think he means it," I mumbled, as tears stung the corners of my eyes.

"See, this is exactly what I'm talking about. Crying the moment someone says something you don't like. Is it any wonder he has to lie to you? Am I meant to feel bad for you? That might work on Michael and Mum, but it doesn't work on me," said Daniel.

"Linda?" I choked on the word, dreading what came next.

"Oh, come on, you know what you're doing, emotional blackmail. That's why she lets you stay. Do you think she is pleased you're ruining his life, always being around? You're a pain Adrian, you're underfoot. Mum's sick of it, truth be told," said Daniel.

"L-Linda wants me gone?" I asked, swallowing around the lump in my throat. Sweat beaded all over me, and I felt like I was going to be sick again.

"How could she not? You, swanning around her home all day, it'd be better for everyone if you just left. Sounds like that Olivier person you abandoned could use your help too!" he said as he took the last swig of the bottle and grimaced.

"How do you know about Olivier?" I asked.

"Oh, didn't you notice? You dropped this the other day," said Daniel as he retrieved a small, perfectly smooth black stone from his pocket.

"My whispering stone," I said. I took a step forward, but Daniel stretched his arm up high out of my reach.

"Is that what you call it? I did think it was weird how it started talking," he said. My heart jumped and my stomach flipped sickeningly. Olivier wouldn't use the stone unless it was important, and I'd missed it.

Mothers, Witches and Queens

"When did it speak?" I asked, panic flooding over me.

"A few minutes ago, not long after your friend left, whilst you and Michael were all over each other like a rash, no doubt," said Daniel bitterly.

"What did she say? Hang on, what friend?" My mind raced, my head pounding. Daniel wasn't making any sense and everyone from the party was still passed out in the living room.

"Oh, I don't know, something about the queen's already in the forest or some rubbish. She sounded scared though," said Daniel. A faint smile played on his lips as he ignored half my question, picking his answers maliciously.

"I've got to go," I said, my breath running short, my legs beginning to tremble. Daniel wasn't going to help me. I could see that and the forest and everyone in it were in danger. I didn't have time to work out his riddles. They were probably just meant to upset me anyway.

"Yes, you should go. Go back to your own family and stop ruining mine. And don't even think about taking Michael with you," said Daniel as he started wobbling towards the stairs.

I wanted to wake him and tell him everything, but Daniel's voice was ringing in my head. You're ruining Michael's life, a pain, underfoot, Mum's sick of it, that Olivier person you abandoned could use your help. Don't even think about taking Michael with you. You're ruining Michael's life, a pain, underfoot, Mum's sick of it, that Olivier person you abandoned could use your help. Don't even think about taking Michael with you. Over and over, it played in my head, all the while a big hot heavy lump was forming in the pit of my stomach.

I stood in the doorway to the living room and took a long, lingering look at Michael, asleep in his chair, surrounded by his friends, and I couldn't do it. I couldn't bring myself to take him into harm's way again.

"I love you, Michael Tombs," I said to him from across the room before gently shutting the door behind me. Swallowing hard as tears tumbled down my cheeks, I grabbed a pen and paper and scratched out a quick note, which I left on his pillow in his room, then slipped out the front door. The rush of cool morning air summoned back feelings of nausea as I hurried across the street to Mr Davies' big oak tree.

3

I groaned and as I opened my eyes, a sharp pain hitting me right in front of the forehead and I squeezed them shut again. My hand moving instinctively to my neck. Something felt off, but I couldn't put my finger on it. I sat up fingering the skin around my clavicle when and realised Adrian was gone. He'd had a bit too much to drink and fallen asleep in my lap whilst we were watching a movie. To be fair, we'd all had too much to drink. Sam, Jess, Jack, and Alex were all littered around the room, still asleep. I eased myself out of my chair, careful not to make a sound, and slipped out of the living room. Still absentmindedly touching my neck.

"Morning, Michael, you look a bit worse for wear," Mum whispered as she tiptoed around the kitchen, buttering toast with all the delicacy of someone diffusing a bomb.

"Morning, Mum, sorry about last night. I didn't plan for

everyone to come round. It was Adrian's idea," I whispered back.

"Listen, Michael, I know I'm supposed to be setting boundaries and punishing you for getting suspended. I'm sure that is what all the parenting books I could never bring myself to read would suggest, but you just seemed so happy last night. It was nice to see you with your friends and a smile on your face. I'm sorry we've been at odds the past few weeks. I think I've been thinking about you going to uni for so many years. It was sort of set in my head like cement," said Mum.

"It's okay. I'm sorry for being such a grump about it all. I'll speak to Dan later today when I'm less hungover. Have you seen Adrian? He fell asleep on me, but when I woke up, he was gone," I said.

"Maybe he had the good sense to sneak up to your room and spend the night in an actual bed," Mum suggested, no longer looking at me. She was staring at the kettle now. I could see the gears turning in her head. She was trying to work out a way to boil it silently.

"Thanks Mum," I said as I made my way to my room, suddenly aware of how creaky our staircase was. I pushed the door open, expecting to see Adrian snuggled up in my duvet. He liked to roll himself up like a burrito when I wasn't around so he was just a tuffet of blonde hair sticking out of a duvet roll, but there was no sign of him. The only thing out of place was a piece of paper folded up on top of my pillow. My stomach dropped as my eyes fell on it. I took a deep breath, told myself not to imagine the worst, that everything was probably fine, and picked it up.

Dear Michael,

Gosh, this feels weird. I want to just talk to you, but you're asleep and well, if I talk to you, I know you'll come running after me. In fact, I'm sure you will when you find this letter anyway. So, I suppose what I'm doing doesn't really make sense, but I don't know what else to do. I guess that means I can't tell you where I'm going. I don't know what to do. I feel like I'm trapped in a cage of wrong choices.

I folded the note closed again, my breathing short and shaky, my throat painful and tight. Suddenly I was pouring with sweat. I took a few more deep breaths and opened the note again.

Like whatever decision I make will always make things worse, and it makes my stomach squirm, although that might have been Alex's drinks. Sorry, I'm rambling. I just can't drag you into danger again for my sake. It's too much to ask and I know if I asked, you'd say yes. Daniel is right.

"Fucking Daniel," I growled to myself.

I'm ruining your life. Oh, and please apologise to Linda for me. I know she doesn't like having me around. I never meant to become an annoyance or emotionally black mail anyone or get in between you and your family. I'm rambling again, aren't I? I suppose I'm putting off leaving.

I'm so sorry and I love you so much. I'll see you soon.

Love Adrian.

I read the note over and over, part of my brain refusing to process the words on the page. It was crumpling in my hands, my fists tightening involuntarily. My mouth started to fill with saliva, my eyes were watering, and then I was being sick. I lunged for the dustbin, grabbing it as I hurled and cried and shook and sweated.

"Is he in there? Oh god, Michael, that smells awful," said Mum, poking her head round the door.

"Did you speak to him this morning, Mum?" I asked. My voice was low, almost a growl. I spat into the bucket, a thick acid film coating my tongue.

"No, Dear, why?" she asked, looking worried suddenly. I watched her eyes flick from my bed, noticing he wasn't there, then to the crumpled note in my hands, but mostly they just lingered on the bin.

"Read this," I said, speaking through gritted teeth as I got back to my feet and thrust the page into her hand. I watched her scan it, her eyes growing wider the longer she looked at it.

"Michael... I don't know what to say. I don't know where he got this idea that I don't like having him around from, but he's wrong," said Mum.

"He got it from Daniel obviously, I could kill him, Mum, I really could," I said as I stormed past her along the corridor to Daniel's room. I grabbed the door handle and twisted it, but it didn't budge. Locked.

"Knock, knock!" I yelled, banging my palm against the

door so hard it swung open, slamming against the wall, the lock splintering the door frame as it went.

"What the f—"

"What did you say to him? Where did he go? Tell me right now, Daniel!" I cut him off mid-sentence as I launched myself across the room, grabbing him and dragging him out of his bed in just his boxer shorts.

"Get off me you psycho," Daniel squirmed, his expression a mix of rage and confusion, his hands on my wrists. He was trying to tear me off him, but I could barely feel him.

"I said tell me where he went right now." My voice dropped to a low threatening growl, Daniel's eyes widening, anger quickly giving way to fear.

"You're hurting me," he said, his voice becoming high and squeaky.

"I said tell me." My voice rumbled through him as I pulled his face up to within an inch of mine. His acrid vodka breath turning my stomach.

"He went through the tree on the Mr Davies' drive, said something about saving Olivier," said Daniel. Without another word, I dropped him onto the floor, shoved past Mum who was standing horrified in the now broken doorway and thundered down the stairs and out of the house. Crossing the street at a sprint, I reached Mr Davies' large oak and snatched at the piece of Excalibur around my neck, but my hand found only air. I reached behind to check if it'd rotated around, but a palpable sense of dread was already overtaking me. My breathing growing short. I clawed at my chest and neck. No chain, no stone, nothing was there. It was gone.

"Shit, shit, shit, shit, shit, shit," I hissed to myself. I turned back towards the house, sprinting upstairs and began tearing through my room. Cushions and stray socks flying in every direction as I grabbed everything in sight to check.

"Michael, I thought you were going to find Adrian?" I heard Mum's voice behind me but didn't turn. I had to find it. I had to find my Excalibur shard.

"My piece of Excalibur is missing. Without it I can't get into the forest, Mum. Have you seen it? Have you put it somewhere?" I half asked, half accused as I upturned a set of drawers, only finding dust and an old pair of pants.

"No, Love. I didn't think you ever took it off," she said.

"I don't. Never," I said, spinning on the spot, satisfied it wasn't in my room, only to find Daniel standing sheepishly behind Mum. Red hot rage boiled through me at the sight of him. I wanted to scream. I wanted to shove him over the banister and down the stairs.

"Daniel, start looking for Michael's necklace, it's a chain with a greyish green stone attached to it," Mum commanded.

"Do I—"

"Not another word!" Mum snapped, wheeling round on him so quickly he stumbled backwards, eyes wide and startled. I walked past them, making sure to give Daniel the dirtiest look possible.

"Where do you remember last having it?" Mum asked.

"At the community centre!" I yelled, as the image of my silver hammer sprung into my mind, poised to smash Jude's stupid face in.

"What was at the community centre? And please, don't shout," said Jack, wincing as he appeared in the kitchen, looking rough.

"My stone's missing, my piece of Excalibur, I need it back," I said as I started lifting every stray corner shop bag and empty biscuit packet in the vain hope that it had found its way under one of them.

"Can't Adrian just get you another?" Jack asked as he yawned and stretched.

"Adrian has gone to the fay forest without me and he's in trouble," I said, checking under the toaster for some mad reason.

"Where did you go after?" asked Jack, immediately becoming serious and focused.

"I don't know. Home," I said.

"Could someone have taken it?" asked Alex, appearing in the doorway.

"How did you know what we're talking about?" I asked.

"Were you under the impression you were being quiet?" said Alex.

"Jude tried to take it. That day at the community centre, but Adrian stopped him," I said, checking inside the kettle and almost chucking it across the room when I didn't find the shard lying at the bottom of the limescale soup within.

"Could he have tried again?" Alex asked.

"I've not seen him since," I said, slamming the kettle back down on the counter, glaring around the room at all the inanimate objects that could be hiding my shard.

"You mean your goth looking friend?" Daniel asked. He'd appeared shamefaced, hovering in the doorway.

"What?" I bellowed.

"Yeah, he was banging at the door, said he'd got locked out by mistake going for a smoke, so I let him in. Was that wrong?" Daniel asked, obviously me dragging him out of bed had scared him into compliance.

"Yes, it was fucking wrong. He was the guy that I told you about, that attacked Adrian at work," I growled, spinning around on the spot, again reaching impotently for my neck. I didn't know what to do. Jude had my shard. Which meant Gwen had my shard, which meant the fay forest was in danger and Adrian was there and I couldn't get there.

"Jude's been texting Jack nonstop since we started ignoring him. We can probably find him and get it back," said Alex.

"He probably won't have it anymore," I said, a chilling feeling of defeat overcoming me.

"But he might," said Alex.

"You think?" I asked, a little spark of hope leaping into my chest in spite of myself.

"Yep, and if he does, we'll get it. It'll be easy. He's obsessed with you. We can trick him," said Alex, a plan already formulating behind his eyes.

Mothers, Witches and Queens

"Okay, but what's Michael going to do?" asked Jack.

"I'm gonna go to Starkton woods. Nimueh mentioned that dryads can see through the trees, sometimes they look into our world. There is a chance one might see me, or a goblin might come through, or another fay, it's unlikely, but there's a chance," I said, blowing on the tiny embers of hope lest they go out.

"Okay, we'll text you when we've got it. If we don't hear back, we'll assume you've already got into the forest," said Jack, who was rapidly shoving things into his rucksack.

"Thanks guys, you're life savers," I said as they headed for the door.

"Well, you and Adrian did literally save mine," said Jack, giving a wink as he unlocked his car and they sped away, probably quicker than was safe.

"Where are they off to?" Mum asked, appearing behind me, wet with sweat, an old shoe box in each hand.

"They've going to get it back," I said, closing the door.

"Oh, good cause it wasn't in theses," she said, dropping the shoe boxes.

"Mum, I need you to drive me to Starkton woods. There's a chance we might be able to get in another way," I said, pulling my shoes on.

"Of course, DANIEL, GET YOUR SHOES ON!" Mum turned from sweet and understanding to a drill sergeant as she bellowed up the stairs. If he were under any illusions regarding Mum not knowing what he'd said about her to

Adrian, they were about to be quickly and unceremoniously dispelled.

"Does he have to come?" I asked.

"He needs to make it up to you and Adrian, so yes," said Mum as she pulled on her most menacing coat, a black leather jacket she'd bought on a whim and only ever wore twice a year. It looked rather odd on top of her nighty.

4

"Mu-Terra and the dryads are searching the forest for any sign of Gwen in case they can spot her and get to her before she reaches The Hut. Wynda and her spies are looking for any hold ups of mirelings that have escaped in case they have any useful information. In the meantime, we shall be taking our forces directly to The Hut, to see if we can't cut Gwen off in case the dryads can't find her. The good news is, the gnomes have managed to develop a poultice that can undo whatever she is doing to the minds of the mirelings. Hopefully, it'll work on any humans and fay she manages to take control of too. Now, are we all ready?" Olivier barked her briefing standing at the foot of Grandfather Tree, a hodgepodge selection of champions and fay assembled before her.

"Have you got room for a little one?" I called, as I wriggled, elbowed and pushed my way through. She looked every inch of her a leader, from her leather padded shoulders and her thick chest plate that made her look somewhat like a barrel, to her heavily toed boots. Her eyes flashed and her jaw set, I couldn't help thinking how glad I was it was her making that speech, not me. She was born for this stuff. I was just born into it.

"Adrian, where's Michael?" asked Olivier, stepping down from her pedestal, which was actually a particularly thick, high arched root of Grandfather Tree. As she made her way towards me, the crowd parted. Her face was steely, but there was concern in her eyes.

"He's caught at home, family stuff," I lied. I don't think she believed me. She didn't look convinced. I had never been that good at hiding my feelings, and heartbreak was proving harder than most.

"You didn't respond to my whispers," said Olivier.

"I misplaced the stone, but someone heard the message, it was relayed. You think Gwen is in the forest? Why is that?" I asked, trying to move the conversation away from me and Daniel and Michael and all my mistakes.

"Mirelings have been fleeing The Hut, some of them out of their minds, gibbering things likes 'she's here', 'she comes', and from what we've been able to make out, it looks like The Hut itself is changing, growing or opening up or something," said Olivier. I swallowed, the matted web of black embroidery thundering back into my head. Penny's predictions. I couldn't let Penny's predictions come true.

"Not to mention the clouds," said Rocco, emerging from

Mothers, Witches and Queens

the crowd along with his twin Ephyr. I'd grown up with the sylphan twins who'd helped Michael and Olivier rescue me from Merlin, but we'd never had much to do with one another. They didn't have much to do with anyone else except each other and no one had much to do with me. Nimueh's reputation saw to that.

"What's wrong with the clouds?" I asked, looking up into the dense green canopy above us.

"You can only really see it from the air, but over The Hut there are these big dark swirling black clouds," said Ephyr.

"They were red," said Rocco.

"They were not red, they just had red flashes," corrected Ephyr. Olivier rolled her eyes and stepped in front of them, blocking the sylphs as they began to bicker.

"Are you okay? You look dreadful and smell like a gnomish brewery," said Olivier, placing a gentle hand on my shoulder.

"I threw Michael a surprise party last night, that's all. Should we get going?" I asked, trying my best not to give away how nauseous I felt, or how painful it was every time Michael's name was mentioned. The image of him asleep in his chair, surrounded by his friends kept repeating in my head.

"Are you sure you're up for this? It's going to be dangerous," Olivier whispered into my ear as she pulled me into a hug and gave me a very out of character squeeze. I knew she was just being protective, but it still stung. No one would ever try to talk Michael out of doing the right thing, because they knew he was strong enough. People didn't think that about me. Then again, I'm not sure I always do either.

"I'm sure. I need to do something to help for once," I said as we pulled away from each other. For a moment hesitation flickered across Olivier's face. I screwed up my fists and ignored the voice in my head telling me she thought I was weak, but then the hesitation was gone.

"Right, everyone, we're heading out. The sooner we set off, the better chance there is that we'll beat Gwen there. That woman never got permission to reach The Hut, so she'll be picking through the forest finding her own way, which gives us a chance of getting ahead of her," said Olivier, raising her voice and commanding the attention of the crowd before she set off, and they followed in her wake.

"Hey, Adrian, you here to help save the day?" asked Ionia, Caspia's sister, another water nymph. She had long white hair tied in plaits that dangled down to the small of her back, flashing blue-green eyes, and pale, white skin with olive undertones.

"Something like that. Where is Caspia?" I asked with a smile, joining her as we marched through the archway of trees out of Grandfather Tree's clearing.

"Oh, they've been a grump ever since Olivier and the council took over running things. They're probably hiding somewhere trying to scrounge up enough information to get Nimueh to give them a sideways glance," said Ionia.

Mothers, Witches and Queens

"I bet they're not the biggest fan of mine then?" I said awkwardly.

"Mixed feelings actually, you get the blame for the council idea and for stepping down, but also get credit for ousting Merlin. Caspia wouldn't know whether to spit or bow and scrape," Ionia said, chuckling and a low, rolling laugh joined hers from behind. My eyes flicked to the source, and I flinched, realising it was Jamie. The hunter type champion that had helped Merlin imprison Michael and me in The Hut. His laughter halted. He must have caught my flinch out of the corner of his eye.

"Oh right, you've met before, haven't you," said Ionia, letting herself fall back a pace so that no one was between us.

"You could say that," I said nervously, my eye drifting to the silvery hatchet glinting in Jamie's hand.

"I owe you an apology, Adrian," said Jamie, as the silvery hatchet popped out of existence, returning to the form of a shard of Excalibur in his hand.

"I think you owe him more than that," Ionia and Jamie shared a look and then Jamie sagged.

"I'm really, really sorry, Adrian. I didn't realise everything Merlin was up to, everything he was doing to you. If I'd known, I never would have fought so hard to keep you as his prisoner," said Jamie.

"But you know now?" I asked, my eyes falling to look at my shoes as my voice shrank.

"Olivier told us. Well, a lot of stuff came out about the

darker side of Merlin after you left. It wasn't all about what he did to you," Ionia explained, putting a reassuring hand on my shoulder.

"You were just doing your job. Don't worry about it, Jamie." I said, offering a weak half smile.

"That's no excuse though, Adrian. I want you to know, I owe you one, whatever you need, whenever you need it, name it and I'll do it," he said, reaching out a hand towards me, before thinking better of it and withdrawing.

5

In retrospect, pink wellingtons, my used-to-be-white-but-now-grey nighty and a leather jacket, wasn't the best outfit to go trawling through the woods in. Unfortunately, Michael had been in such a state I'd sort of lost track of what I was wearing. That, and tracking down poor little Adrian did feel rather urgent. I hated the idea that he thought I was annoyed at him being around or didn't like having him at home.

"Mu-Terra, let me in, I can help! Anyone, just open a tree!" Michael yelled into the woods at large. He'd been going at it since we got here, and his voice was growing hoarse now.

"And you're telling me he's not barking mad?" Daniel asked snidely, as he trudged along behind me. I was beginning to regret insisting he came along.

"I am Daniel. Now, make yourself useful and stop pouting. You've got no one to blame for this situation but yourself," I said.

"And how exactly do I make myself useful? Just shout at trees and hope for the— WHAT THE HELL IS THAT!" Daniel yelled. I wheeled round on the spot, stumbling over a root, and clattered into him. What looked like an angry green ball of teeth was charging out of a tree, followed by an angry, slightly more human looking, little green man, which I knew to be a goblin. Unlike the ones I'd seen by the lake however, these creatures didn't have sickly yellow eyes like someone with jaundice. Theirs were glowing red.

"Michael! We have a goblin problem!" I yelled, as I pulled Daniel behind me and began pushing him backwards, doing my best to keep an eye on the goblin and his mut.

"BACK OFF!" That alien voice that wasn't Michael's boomed out of him, scattering birds from the trees, echoing through the forest like a bomb. For a split second I felt relief, then the next thing I knew I was being shoved to my knees in the bracken and dirt as a gnashing red eyed mut launched itself through the air towards me. Daniel was screaming, he must have pushed me clear before the mut had attached its teeth to his arm. Its jaws were almost up to his elbow, the first trickles of red already dibbling down his arm.

"HELP ME!" wailed Daniel, waving his arm around.

"Mum, duck," Michael commanded, and I did, just in time for a sharp stick to sail over my shoulder, lodging itself in the ground next to Michael's foot. I craned my neck around and caught sight of Michael launching himself through the air, tackling the diminutive green man to the ground, before lifting him by the neck and viciously slamming him into the tree he'd just appeared through.

"Hold on Daniel!" I said, taking a cue from my son's brutality. I grabbed the thickest branch I could lay hand to and a large rock. With all the force of a butcher cutting through bone, I shoved the stick between the roof of the creature's mouth and Daniel's arm, sending a spray of teeth and blood skittering to the forest floor. Next, I smashed the rock down on the creature's skull, eliciting a pathetic whimper and a sickening splintering sound. Luckily, it was the stick and not Daniel's arm.

"Get it off, get it off, get it off!" Daniel whimpered, tears streaming down his cheeks as he collapsed to his knees. I prised the thing off as gingerly as I could and winced as more blood began to pour down Daniel's forearm.

"Oh god, I need something to stop the bleeding with," I said, frantically rooting through my pockets whilst praying that hundreds of hours of Grey's Anatomy had taught me some medicine by osmosis.

"Here, use this," said Michael, pulling off the tight pink polo Adrian had given him and handing it to me, like he was in some sort of Hollywood action movie. I did my best to tie the thing tightly around the bite marks, whilst also trying desperately not to notice how deep they were, as I thought I might be sick.

"I wanna go home," Daniel whimpered.

"We will, Baby, come here," I said, scooting round behind him to give him a hug as I kissed his head. There's no getting away from it. Your kids' head smell just never gets old, even when they're a grumpy twenty-something-year-old.

"We can't," said Michael, as he stood over us, panting and sweating and looking around the forest wild eyed.

"Look Michael, I know you want to find Adrian but—"

"It's not that. Didn't you see their eyes, the way they ignored my commands?" he asked, as he helped Daniel and me get up. The way he pulled us to our feet, you'd think we were the size of high school cheerleaders.

"I noticed they were red," I said, as Michael looped Daniel's good arm over his shoulder and helped him start walking towards the car.

"That means Morgana has control of them. That's how Gwen's eyes looked, and I'm guessing that's why the voice didn't work on them," said Michael.

"So, what?" whined Daniel, struggling to walk. The shock seemed to have sent his legs all wobbly.

"So, if Morgana is controlling them and they're coming here that means she's sending them after someone. I'm guessing that someone is me and Adrian, and she knows where we live, she stalked us when she was controlling Gwen, remember?" said Michael.

"So, where do we go?" I asked, doing my best not to panic as I rubbed Daniel's back in a circular motion and crossed my fingers behind my back, hoping his bleeding would stop.

"There is only one thing I can think of," said Michael as he helped Daniel into the back seat.

"Where to?" I asked, getting behind the wheel.

"To the witches," said Michael.

"To what?" Daniel blurted out from the back of the car.

6

We'd barely set foot on the path when Olivier called us to a halt. The body of a goblin came flying from the undergrowth and was slammed into a tree by a powerful jet of water. Once pinned to the tree, the water snaked up across its chest and began forcing its way into the nose and mouth of the goblin. The creature choked and spluttered for a couple seconds before its eyes, which were glowing a disconcerting red, rather than their usual sickly yellow, rolled back into its head and its body went limp.

"Hello, Olivier," said Nimueh, emerging from the brush line. She clenched a fist and drew all the water around the goblin's body back into herself, ripping some out of the surrounding grass for good measure, leaving it cracked and brown. A few awestruck whispers left the crowd, the odd deferential 'Lady Nimueh' muttered. I'm sure I even heard a couple gasps. I couldn't help rolling my eyes.

"Hello, Nimueh, nice of you to show yourself. I've been looking for you for a little while now," said Olivier, taking a step towards her half-sister.

"Yes, but you've been looking for The Hidden Queen too, haven't you? And trying to run the fay forest. That was always your trouble, Olivier, lack of focus," said Nimueh, with just the slightest unkind smile on her lips.

"Is there something you need Nimueh? Only we're in a bit of a rush, if we weren't I think I'd have you arrested," said Olivier, delivering a jab of her own.

"Oh, just something I thought you might like to know," said Nimueh, her voice dripping with smugness.

"Spit it out," said Olivier.

"I know how the little human woman with the broken hand got into the forest," said Nimueh. As she spoke, her eyes flicked from Olivier to me, just for a second. My stomach lurched. I'd been hoping she wouldn't notice me, and now she had. Somehow, I just knew that whatever she was about to say had to do with me.

"How?" asked Olivier.

"Oh, I'm not giving you all my secrets for free. I want my lake back and your word that you'll vouch for me when I come before the council," said Nimueh. She put the emphasis very clearly on 'my'. Olivier hesitated and again Nimueh's eyes flicked to me, the cruel smile she sported growing as our eyes met, my breath becoming a little shorter, a little more panicked. Before I knew it, I was pushing through the crowd towards Olivier, placing a hand on her shoulder, whispering into her ear.

"Give her whatever she wants," I said.

"Done, so how did she get in?" asked Olivier, without another moment's hesitation.

"She used an Excalibur piece, a champion in Starkton must have misplaced theirs," said Nimueh.

"How do you know that?" I asked, stepping out of the crowd to stand level with Olivier.

"I saw her do it with my very own eyes and I thought you should know. I'd hate to think of the poor defenceless champion back in Starkton, unarmed and alone," said Nimueh. She didn't hate to think of it, she clearly loved thinking of it.

"He's not defenceless, he's a prince, he has the voice," I snapped, giving up the pretence that we weren't talking about Michael. I didn't want to play along with her nasty little games anymore.

"Of course, of course, assuming the voice works on a creature under her spell, those eerie red eyes, I dread to think," said Nimueh.

"That's enough Nimueh, you've dripped your poison, now be on your way," said Olivier.

"Not until you give me access to my lake," said Nimueh, taking another step towards us, the smile melting into a determined, jaw clenched glare.

"Fine!" I said, as I reached out through the forest and found the lake, picturing it in my mind's eye, glistening in the dappled light. Excalibur like an emerald iceberg in its centre, coloured by the trees all around. Deep inside me I felt my connection to that place. I took Nimueh's hand and shared it with her.

"Finally," said Nimueh, with a tremor of excitement in her voice as she withdrew her hand.

"Satisfied?" asked Olivier.

"It's a start," said Nimueh, stepping past us both, as she began her walk down the endless yellow path of the forest and quickly melted into the scenery.

"Onward," said Olivier, without wasting a second. She took up her march again, but quicker now, I had to almost trot to keep up.

"You don't think she's right, do you?" I hissed.

"About what?" Olivier hissed back.

"About creatures under Morgana's control being immune to the voice," I said.

"How would she possibly know that, Adrian? She's just trying to scare you," said Olivier, giving my hand a quick squeeze.

"Okay, yeah, you're probably right," I said. I was trying to convince myself as much as anything, but a little voice in my head did keep reminding me that Nimueh spent time in Merlin's private quarters. Perhaps she knew more about Morgana than she ever let on. I shut my eyes and tried to shake the thought out of my head, but to no avail. I let myself drop back, melting into the crowd until I caught sight of Jamie.

Mothers, Witches and Queens

"You said you owe me one, whatever I need, right?" I whispered as we fell into lockstep.

"Yep, whatever you need," said Jamie, looking down at me slightly nervously.

"Well, if I say the word, I need you to grab as many fighters as you can and go to Starkton. Michael might be in trouble," I said.

"But what about the mission?" asked Jamie, letting his voice drop to a whisper too.

"You said whatever I need, whenever I need it," I hissed. Jamie's brows furrowed, and his face screwed up into a frown, until at last he nodded his assent.

7

Luckily, the Starkton community centre was right on the border of the Starkton woods, so it didn't take long for Mum to drive us there. Although the journey felt longer with Daniel moaning and groaning in the back of the car the whole way.

"You know who could have healed you?" I said, craning my neck around to look at him as he cradled his arm wrapped up in my ruined polo.

"H-healed me?" Daniel asked, confused.

"Adrian, the boy you chased off into mortal peril, he could have healed you. In fact, he would have, with no hesitation, even though you've been awful to him," I said.

"Come on, Michael, that's enough. Daniel is in a lot of pain," said Mum.

"Well, he wouldn't be, if he'd been nicer to Adrian." I huffed, crossing my arms as we pulled up outside the centre.

"This is where witches live?" asked Daniel, as he struggled to climb out of the car.

"We don't live here, just practice," said Enid as she squelched up behind us in her wet waders, with a couple of large fish slung over her back.

"I thought we were going to see witches, not fisherwomen," said Daniel, doing an impressive amount of limping for someone who'd hurt their arm.

"Are you labouring under the misapprehension that the two are mutually exclusive?" asked Enid. Without turning back to face us, she let herself into the building, leaving the door open for us. "You coming or what?"

"Let's get inside," said Mum, helping Daniel up the stairs. I took a cursory glance over my shoulder at the tree line before following them in.

"Well, this is lovely," said Mum, admiring the various hanging plant baskets and crystals that were haphazardly scattered around the witch's coven meeting room.

"Looks like we're all here then," said Liz. Further inside were Penny and Terrance, sitting cross-legged on cushions. Liz was in front of them, her legs in full lotus, all of them with their eyes closed. Enid was flicking fish scales into a silver bowl in front of Terrance's window of potted plants. There was another woman I didn't recognise. She had dark brown skin and was wearing a dusty apron with multiple pockets on the front, full of what looked like files and chisels. Her hair was one large, well-kept, bouncy black afro.

"Jude and Gwen aren't," said Penny dejectedly.

Mothers, Witches and Queens

"Yes, well Gwen is in the fay forest being possessed by literally Morgana, and for all we know, Jude is too, so I think it's safe to say, they're not coming," Liz snapped.

"Do any of you know first aid? My son's arm got bitten," said Mum, shoving Daniel into the centre of the room like a mother pushing her child to go play in the playground with the other kids.

"I do, I'm Jade, by the way," said the stranger in the apron.

"What bit him?" asked Penny, again risking Liz's wrath by taking a peek at Daniel's arm, bandaged with my polo.

"A goblin mut," I said. Penny's eye flitted to me and her mouth dropped open before she averted her gaze again.

"Where did your shirt go?" she asked, as I became acutely aware that I wasn't wearing one. Somehow being half-naked in a room full of witches felt a lot more vulnerable that it did in the woods.

"What's a goblin mut?" asked Jade, as she gingerly unwrapped Daniel's arm.

"How do you know he doesn't have a shirt on?" Liz asked, with all the accusation in her voice of a librarian shushing someone, although she'd opened her eyes too.

"It is impossible to meditate with you all bickering," said Terrance, giving up all together as he fell out of his cross-legged position and got up to go inspect his succulents.

"You're right, Terrance," said Penny, producing a needle

and a disk of tightly drawn material that she began sewing into absentmindedly.

"I expect it's like a dog, but a goblin one," said Enid, as a fisheye plopped into her silver bowl.

"Looks like you got off lightly," said Jade, giving Mum an encouraging nod to approach.

"Oh, my goodness, I was sure it would have gone to the bone. That thing's teeth were at least an inch long," said Mum, taking Daniel's arm in her hands and inspecting it closely. I joined her and to my surprise, in place of the deep, bloody gashes I'd expected were just some fairly nasty scratches.

"How's that possible? One of them bit me once and the wounds were deep. Adrian passed out trying to heal them," I said, shuddering at the memory of those long needle-like teeth sinking into my shoulder.

"And you said there might be more of these things coming?" asked Penny, her needling speed increasing as the anxiety in her voice rose.

"Yep, and I don't have my Excalibur shard, and my powers don't work on them," I said. I should have felt nervous. This was worth being nervous over, but somehow, I was just numb.

"We need to hide," said Penny.

"Are you mad? We need to defend ourselves. We're a coven and we're in our place of power," snapped Liz, before shutting her eyes tight and beginning to mutter under her breath.

Mothers, Witches and Queens

Terrance inspected the row of plants in the window. "What we need is reinforcements," he said. "Are you feeling okay? Yours and Adrian's succulents are looking a bit piqued."

"They're hungover. Do you have a kettle, Terrance? I think everyone could do with a cuppa," said Mum, handing me back the bloody polo, which I didn't particularly want to put back on.

"This way, Mrs Tombs," said Terrance, leading Mum into the back room, leaving Daniel standing agog in the middle of the room, opening and closing his mouth like a fish on a line.

"Can't Adrian help us?" asked Penny anxiously, as she sucked the finger she'd just pricked.

"He's in the fay forest, trying to stop Gwen getting to The Hut. He thought I'd follow him, but it looks like Jude swiped my shard and Adrian took the whispering stone we use," I said. Penny's eyes darted guiltily away, whilst Enid sucked her teeth disapprovingly.

"What's a whispering stone?" asked Jade, her eyes suddenly alight. They were a warm dark maple colour.

I described the stone to her. "Perfectly round, like a skimming pebble. The fay use them to communicate with each other, a bit like phones."

"Oh, now you've got her attention," said Enid, chuckling to herself knowingly as she split a fish down the centre, spilling its entrails into the bowl. A sickening squelching sound echoed through the room, followed by an awful fishy smell, reminding me that I'd thrown up recently and my teeth were beginning to feel furry.

"What does she mean?" I asked.

"She's referring to the fact that most of my practice revolves around crystals and stones," said Jade, stooping to pick up a dusty little chest studded with all sorts of odd stones.

"She's like a magpie, she likes shiny things." Enid chuckled again, then her eyes went wide, and she dropped the fish bodily into the bowl.

"What is it?" asked Penny, looking at her nervously.

"They're coming, lots and lots of them are coming," said Enid, sounding nervous for the first time ever as far as I could recall.

"Like this?" asked Jade, spinning round with a perfectly rounded, shiny, black pebble in her fingers. Apparently so absorbed by her box of rocks, she'd missed the news that had drawn the attention of myself, Penny and even Liz, who'd halted her muttering.

"Tea everyone?" Mum asked, emerging into the room, with a platter of chipped, mismatched mugs and two teapots.

"Yes please," said Liz, elaborately unfolding herself from her position as she scuttled for the tea tray, taking one in her now shaking hands and gulping it.

"What did we miss?" asked Terrance, watching Liz nervously.

"A whole swarm of those needle toothed buggers are

heading our way. Terrance, Liz, barricade the doors, I'll get the salt," said Enid, who'd transformed into something of a general and was hobbling off into the kitchen.

"She used to be a traffic conductor," said Liz knowingly, before gulping at her tea and setting the empty mug on the tray. She grabbed a chair and carried it out of the room towards the front door, Terrance following in stunned silence.

"Barricade? Shouldn't we be leaving right about now?" asked Penny, getting to her feet as she began winding up her thread.

"And go where?" snapped Enid.

Anywhere but here. She knows where we are. She's sending those monsters here, so let's leave," said Penny, looking around the room desperately for support.

"You've had the same dreams as all of us, Penny. We knew where to find Adrian and Michael, and we didn't even look for them. Do you really think there is somewhere we can hide from this Morgana person? Heck, she's inside Gwen's head. She probably knows where we all live, just like Gwen does," said Liz, crossing the room to pick up another chair.

"Not to mention, explaining a load of goblins battering down your door to the neighbours might be tricky," I added, hopefully helpfully.

Penny opened her mouth to speak again but paused. Her brows creased, her mouth closed again, and she returned to her needlework. It wasn't immediately clear how that was going to help, but at least she wasn't arguing anymore.

"Would this work?" asked Jade in a much firmer voice, grabbing my attention back to her little stone.

"I mean, it looks like one, but they're magic. They're not just ordinary stones," I explained exasperatedly as I joined Terrance and Liz in barricading the front door, though what good it would do, I'm not sure.

"I'm a witch and I work with stones. I think I can make it magical. Now put that down and follow me," said Jade, almost dragging me back to her gem encrusted chest. She started fishing out what looked like large chunks of clear crystal, along with some smaller black ones and loading me up with them.

"What do I do with these?" I asked, looking at them curiously.

"They're quartz and black tourmaline. The black tourmaline is protective, and quartz can amplify the effects of other crystals. Put one either side of each doorway, then one of the black ones equidistant between each of them," she explained, before holding the small perfectly round stone against her chest, which I now noticed was laden with a tangle of gems on silver chains.

"What's she doing?" muttered Daniel, managing the first words he'd spoken since we got inside. Mum had been pouring tea into his mouth and it seemed to have livened him up.

"I believe it's called setting an intention dear," said

Mothers, Witches and Queens

Mum, as she went round the room dropping off mugs of tea to the coven.

"That's correct, Mrs Tombs, very impressive," said Terrance, sounding genuinely impressed, but in a kind of patronising primary school teacher sort of way.

"How do you know that?" asked Daniel incredulously.

"I've been googling things, this witch business. I thought it was all quite interesting," said Mum, as I left the room to go drop off my crystals. Although what good it would do us, I wasn't sure. I was three doorways in when Mum appeared behind me and tapped me on the shoulder.

"How are you doing, Dear?" she asked, kneeling next to me and taking half my armful of crystals.

"I don't know," I said shakily. I'd been doing my best not to feel anything. I was worried that as soon as I did, I'd break down and I couldn't afford to breakdown right now.

"I say, look on the bright side," said Mum, as she began placing crystals at the back door.

"What's that then?" I asked, trying to ignore the twinkle of hope she was stoking inside me.

"If Gwen's goblins, or Morgana's or whoever… if she's sending them here, to get us, they can't be there, to get Adrian, and he'll be with Olivier. She'll look after him," said Mum. She was smiling, and I realised, as my chest loosened just a little, that I was smiling back.

"I just can't believe he went without me," I whispered, letting myself fall backwards and leaning on my elbows. Mum's little spark of hope had broken the dam and now I was feeling. Feeling the dread and hope and the abandonment and the anger and the yearning.

"He was just doing his best to keep you safe, just like you have for him. He left you behind out of love," said Mum, wiping the tear tumbling down my cheek with her thumb.

"Do you think we'll see him again?" I asked, choking on a sob at the thought of never seeing him again. The dread I'd been numbing myself against bubbled up and spilled out of me.

"Of course, Darling, come here," Mum said, pulling me into a hug, as she began soothingly rubbing my back.

"Everything okay in here?" came Enid's rather strained voice. I peeked over Mum's shoulder to find Enid struggling with a large bag of salt with a small hole in the bottom that she was using to create a trail of white around the borders of the room.

"That looks heavy," I said, letting go of Mum.

"It is, you're a strong lad, you take it," said Enid, giving me an appraising look up and down and then sucking her teeth before handing me the bag. I don't think she approved of my shirtlessness. To be fair, I wasn't loving it either.

"Line the edges of all the rooms we want to fortify, don't leave any gaps," said Enid.

"What's it for?" I asked, watching her hobble out.

"Well, in theory, it's supposed to keep evil spirits out, but I'll settle for feeling like I'm being proactive at the moment," she said. Without turning to face us again, she disappeared back into the main coven room.

"Do you think it'll work?" I asked, as I dragged the line of salt around the edges of the room.

"Can't hurt. Hey, maybe it'll stop us slipping if we get snow," said Mum, chuckling to herself.

"Yeah ma—" Something slammed into the front door, rattling the pile of chairs and benches that had been propped against it. Mum and I jumped out of our skin and I scattered salt everywhere.

"What on earth?" said Mum. She crept up to the window, just as another chair-shaking bang erupted from the door.

"There are goblins outside," she said, peeking through the window for a second before ducking down below it.

"Everyone back inside!" said Enid, her head popping back out of the coven room door. I hastily finished salting the perimeter of the room and followed them both inside.

"What do we do?" asked Penny, scrambling to her feet as she discarded her weaving and made a beeline for the window, only for Enid to grab her.

"Nobody stand by the windows. They could break the glass," warned Enid.

"What do we do? What do we do?" Terrance had started panicking in the corner. Jade was still holding her stone lovingly to her chest and, to my surprise, Daniel was making the rounds with a teapot, topping people up.

"Wanted to be useful," he said with a shrug, cradling his

scratched-up arm as he presented me with a half mug of lukewarm tea.

"Erm Penny, why did you sew this?" asked Liz, picking up the discarded disk of needle point.

"Does it really matter right now Liz? I was barely even paying attention to what I was doing. We are about to get eaten by goblins!" Penny snapped.

"Erm yeah, I'm guessing it does," said Liz, showing the room the swatch of fabric. On it was stitched a few words in large, swooping black letters that I could hardly read.

Morgana is already free, Adrian is walking into a trap, he must be warned. She is sending goblins to destroy the coven before the seventh in seven is awake. Be careful.

P.S I'm sorry sisters, she was too strong for me.
Blessed be, G.

Tears tumbled down Penny's face, her voice trembling as she took the note and read it aloud.

"I don't understand, who's G, I thought her name was Penny?" said Daniel, confusedly.

"It's Gwen. She's sent us a message," said Enid, her jaw locked and voice steely, fighting the tears welling in her eyes.

"That means she..." Terrance gulped and couldn't seem to finish the sentence, his mouth falling wordlessly open.

"She's gone," said Liz, shortly, a single tear tumbling down her cheek.

"She said Adrian was walking into a trap... we have to warn him, I have to, somehow, speak to him," I said. My voice was shaking, I whirled round looking at Mum wide eyed and panicking.

"The stone's nearly ready. I just need a few more minutes," said Jade, still clutching the stone to her chest, which was now wet with tears. Barely flinching as the sound of a shattering window in the next room echoed through the community centre.

"We haven't got time to mourn Gwen now, there are quite literally, goblins at the gate," said Enid, pushing her palms into her eyes and rubbing them. There was another bang at the door which sounded like it sent chairs clattering to the ground.

"So, what do we do?" asked Penny, her voice wobbling, snot bubbles popping out of her nose.

"We hold fast, we buy time for Michael to get word to Adrian, we make Gwen proud," said Enid, hastily wiping away another tear. I nodded, steeling myself and scanned the room for anything I could improvise as a weapon.

"They'll be inside soon. Get behind me," I warned.

"You must be joking, you get behind me boyo," said Mum, pulling me back and away from the door, clutching a kettle in her hand like a battleaxe.

8

The trek to The Hut was harsher that I'd expected it to be. Of course, I'd expected that our permission to reach it would have been revoked. I hadn't expected the forest to have taken on the dense thorny, murky, humid nature of the mireling swamps though. Each step was heavy as we dragged our feet through the sodden earth. The air was thick and hard to breathe, it sat on our skin like oil, and made our clothes stick. The sylphs were struggling most of all, used to the light, fresh air of the fay forest, used to their feet barely touching the ground from one step to the next. Adrian, Ionia and I had done our best to draw as much moisture as we could out of the ground and the air as we walked, but we could only hold focus for so long. Adrian's mind especially was elsewhere, always looking back over his shoulder.

"Tell me what's on your mind," I said in a low voice, barely audible over the chorus of panting from everyone behind us. Looking back at them all, I couldn't help thinking any element of surprise we may have hoped to achieve was doomed. There was nothing silent or subtle about a couple of dozen fay hacking and slashing and wheezing their way through a swamp. Not to mention the fact that cutting a path wide enough for us all to walk more than one by one was eating up time and energy we didn't have.

"Michael… he's defenceless, if Morgana sends anything after him…" said Adrian, panting heavily, just barely managing to pull my focus away from our bedraggled troop. He was almost grey now. He'd looked ill when he arrived, but the effects of the swamp had exacerbated things.

"And why would she do that?" I asked, pushing my fringe off my forehead where it had plastered itself.

"He's a prince. That could be a threat to her. I bet Nimueh's right and the creatures under her spell are immune, but Morgana can't possibly keep the entire forest under her spell at once. No one's that powerful," said Adrian, hissing painfully as a low hanging thorn nicked his ankle.

"Let me heal that," I said.

"It's just a scratch. Don't change the subject," said Adrian softly, pulling his sock up over the cut. I could almost laugh. He wasn't my son but sometimes I couldn't help but see flashes of me in him. He was kinder than me, and softer too, but there was a streak of pragmatism somewhere deep down in that blonde mop of his. It was the part of him that could negotiate with hags and usurp Merlin. I let this distract me enough that I cut my finger on a thorn, reaching out to push some of the blackening overgrowth out of our way.

Usually, in the fay forest the canopy blanketed the sky high above us, creating a green veil. Now, in this changing swamp, the whole world felt closer. The wild plants overhead were only a few feet above us and dropped thorny vines down into our path.

"You're right. I suppose he could be a threat if he could get to her, but she has his Excalibur piece. So, he can't," I said.

"For now, but she knows we have more. She knows it's only a matter of time before we get another piece from the lake," said Adrian. His breathing was getting shorter and shallower. He was starting to panic.

"Adrian, what is it?" I asked.

"Now is the perfect time, don't you see it? Michael is a threat to her, and right now he doesn't have his shard. If there was ever a time for her to strike at him, it's now. He needs help now. Jamie, I need you!" he said, whirling around on the spot to face the crowd. Only his foot got stuck in the mud, so he twisted himself over and fell to his knees, sinking a couple of inches into the almost black swamp ground.

"Jamie?" I asked, a little taken aback as I helped him to his feet. The mire of the swamp coating his lower half as he pulled himself out of the mud.

"What d'you need?" asked Jamie, emerging from the throng of sweaty fay. Once upon a time, Jamie had been one of Merlin's most loyal champions although with the help of Ionia, he seemed to have turned over a new leaf. He was tall and lean but broad shouldered, with long brown hair tied into a bun, sporting the shadow of a dark beard, and sweating buckets.

"I need you to go and find Michael and make sure he's safe. Take the group with you. Olivier and I will carry on together," said Adrian. He was doing his best to sound authoritative, a tricky task when you're winded.

"Now hang on a minute. I can't let you send my whole force away. We need them for Gwen," I said.

"We don't though, either way. She's not got there yet, and then all we need is one of your mushrooms to knock her out. Or she has and we won't be enough, anyway. Look at us, we're exhausted, we can't siege The Hut. Our only hope is to catch her by surprise before she reaches her body. And a big crowd of panting fay doesn't help that, in fact, it hinders it. Surely you've already realised this?" said Adrian. I wanted to yell, to challenge his insubordination, but in spite of myself, I was smiling. He was right, and he was smart, when he actually applied himself at least.

"Okay, that I concede, but how are they going to help Michael if they don't know where he is?" I said, struggling for a hole to poke in his logic, to test him as much as anything.

"Jamie is a hunter. You can find him, right?" asked

Mothers, Witches and Queens

Adrian, turning his big, hopeful, sparkly blue eyes on Jamie. I couldn't help but roll my own as Jamie stammered out an awkward yes. I'm sure Adrian didn't know he was doing it, but he could make himself very hard to say no to.

"Just need to have a good place to start," said Jamie, clearing his throat with a somewhat performative grunt.

"If I know Michael, he'll have gone to the woods in the hope of some fay coming through that he could hitch a ride with," said Adrian, leaning awkwardly against a thick black vine to take the weight off his cut leg. He recoiled in quiet disgust a moment later, dragging a few strands of sticky tar-like blackness with him as he went.

"That's some pretty desperate logic," said Jamie sceptically.

"Trust me, with these two if there is a chance at all, they'll take it," I said with a chuckle, although my voice came out cracked and hoarse, must have been the panting.

"Okay, enough chitchat, get going. They could already be in trouble," said Adrian. Jamie gave a sort of awkward salute that he seemed to think better of halfway through. What followed was a procession of roughly three water nymphs, five gnomes, four sylphs, and two champions, following four dryads each through doorways opened in the biggest trees they could find in the vicinity. Adrian and I watched them go, taking a breather on a handy stump.

"Do you think he'll be okay?" Adrian asked, rubbing his eyes, which I was only now noticing had become red and sore looking.

"Well, we've sent every fay and champion I could muster at short notice to help him, so I certainly hope so," I said, forcing myself to my feet and offering Adrian a hand, heaving him up with me. Together, we began trudging up a particularly steep track of the marsh.

"How are you feeling?" he asked, as we got within meters of cresting the hill.

"Like my body weighs about twice as much as usual," I said, clearing my throat, which was becoming thick and gravelly.

"Have you hurt your leg? You seem to be limping," said Adrian, reclining against a tree before quickly pulling away, having accidentally impaled himself on some sort of prickly ball, which he gingerly picked out of his shoulder.

"Actually, now you mention it, it's gone a bit numb. I hadn't noticed," I said, leaning down to inspect my leg, but finding no cuts or bruises. Although I did make myself dizzy as I stood up.

"Lift your foot up," said Adrian, kneeling down in the muck to inspect me. I did as I was told, like an obedient horse. What followed was a rather dramatic gasp.

"What is it? What is it?" I said, a brief panic getting the best of me as a rush ran through my system.

"There is a huge thorn in your boot. I'm gonna pull it out," said Adrian.

"No, wait do—" He already had. I felt something shift, like a nerve had been released. Pain radiated up my leg, and I slumped down on my knees.

"Oh, my god you're bleeding. Hang on," said Adrian. I couldn't speak, I couldn't form words, but I knew what he was doing, and I wanted him to stop. I don't think it had dawned on Adrian yet that we'd managed to wonder ourselves into such a perilous situation. Suddenly there was pressure at the base of my foot and then soothing cool water and the pain ebbed away until I could speak again. Already I was regretting not holding back at least one dryad.

"Adrian, stop it, save your strength." I croaked and coughed, spitting up some sort of strange bile. I blinked, looking around. The air, which had been steamy now seemed to have some sort of pollen floating in it, like a white grey film. I dreaded to think how long we'd be breathing it in.

"I'm okay." Adrian's voice was hoarse and cracked like mine, but smaller. I heaved myself round and turned to face him, plopping down in the mud. He looked exhausted. His eyes weren't just red, they were bloodshot, his skin was shiny and grey with oily sweat, and he clearly was having even more trouble than I was catching his breath. To my surprise, as I took in the awful sight of him, he started to crawl.

"What are you doing? You need to rest," I said.

"I just want to get to the top of the hill," he said, staggering to his feet as he painstakingly trudged the final few steps and again sank to his knees. From behind him I could see the trickle of red running down his leg. He was kneeling among a bed of suspicious looking purple lily pad-like plants, suspended in the black mud. Looking around us, I realised that they'd spread back along our path like a carpet.

"And then what?" I asked, my heart pounding in my ears as I dragged myself to the top of the hill after him, careful to avoid the purple lily pads, which I'd immediately felt wary of.

"I think we're too late," he said, ignoring me as I sunk down next to him and shuddered at what lay before us. The Hut, but not as we'd known it, no longer the gnarled and twisted boulder-like knot of roots. Now it stretched up high into the sky, like a perverse mockery of Grandfather Tree, blackened and twisted, with jagged thorns as big as people. Huge branches reaching out in all directions, like the bony hands of giants without a single leaf to speak of between them, and above it, a twisting roiling swirl of clouds.

"Ephyr was right, black with red flashes," Adrian croaked, crawling over to a tree to rest against, whilst I struggled defiantly to my feet. I'd never been a very good loser.

"You just rest there Adrian, I'll come up with something," I said, doing my best not to let him see that every time I looked at him a terrible heart pounding dread rumbled through me. I was fighting to keep the words out of my head. *He looks like he's dying.* I quietly sniffled, rubbing my eye with my fist before a tear could form, when a whisper issued from Adrian's pocket. He rummaged around in it sluggishly and produced a whispering stone.

"Adrian, I don't know if you can hear this, but we could

really use some help right now, we're at the community centre on the edge of the woods, and Morgana's goblins are here, and the voice doesn't work on them. And you if you can hear this, you've got to stop. Morgana has set a trap for you."

Adrian's bloodshot eyes peeled wide as he and I shared a look. He did his best to clear his ragged, croaky voice before he spoke into the stone.

9

"Don't worry, Michael, help is on the way." Adrian's voice rumbled out of the stone sounding cracked and raw.

"Did he sound sick to you?" I asked, my eyes darting to Mum frantically, both of us flinching as the sound of splintering wood echoed from the entrance hall. Now only one door stood between us and the goblins.

"We've got bigger problems than Adrian's sore throat," bellowed Enid, as the door finally burst open and two red-eyed goblins stepped inside, brandishing long, lethal looking spiked sticks.

"Stand back," Mum commanded, about to charge, when I noticed a flicker of yellow in the goblins' eyes.

"Wait!" I shouted, grabbing her by her leather sleeve and pulling her back as the goblins paused in the doorway.

"STOP WHERE YOU ARE!" I let the voice ring out of me like a hammer on church bells and watched the goblins halt their advance. Their eyes flickering from fiery and red, to glazed over and milky yellow.

"I thought you said the voice didn't work on them," Liz hissed, adjusting her grip on a particularly large terracotta pot.

"It didn't," I hissed back as we all stood poised, ready to launch on the two goblins in the doorway. The sounds of more scuttling and chirping issued from behind them as their sabre-toothed brethren fanned out through the community centre looking for us.

"It must be the crystals," said Jade, more excitedly than seemed appropriate.

"And the salt," added Enid.

"Weakening Morgana's hold on them enough for the voice to get through," I breathed.

"That stuff actually works?" Daniel asked, sounding genuinely shocked.

"Honestly, Daniel, I don't know how you can still have doubts in the face of all of this," said Mum, her knuckles white from her grip on her kettle.

"Did that one just move?" Penny hissed. My eyes darted back just in time to watch the goblin's eyes flicker back to red as it turned its saliva-dripping, ear-to-ear grin towards us and began to advance.

"STOP!" The voice boomed, and it froze, its eyes flickering back to sickly yellow, only for the goblin beside it to begin its advance again.

"STOP!" The command thundered out of me once more,

freezing them both with their sharpened sticks outstretched towards us. The chirping and scuttling sounds outside the room turning to yammering hoops as the other goblins heard my voice echo through the building.

"Well, this isn't going to hold them for long," said Enid, brandishing her filleting knife like a gladiator facing down a lion, in waders.

"Back door, Terrance, get the back door," said Liz, as another goblin skittered over the heads of the front two, sending a crystal clattering across the floor towards us. The first two goblins' eyes flickered back to red. The creature launched itself off its companions' heads, kicking them both in the eyes as it thrust its spear towards Mum. I darted forwards, grabbed the stick out of the air and used it to swing the goblin with a thunderous crunch into the wall. First blood seemed to send the other two into a frenzy. One leapt for me, but Mum brought the kettle down over its head, sending it jaw first into the floor of the community centre.

"FOR GWEN!" Liz screamed as she brought the pot down on top of the dazed creature's head, sending terracotta shards in all directions. Goosebumps prickled down my arms as an echoed war cry burst from the whole coven as they plunged into the fray.

A second goblin lunged for Enid but was temporarily stunned by a large chunk of quartz, which sailed through the air and smashed into its head right between the eyes. This gave Enid just enough time to plunge forward with the filleting knife. A third charged past her towards Jade, only for Penny to catch it in a large knitted blanket, leaping clear of its spear jutting out of the rather open weave. I sprinted forwards and booted the thing with such force it sailed clean through the air, smashing through the window with an ear-splitting yelp.

"I told you quartz was for protection!" yelled, Jade as she began frantically lobbing small, sharp looking stones at the goblins now pouring through the doorway.

"Come on, come on," Terrance screeched from the kitchen, holding the emergency fire exit open for us. Daniel darted out first, followed by Penny and Liz, whilst Mum, Enid and I locked eyes with the advancing swarm of goblins. All the while Jade lay down covering fire in the form of a hail of tiger's eyes and jagged amethysts.

"DROP YOUR WEAPONS!" The voice rang out of me, but to no avail.

"Worth a try," said Mum, chucking the lid of the kettle like a heavy frisbee into the eyes of another fanged green charger.

"I'm out of crystals," Jade wailed as she scurried for the door.

"I think that's our cue to leave," said Enid, falling out of the way of a launched spear just in time for it to pin her bucket hat to the wall behind her. At which point she began frantically crawling backwards, her knife arm outstretched towards the oncoming goblins.

"Adrian said help was on the way, right?" asked Mum,

Mothers, Witches and Queens

as she chucked the whole kettle into the face of the next assailant and stretched her arms out, forcing me back with her towards the exit.

"He did," I said, snatching a spear out of the air and chucking it back at an unusually large and chunky looking goblin's foot, pinning it to the floor, before both of us darted out into the dusky evening light. Terrance slammed the door behind us. Penny, Jade, and Liz were busily propping up old bits of brick and pot against the door, for what good it would do us.

"Erm, guys..." came Daniel's voice, high and squeaky, from behind us. I turned, looking for the source only to find myself facing down dozens of blinking red eyes, breaking the forest line, yelling and hooting as they went. Mum's thick arm thrust into my eyeline as she grabbed Daniel and me and yanked us back.

"Get behind me boys," said Mum. There was a wobble in her voice that prickled my eyes.

"Help's on the way," I said to no-one in particular, reminding myself, begging myself not to panic. Cold rivulets of sweat ran down my back as little gnashing green men emerged from the shadows.

Once the blazing red eyes of the goblins had settled on us, a shrill cry rang out and they broke into a sprint.

"This is bad," Terrance squeaked.

"Understatement," Liz said, as a slam at the door behind us made us all jump.

"What now?" asked Daniel in a desperate voice. One

that told me he already knew none of us had an answer for him.

I squeezed my eyes tightly shut and crossed my fingers, taking a shaky breath in as I tried to imagine Adrian's face, with his twinkly blue eyes and his kind smile, without a care in the world.

"I love you," I whispered. I took one more deep breath, braced myself for what was to come, opened my eyes found and found a large round green head and teeth flying straight for me. I ducked and looked back over my shoulder, to see a silvery axe lodged in the goblin's back. I turned back to the crowd of goblins just in time to watch several thick, root-like ropes burst out of the grass, dragging charging goblins to their knees.

"What's happening?" yelled Enid, as the rest of the witches looked on in shock. I blinked as a tear rolled down my cheek, watching dryads, sylphs, water nymphs and gnomes alike explode out of the tree line, brandishing staves and sickles and hammers.

"Adrian sent help." I choked on the words as more tears streamed from my eyes. I turned back, grabbing the silver axe, which popped into a large hammer in my hand, and charged for the goblins. I caught the first on the chin with the upside of my hammer, sending him sailing through the air like a golf ball. He landed with a crunch behind me as I bounded forth, some sort of primal scream ripping out of me as I went. My skin tingling and my heart pounding, adrenaline coursed through my system like electricity as I slammed into a goblin before it could aim its spear towards a water nymph I vaguely recognised. Only for her to fire a jet of water past my ear into the mouth of a mut that had jumped for the back of my neck.

Behind me, a rallying cry of "FOR GWEN" erupted as the witches charged. A wall of giant mushrooms burst from of the earth, shielding them from a flight of spears. I scanned the field for gnomes and found two, with their hands plunged into the dirt, their eyes on the giant mushroom wall. I sprinted forth, releasing a primal growl that stunned a large skittering spider that was heading for them from behind. It was still for just enough time for my hammer to become a shield in mid-air, which I slammed with a crunch into its eight, scarlet red eyes.

Within what felt like mere seconds the goblins had all been repelled or crushed or bludgeoned or skewered or rooted to the floor. As silence fell, I realised I could barely breathe and sank to my knees with a euphoric grin on my face.

"You alright Michael?" Mum asked, as she staggered towards me sporting a few bruises and a slashed leather jacket but looking otherwise unscathed.

"He saved us, Mum. Adrian saved us," I beamed, happy tears still streaming down my face, getting caught in the little knot of hair on my chest.

"Well, I can see what Adrian sees in you," said a vaguely familiar water nymph as she plopped down next to me. She was shiny with sweat, and covered in mud from the knees down, like she'd come from a jungle or a swamp or something.

"Where is he anyway?" I asked, my eyes whirling around the scene, expecting to catch him emerging from the forest line or the fray any second now.

"He stayed behind with Olivier," said the water nymph.

"To do what? I told him it was a trap. Why didn't he come back with you?" I said.

"What are you talking about? You didn't send any messages," came a familiar male voice from behind me that I also couldn't seem to place.

"Yes I did. Just now, I sent a message. Adrian said help was on the way and then a minute later, here you are," I said, turning around to find myself facing one of Merlin's champions, Jamie. My grip tightened on my shield as I rose to my feet, my eyes narrowing towards him.

"Peace, peace," said Jamie, raising his hands above his head in surrender.

"You know you're about to hit him with his piece of Excalibur," said the water nymph sitting behind me.

"I'm working for Adrian. He sent me to find you, half an hour or so ago," said Jamie, lowering his hands, but keeping his distance from me.

"So where is he n—"

"Michael, my eyes are getting quite heavy now," Adrian's voice cracked out of the stone. I plunged my hands into my pockets, grabbing it.

"Adrian, where are you?" I whispered into the stone.

Mothers, Witches and Queens

"I'm at the top of a hill, looking at The Hut, its changed." He sounded hazy and distant, the gap between each word making it sound like he was having to concentrate to speak.

"Okay, we'll come get you, we'll get a dryad to come get you," I said, pleading into the stone for him to be okay.

"You can't. We're not where they left us. You'll just come out somewhere in the swamp." Adrian yawned out of the stone.

"That can't be right," I almost yelled.

"It is," said the water nymph behind me, a note of panic in her voice.

"I think Olivier has fallen asleep. She hasn't spoken or moved in a while. Are you still there Michael?" Adrian's voice whispered out again, sounding dazed and confused.

"ADRIAN AND OLIVIER ARE IN TROUBLE," Jamie yelled, waving his arm for attention.

"Adrian, I'm here, Love, I'm here, stay with me, stay awake for me Adrian." I choked back a sob before I spoke, fighting to keep my voice level, and lively for him.

"Michael, I wanted to say goodbye, better than I did this morning... You were asleep then... I shouldn't have left you," said Adrian. His speech was broken. He'd stop and start like he was forgetting his place in the sentence.

"No, no goodbyes, Adrian, don't you dare say goodbye to me," I said. I broke into a cry and sobbed into the stone. Mum and the witches flocked around me.

"Don't cry, Michael, I won't say goodbye, but my eyes

are closed now. I'm quite cold, I keep shivering. I'll just say, see you later… Michael … I love you," said Adrian. There was a thud that followed, and the crackling whispering sound ceased. I snapped round to the crowd that had formed around me and found a dryad.

"TAKE ME TO HIM RIGHT NOW!" The voice exploded out of me without me meaning for it to. The dryad's eyes glazed over and his brow furrowed, frozen in a strange stiff motion, reaching towards me, his mouth falling open wordlessly. His thick arms twitched, as black dreadlocks fell in front of his face for a moment.

"He can't. None of us can. We don't even know where they are or how far they've got since we left," said another dryad, cowering away from me as I turned my gaze on her. She was wearing a torn green dress that was muddy around the hem. Her skin was almost black, with hints of slivery grey, her head shaved bald.

"I think I know where they are," said Penny, emerging from the crowd and taking my hand as she began to drag me towards the centre. I didn't resist following her into the coven room, where she pointed to a wall. I followed her finger to a woven image that I'd seen once before. In the foreground stood a blond figure with their back to me, beside them a twisted dead looking black tree, which propped up another blonde character. They were both looking down into the background of the picture, which contained a huge, impossibly large mess of twisted thorny

Mothers, Witches and Queens

black and brown branches. My stomach lurched as I realised, I was looking at Adrian and Olivier and The Hut.

"Take me there, take me right now!" I pleaded with the dryad woman as the crowd filtered in.

"That's not how it works. We can only go to the tree we left, or the grove," she explained, gently resting a hand on my shoulder. The look in her eyes was saying, 'I'm sorry'. They were the eyes of someone giving up. I felt like I might be sick again.

"Pendula is right, Michael," said the water nymph I couldn't quite place, in a heavy, defeating tone that made me want to scream.

"Oh my god, look at his succulent," said Terrance, as he all but tumbled over two gnomes entering the room. My eyes darted to the window and peeled back in horror at the sagging, deflated, brown lump from which Adrian's name tag dangled. And then it hit me, Terrance, and his magic plants.

"Terrance, open a tree, any tree, and take me to this one," I said, jabbing at the sewn image of the tree that I presumed Adrian was currently propped against.

"Oh, Michael, I'm not sure. I'm not sure I can do that," he stuttered nervously.

"It's worth a try at least Terry," said Liz.

"Liz, I read succulents. I don't create magical portals in trees!" he snapped, before giving me an apologetic glance.

"But once upon a time you didn't read succulents, you just worked in a garden centre, and then you did read succulents, so why can't you be the person that walks through trees Terrance?" Liz beamed encouragingly at him.

"If there is anyone I know who could get a tree to open up for them, it would be you, Terrance," said Enid, hobbling across the room and giving his hand a tight squeeze.

"Terrance, come on, give my son a bit of hope," said Mum, placing a hand on Terrance's shoulder. I watched a shiver run down his back in real time, the way his eyes lit up, sparking and unmissable.

"I can try, but I need a cup of that tea of yours," he said, going to the corner of the room and plunging his hands into a bag of soil.

"What are you doing?" I asked, bewildered.

"This is my process," he said, rubbing the dirt into his hands, like it was soap.

"And the tea?" I asked, watching Mum disappear into the kitchen.

"Just a theory I'm working on," said Terrance mysteriously.

"Okay, let's find a good tree," I said, deciding to ignore Terrance's foibles and hold on to my little spark of hope as tightly as I could.

"I want a big one. I'm picturing a really thick trunk," said Terrance, walking almost in a daze, his hands already outstretched.

Will this do?" I asked, guiding him out of the centre towards the thickest tree in the tree line. I think it was an oak, I wasn't sure and didn't care. I just needed to get to

Mothers, Witches and Queens

Adrian. The sound of his stone, the last thud we heard from him echoing through my mind.

"Should do," muttered Terrance as I became aware of Mum, a ball of elbows and knees muscling her way to the front of the crowd of witches, fay and champions that had formed behind us, with a particularly chipped mug in her hand.

"Last cup, back of the cupboard," she said by way of explanation as she handed it over.

"It'll work," said Terrance. He practically inhaled the tea before placing a hand either side of the tree and starting to take slow deep breaths.

"Imagine a crack opening up in the bark. Imagine it, brown and then black and then dark green, then green, then Adrian leaning against the tree coming into view," said Penny speaking softly just behind Terrance. I stood, holding my breath, staring at a spot on the tree, voices in my head repeating unhelpful phrases ad nauseum, like 'a watched pot never boils'. Suddenly, a crack rang out. The bark peeled back into brown, then black, then a green hole, dappled light, murky steam, opening a yawning, creaking gash in the tree.

"It's working, I'm doing it, I'm doing it!" tears of joy streamed down Terrance's face as his trembling fingers plunged into the bark as if it were water and pulled the portal open wider. I took a deep breath, nodded my thanks to Terrance, then I plunged my foot through it.

"I'm coming Adrian!"

10

I pulled my knees up to my chest, yawning and stretching, enjoying the soft, humid warmth of the forest. Olivier was still kneeling before the huge, twisted tower of black thorns, but then she slumped forwards. It had been nice hearing Michael's strong voice. He'd sounded scared, but I couldn't remember why. Something slipped from my hand. A stone, a nagging little voice in the back of my head, wanted me to pick it up. It was an important stone, but my arms were so heavy, and I was so warm.

"Stay awake!" Olivier's head snapped up, her voice piercing, jarring me back out of the haze. I did my best to take another slow deep breath, my throat sore and rattling.

"I am awake. I was just talking to Michael, but I've dropped the stone and I can't seem to find it," I said as I lazily patted myself down, my vision blurring before my heavy lids dropped closed again.

"Don't worry about that, just stay awake, Adrian, and you'll be fine." Olivier gave a grunt, followed by the sound of rustling leaves and squelching mud.

"I thought you'd already fallen asleep, anyway," I said, letting my head drop down and my chin rest against my knees, that I'd pulled up to my chest. I couldn't seem to get warm now. The swamp was sticky and humid, but shivers were wracking my body. I had to clench my jaw to stop my teeth chattering.

"I wasn't asleep, I was just thinking about next steps," said Olivier. She sounded strained.

"I don't think I can take any more steps. I'll just sit here for now… I'm sorry if I've been a bit of a let-down," I said. A tear rolled down my cheek as the idea of what was happening to me danced on the edge of my mind. I already knew. Part of me did anyway, but it was the deep down part and I felt so floaty, like I was only right at the top of my thoughts. Trying desperately not to look the reality of the situation in the eye. My breath had slowed now, to tiny little rattles.

"Don't worry, Adrian, you'll feel better soon, I promise," said Olivier. Her voice sounded small, like it was coming from far away. I was only vaguely aware that she was with me, and I couldn't seem to speak anymore. I wished I'd told her I loved her, whilst I still could. I couldn't feel much of any anything anymore, not hot, or cold, or sticky, like I was right on the edge of falling asleep, and I couldn't for the life of me remember why I

Mothers, Witches and Queens

shouldn't. "Just hold on Adrian, hold on, they'll be here soon," As Olivier spoke, her voice got louder, and crisper, and I could feel her leant against me, her weight on my side. Her hand on the back of my neck, a fresh, soothing, cooling feeling washing over me. Suddenly my lungs filled with air, and my eyes fluttered open again, feeling lighter.

"There you are, looking better already," Olivier croaked, I turned to face her and my stomach flipped. She was pale, a dark, almost blue grey colour, pouring with sweat, yet her lips looked so dry. Her eyes were huge, bulging, but dull, and somehow seemed to have sunk back into her skull. I felt like could see every bone through her stretched skin.

"Stop it! Olivier… Please… Stop." I could hardly speak, could barely get a word out between the sobbing as I cried like I'd never cried before. My whole body shaking, almost convulsing. I reached up to her wrist to pull her hand from my neck.

"Don't you dare," she said. Her voice creaked out of her like the splintering of dry wood, shooting me her signature stern glare, through her bulging bloodshot eyes.

"But… but…" I couldn't speak, I couldn't get a word past the whimpering sobbing, breath-stealing, cries.

"Just listen. I've got some things to say that I should have said before now." I nodded soundlessly as she took a slow, painful swallow.

"Adrian, I've not lived a life of great love. I lived a life of great privilege. It was my privilege to dedicate myself to caring for the forest and the fay. That made me happy for a long time, and I was good at it. Until I met you, the greatest joy of my life has been my time with you, time spent loving you. You may not be my son, but you are my boy, and I leave the rest to you. I need you to look after them all for me, Adrian. I know you can, my darling." She took one last painful gulp of air, cracked a smile, and her eyes slid shut, her head falling forward, resting against my shoulder as I felt her hand slip from my neck.

"Olivier, wake up Olivier, wake up," I said. I lifted a trembling hand to her sallow cheek and pushed water into her, or tried to at least. It just pooled around my fingers and ran impotently down her face.

"No," I whimpered. I grabbed her, pulling her into my lap, cradling her in my arms. She was so light, she felt hollow.

"Wake up, Olivier, please, for me, just wake, please… Please…" My voice cracked and I let out a wail like a wounded animal, collapsing forward, draping myself across her. I fell onto my side, still holding her in my arms. I don't know how long I lay there. Time slipped away as I sobbed.

"Wake up, please wake up," I repeated over and over until the words lost all meaning. My eyes grew heavy as the crushing, screaming grief gave way to numb exhaustion. I was barely awake when I vaguely registered a foot stepping out of the tree I was slumped against and slipped into sleep.

PART IV

SEVENTH IN SEVEN

1

I'd been sitting by his bedside for hours when it happened. Of course, Ionia had healed him the second we got him back, but he still hadn't woken up. She said he was just tired, that he'd need sleep. For all the good it can do, nymph magic is no substitute for sleep, that's what she'd said. So, we'd taken him home, bundled him in a blanket Penny had weaved back when she first started dreaming of us, and I'd been by his side every hour since. A row of undrunk cups of tea were lined up beside my chair. Mum didn't know what to do, because there was nothing to do. I just held his hand, put on a brave face and talked to him about happy things. I promised we'd never be apart again, begged him to come back to me. Stopped begging, stopped crying. I'd just kiss his cheek and hold his hand and pour every ounce of will and hope and anything else that might do any good into him. Whilst desperately trying to get that image out of my head. Adrian lying there, soaked with sweat and mud, legs cut to ribbons and skin the colour of ash, cradling her. holding onto her, what was left of her. Thin and dry and cracked and gone. And there it was again, in my head again. It would be in my nightmares, if I slept.

And then it happened. His finger closed, just a little, around my own.

"Adrian? Adrian, can you hear me?" I said. Tears tumbled freely down my face as his shining blue eyes fluttered open and his face came back to life.

"Michael?" said Adrian. His voice was small, but it was there.

"I'm here, Adrian, I'm here," I whispered, that was all my voice could manage as I leant towards him. I had to be close to him. If I wasn't, I didn't know what I would do. Burst into flames, melt into a puddle or lose my mind completely. I had to be close to him and not let him get far away again.

"Where am I?" he asked, blinking sleep from his eyes as his hand slipped into my hair and he scrunched it gently, sending warmth rushing through me. A little smile broke across his beautiful face as I drew closer. I didn't know whether to cry or jump for joy and I had to try very hard not to squeeze the life out of him.

"Our bedroom, you're in bed. How do you feel?" I asked, gently squeezing his hand.

"I don't remember… going to bed," he said. His beautiful face creased as his brow furrowed.

"D-don't worry about that, everything's fine now," I said hastily. I didn't want him to remember, not yet, for now he didn't have to know. Let him just be happy, just for a little while.

"I remember I was doing something important, something urgent," said Adrian, as the peace drained out of his face, replaced by a focused stare.

"That's okay, we... we can do it later," I said, even though I knew I'd lost the battle. It was all coming back to him, in all its awful detail.

"Olivier! Where is Olivier? She needs my help. I've got to help her!" Horror chased concentration from Adrian's face as I watched the awful memories scream into his mind. Suddenly he was a flail of limbs, scrabbling to get his legs underneath him as he leapt out of bed like it had given him a shock.

"Adrian, wait," I choked, more salty tears tumbling into my mouth.

"I can't, there's no time," he said. I winced as he staggered clumsily to the door. He hadn't recovered yet, not properly.

"Adrian please..." I said. My voice trailed away as he all but fell into and through the door, wearing just some bed trousers and a dressing gown.

"Michael, please, help me. I have to get to her, to help her," said Adrian. He turned to me. Already, urgency and panic were morphing in his voice. The memory must have been coming into clearer focus.

"Adrian, you can't," I said. I struggled around the lump in my throat as I offered him a hand and pulled him up and held him to my body.

"But she needs help," he whimpered. I shook my head wordlessly as he started to push away from me, struggling. He was so weak, he could barely fight at all.

"Let me go to her…" he said, bursting into tears as he started to pound feebly against my chest.

"No," I whispered, holding him, rubbing his back as he struggled in my arms.

"I can save her," he said, sobbing.

"She's gone, Adrian," I said softly.

"No! No, no!" He slammed his fists against me with his last burst of strength and then collapsed into my arms sobbing.

"I'm so sorry," I whispered, tears streaming down my cheeks as I held him to me and kissed his head.

"No, no, no, no, no…" he whimpered, his voice trailing away to nothing as his legs gave way beneath him and I lowered us both to the floor. His hands no longer fists, gripped my clothes as he cleaved to me, his body trembling all over. I stroked his hair, kissed him and wished, silently, that he'd be okay.

2

Olivier died. No one had managed to actually say those words yet. Michael had told me she'd gone, that was the closest anyone had got to saying it. That was just before I collapsed in his arms and cried myself to sleep. I couldn't sleep anymore, though. Now I was in Michael's living room, in that same blue grey half-light he'd been sleeping in, when I'd left him yesterday. Linda and Michael were up too. Linda had made so many cups of tea she'd run out of tea bags. Now they both just looked worried. They were worried about me, because I'd collapsed in Michael's arms and cried myself to sleep, and now I was up before the sun sitting in the living room staring at nothing. Apparently, we were on the special occasion loose leaf, which called for the special occasion teapot. It didn't seem very special, just inconvenient, and probably difficult to clean. Olivier was dead, and I was thinking about the special occasion teapot.

Linda had a special occasion, loose leaf stuck between her teeth. I couldn't seem to feel that she was dead. I had done, before. I'd felt it like panic, like something I had to stop, but that was like trying to stop the sunrise at midday.

"What happened to her... body?" I asked. My voice sounded distant.

"Once they realised she was... that they couldn't help her, they said they'd take her back, to take care of things. The erm, the sylph twins, I think it was," said Michael. He was struggling. His warm amber eyes were pink and blood-shot and sore looking. He had streaks left behind by tears tracking down his cheeks.

"They'll be singing the song of the lost. Last time I heard that, Cynthia had died," I said, matter-of-factly.

"Cynthia?" Linda asked.

"You remember the day I brought Adrian round for the first time, when his sister had died?" Michael asked, weakly.

"Oh, I do, you poor..." Linda cut herself off. She'd called me a poor dear so many times it had lost all meaning.

"She wasn't really my sister. She was a champion, like Michael would have been, if I'd done what I was supposed to. Olivier's champion. It was because of her that I knew I couldn't let them have Michael," I said.

Michael offered me a smile, reaching out to me, trying to find me in the dark. I didn't smile back and after a moment, his face fell. Somewhere off in the distance, I felt bad about that. Achingly stomach twistingly guilty and I

Mothers, Witches and Queens

hated myself for not giving him what he needed. For not letting him know things would get better. But that was all so far away, so distant that it was almost as if they were someone else's feelings, not mine. I didn't give him what he needed because I couldn't.

"I think that was the day I really knew I loved you," said Michael, looking down, talking to his feet. Part of me had fallen for Michael the second I set eyes on him, but that day was special.

"I remember you wrapping your arms around me. I never wanted that to stop," Michael smiled again, this time just for him. He smiled at the floor, escaping into a memory. I couldn't do that right now. I had to be here, in this room, in this blue light, looking at them, and the teapot with the rainbow polka dot pattern on it. And the brown blanket lazily thrown over the sofa, and the cushions splayed out across the floor where Michael's friends had slept the night before. The night before, the night before, the only memory my mind wanted to conjure anymore, which I didn't want to escape into right now.

"More tea, Adrian? There is still some in the pot," said Linda, breaking the silence that had settled.

"What do you do in the still world when someone dies?" I asked. I heard the word before I thought to say it, and for a second a cold shock ran through me, and I thought I might be sick or throw my mug across the room or sink to my knees and wail at the sky until my throat bled. I didn't do any of that. I just sat there.

"We have a funeral, we… we gather up the folks that knew them, and loved them, and we talk about that, and we bury them or whatever else they wanted done with their remains. They do all sorts these days," said Linda.

"Do you sing?" I asked.

"There's music," Linda nodded.

"I'd like to sing," I said, getting up from my chair. I padded through the cold morning of the house to the kitchen where Michael had left his school bag and found a pad and pencil.

"Won't there be a funeral for her in the fay forest?" Michael asked, as he and Linda followed me.

"We don't call it that. We do bury people though. Anyway, they will have done that as soon as they got back. I missed it. Slept through it," I said. Some part of me knew I should feel guilty for that, but I didn't.

"Adrian, that's not your fault. You were hurt and exhausted," said Michael. He was right behind me now. I could feel his breath on my neck as I scribbled down words in his notepad. He wanted to hug me and hold me and chase all the bad feelings away, but he didn't. He must have been tying himself in knots, worrying about being respectful and giving space and what I needed. We spend so much time tying ourselves in knots.

"It doesn't matter, I don't want to do it their way, I just want to do… something," I said.

"We can do whatever you want," he said, finally

plucking up the courage to place a hand on my shoulder and give it a squeeze.

"Will you come with me? To the fay forest, to do something for her?" I asked, turning now to face them both.

"Of course, we will," said Michael, a little life lighting him up again. I think he was happy to do something for me.

"Text the witches, and wake Daniel. I want there to be people there. She deserves to have people there," I said, grasping onto the idea that I was fighting for her. As long as I held onto that, whatever else was threatening to spill out couldn't. I could feel it, at my throat, and tickling my nose, and stinging behind the eyes. Something else threatening to be felt.

3

I squinted into the glare of the early morning sunlight, as Penny and Enid piled out of Enid's ancient Jeep. They were the only people in the witches' group chat that were actually awake and Adrian didn't seem in the mood to wait. It felt a bit feeble, just the six of us, but I didn't know what else to do.

"How is he?" asked Penny. She was dressed in a cable knit black jumper and skirt, her hair tied up with a knitting needle sticking through it, which I suspected she'd forgotten was there.

"I don't really know," I said. It was painful to admit, but true. I'd never seen him like this.

"He just has to get through it, whatever way he can," said Enid, giving my forearm a tight squeeze. For once, she wasn't wearing waders. I was surprised to find that she wasn't in camo and fishing gear. Instead, she appeared in a rather tight black dress that cut off just above the knee and a red satin blouse that matched her heels.

"You look... shall we go inside?" I said, not sure how to describe how she looked.

"No need," came Adrian's voice from behind me. He was wearing the gnomish clothes he'd worn as a uniform at The Fun Gi: The green blousy thing that mum was jealous of with the wide brown trousers. I'd always thought he looked beautiful in it, even if they were just work clothes. I wanted to tell him that, but somehow that seemed feeble too.

"I think we're ready," said Mum, following him out in a shoulder to toe black coat, with Daniel in her wake. Bleary-eyed and looking confused in a black suit that I think was his old college uniform.

"Let's go," said Adrian, striding past the rest of us across the road to Mr Davies' oak tree in the drive.

"Sorry the others couldn't make it Adrian. I think they're all still asleep," said Penny in a soft, small voice as we crossed.

"It's fine, now take my hand, I'll take you through," said Adrian, taking Penny's hand and walking her through the tree. I just about managed to catch Enid's expression as they vanished. Her eyes practically popped, but only for a moment before she composed herself again. Although she did make sure to be the next one he took through.

Mothers, Witches and Queens

"Will it hurt?" Daniel asked, looking at Mum nervously.

"It's as easy as stepping into the garden," said Mum, giving him a wink, before Adrian took her hand and led her through, followed by a still quite nervous looking Daniel.

"Adrian, can we talk, just for a moment?" I asked when he stepped back through one last time and it was just us, alone. He looked up at me with those eyes of his and something was missing. All the shine and brilliance were there, but it was different, cold almost, more like Nimueh maybe.

"What about?" he asked shortly, looking back over his shoulder at the tree.

"How you're feeling, what we're doing right now, anything really, just talk to me," I pleaded, a little desperation bleeding into my voice against my will. Adrian blinked up at me wordlessly. He opened his mouth, just for a second, then closed it again. His brow furrowed as he looked back over his shoulder to the tree again, shifting from one foot to the other. He seemed trapped, almost. I couldn't bear his discomfort. "We can talk later, we shouldn't keep them waiting." I said, letting him go. He nodded and quickly took my hand, my heart fluttering just for a second at his touch as he led me through the tree.

The forest was just as awe-inspiring as always. The look on Penny's face as she breathed in a wildflower the size of her head was a good reminder of that. Not to mention Enid almost toppling over as she leant so far back to take in the endless canopy. It was almost enough to make me crack a smile. There was something more though, something more than the dappled green light and the loamy smell and the gentle cool breeze and the flowers wafting along the path. It was a song, not quite like the war song I'd heard once before, or the life of the forest that Adrian had sang for me once at our lake. This one was different. It had less energy. It sort of moaned through the trees, and I could see Adrian shrink as it hit his ear.

"Are you okay?" I asked, leaning down to whisper to him, giving his hand a little squeeze.

"Let's get moving," he said, his hand slipping from mine as he started down the yellow spidery path of the forest. I blinked my eyes and looked up at the canopy and tried not to cry.

"You okay, Mikey," Mum whispered, her hand sliding into Adrian's spot as we followed him down the track.

"I'm fine," I lied. How I felt was complicated and hard to put into words and I wasn't sure I wanted to try, but I could feel them. Mum's big kind eyes burring into me.

"It's okay not to be fine you know," said Mum, squashing herself into me, almost like a big coat-wearing cat.

"I know he doesn't..." I began, "but it just feels like he..." I didn't want to finish that sentence.

"Hates you?" Mum asked, finishing it for me.

"How did you know?" I asked, furiously blinking away another tear.

"After your father died, I think we all had days like that.

Mothers, Witches and Queens

He doesn't hate you, Darling, he's just hurting, hurting so much he can't even feel a lot of it right now," said Mum, offering me a little smile.

"You're sure?" I asked, giving into desperation.

"Michael, I've seen a flicker of a smile on that boy's face once since we found him out in that swamp, just once. Do you know when it was?" Mum asked.

"When?" I asked, wondering how I could have possibly missed it. I hadn't let him out of my sight for a minute in case he needed something or wanted something. I'd been hoping he might have wanted me.

"He was talking about the time you took him home, after Cynthia, about how you wrapped your arms around him. You started smiling and just for a second, so did he. So, hold on to that and let all the other things just wash away," she said.

"Thanks, Mum," I said, giving up my fight as a little tear tumbled down my cheek. When Dad had died, I remember feeling alone, and that made me angry, angry that people didn't know how to be around me anymore. It was like I'd become just the grief, like the rest of me wasn't there anymore. I hoped I didn't make Adrian feel like that.

"We're here," said Adrian, coming to a stop in a mushroom laden clearing before a cave, the old gnome cave we'd met Olivier in once. Standing by the entrance was a shock of red hair, attached to a little elf.

"Cherry, how did you know we'd come here?" asked Adrian.

"All I had to do was think about where Olivier would most want to go. I knew eventually you'd turn up here," said Cherry, clasping both tiny hands around Adrian's.

"You did?" asked Adrian, his voice suddenly high, almost choking, like he was holding something back. Before I knew it, I was by his side, smiling down at Cherry, smiling up at Adrian, both his little hands reaching up to wrap themselves around one of his.

"Oh, of course. The others already put her to rest, but I thought you might like to do something of your own for her. Please, come inside," said Cherry, shooting me a wink almost too quick to catch before he led Adrian by the hand inside the cave. I could barely believe my eyes as I followed them in. Along the edges of the cave were hundreds of tiny phosphorescent mushrooms, lighting the walls, all of which were painted in blue waving patterns, as if to look like the shimmering surface of a lake.

"Cherry, how did you do all this?" I asked, as Adrian stopped dead in his tracks, turning on the spot.

"I have my ways," said Cherry mysteriously, tapping his long nose.

"This is beautiful," said Mum, leading the rest of the group into the cave.

"Linda, I presume, pleasure's all mine, please take a seat," said Cherry, leading her to one of the many moss-covered rocks that were dotted around the cave floor.

"How does that little man know my name?" asked

Mum, as I was seated on the boulder in front of hers, mine being the closest to the entrance to the cave.

"I'm... not sure," I whispered back, trying to remember if I'd mentioned her name in Cherry's cottage. I didn't think I had.

"Take a seat here, Adrian, next to Michael," said Cherry, leading Adrian to the boulder next to mine. I reached out a hand, but hesitated. Just as I did, Cherry caught my eye and gave a quick, encouraging nod. I took a breath and gingerly placed my hand on Adrian's. He didn't pull away. In fact, it even looked like his shoulders relaxed a little.

I'm going to begin now," Cherry said to Adrian, who turned to me and gulped.

"You'll be okay," I said, hoping it was the right thing to say. It seemed like I should say something. Adrian just nodded and turned to Cherry, who'd gone to stand in the centre of the cave before our little troop.

"Hello everyone, I'm Cherry, Adrian and Michael's friend, and I'm here to help. Today we're helping each other remember a very special fay named Olivier. Some of you didn't know her, but suffice to say, she was terrific. I've known a lot of fay in my time, more than most I'd wager, and Olivier was one of the best. Fierce and loyal, and smart and kind. I could go on, but I won't because someone else here, someone who misses her terribly, needs to speak. Adrian, the floor is all yours."

Without another word, Cherry offered a little bow to Adrian and disappeared back into a more shadowy corner.

Adrian didn't stand at first, he just glanced around the cave, as if looking for someone, then slowly got to his feet, took two small steps forward and turned to face the little group. He had a piece of notepad paper screwed up into a ball in his fist.

"Olivier was my aunty, my mother's half-sister. She was part gnome, and part water nymph. She was... she was a part of the Excalibur system... She was..." Adrian paused, his brow furrowed as he fidgeted with the paper. His eyes flitted around the cave again until they fell on me, wild and scared looking. I didn't know what to do. I just nodded, and smiled and held his gaze.

"She was my friend, my only friend for a while, I think." There he was again, my Adrian. His eyes lit up and twinkling and feeling again, like someone had lit a candle and led him back. I couldn't fight the smile that cracked across my face, as it felt like he was talking right to me.

"The beauty of Olivier was that she was always there. She was the cottage at the end of everyone's street. Of course, every death is hard, and every person is missed, but... Not like this. Oliver knew everyone, and everyone knew her. She was reliable, she was..." All that coldness had melted away and with it came a flood of tears. Adrian paused, his voice strangled by sobs for a second. I was about to stand, to walk to him, to support him, when he looked up into the ceiling and let go a laugh. I was stunned back onto my boulder.

"Her last words... Her last words were... They were

spent, telling me that she'd spent her life caring for the fay forest, and now... Now she needed me to pick up where she was leaving off." He looked forward again, tears tumbling like someone had turned on a tap and let out a little sob. My eyes stung, my throat was thick, and my nose tickled. I wanted to scoop him up and take his pain away. I didn't know, I hadn't even thought, but of course he'd have heard her last words, alone in the swamp, watching her die. Suddenly I was furious with myself. Why didn't I think? Why wasn't that obvious?

"I don't think... I don't know if I can do that for her. Anyway, I wrote her a song. In the forest we sing to mark the big occasions, birth, death, war, love, but we don't have words like humans do. I wanted to write her something with words. To speak to her, one last time. I'm going to sing it for you now."

Adrian unfolded the paper ball, his hands trembling, and blinked away his tears. He took a few slow, shaky breaths, then set his eyes forward, past us all, as if he'd seen something there, something he could sing to, and he began to sing.

> From the woods
> And the trees
> To the ground
> Now lay at ease
> We remain
> And think of you
> You'll be with us

Through and through
From the sky
From the river
You'll be far
but always here
I'll think of you
On summer breeze
Beneath the ground
You lay at ease
I'll come along
Soon enough
To be with you
When I've had enough.

His voice was rich and deep, but not as steady as normal. It wobbled and trembled. I could see him straining, veins in his neck, jaw set rigid, hands shaking, tears tumbling, holding fast to that paper like it was a life raft. As he reached the last lines, he looked as though he was going to collapse, his voice getting tight and squeaky and, as the last note echoed through the cave, he threw down his paper and swallowed hard.

"Thank you all for coming." He almost choked on the words before he all but ran out of the cave. I got up and followed him, ignoring the streaming eyes of everyone else in the cave as I passed. The last lines ringing in my head like an alarm bell. What did he mean? That he'd be with her soon enough.

"Adrian, wait! Please," I called after him once we were

Mothers, Witches and Queens

clear of the cave. He stopped, his shoulders were shaking, his breathing short and ragged.

"Please talk to me," I begged, panic cracking in my voice.

"What do you want me to say?" he said, wheeling round on the spot, his face red and angry, like I'd never seen it.

"Whatever's on your mind, whatever you want, how you're feeling, how you wish you felt, anything at all," I said quickly, closing the gap between us.

"Well, I don't know what I'm thinking, and what am I feeling? Half the time I'm not even feeling anything and then the rest of the time it's like there's so much feeling inside me that it's going to rip me wide open to make room." He was waving his arms wildly, his eyes red and teary, his hands flexing into fists and unflexing as he shouted into the forest.

"Adrian I—" I wanted to tell him it would be alright, that it'd pass, that what hurts now will hurt tomorrow, but maybe in a week you'll forgot you're in pain, just for a little while, and then in a month maybe you'll go a whole day without it hurting. That it'll always be there, somewhere, and that right now it feels like you can't possibly live with it, but you can, and that it'll get easier.

"It's true, you know, the very last thing she said to me, her very last words, as she pushed her life into me, to save mine. I physically watched her giving her life, to save mine, as she told me that I needed to look after everyone now, because she couldn't do it anymore. That's how much better she was than me. She died saving some undeserving brat whilst begging him to keep looking after people. Selfless to the end, Olivier. Well done." He looked up, shouting into the sky as he addressed her. I knew some of these thoughts had lived in Adrian's head before, but never like this. They'd never hurt him like this before.

"Adrian, you're not a brat. You're—"

"Oh, I am, I am a brat. I sent her troop away. I demanded that they go and save my boyfriend and left us stranded there, in that poison wasteland. I ran off that morning, ran off from you, and I got Olivier killed. That was all me, and what do I get in return? I get my life saved. I get the perfect boyfriend waiting at my bedside, just desperate to love me, and I can't even let him. What did Olivier get? A lifetime of duty, a disappointing nephew, and a death sentence, that's what. She's gone. You're all stuck with me now! Sorry for the let-down!" He was yelling at the small crowd that had assembled behind me now. All the attendees of her... whatever it had been. His face was red, and veins were popping all over his neck. I could hardly bear to watch. It was worse than watching someone writhing in pain. Like he was tied up in one big angry knot.

"Adrian... I'm sorry, I'm so sorry," I sobbed.

"Don't be. You did nothing wrong, you never do, you needed help, and I chose to send it to you. I chose you and she died. I ran away from you and she died. I messed up and she..." He'd been jabbing himself in the chest with every 'I'. It was painful to watch. He was doing it with such force that it was bound to leave a bruise. Then all at once he seemed to run out of steam.

"Adrian?" I took another step forward, worried that at any minute he might just collapse again.

"I can't be here, I've got to go," he said, as he turned his back and tore off down the yellow winding path.

4
———

Adrian was grieving hard. He was grieving like a dog gnashing its teeth at a nasty thorn in its paw. I'd never grieved like that, not even for David. I didn't have it in me to feel all of that at once. Adrian didn't seem able to stop himself feeling it anymore. He'd done his best. He'd been like a robot this morning. I guess this was what happened when the dam breached and Michael was being washed away in it. My poor boy. Adrian had turned tail and ran, with all of us there watching, like it was some sort of grotesque spectator sport without any winners. I was about to put my hand in Michael's, be his shoulder to cry on when Daniel walked straight past the awful gawping lot of us and pulled Michael, quite roughly, into a tight hug. My boys in each other's arms, not saying a word. What I wouldn't give to show David that.

"What do we do now?" asked the girl behind me, Penny,

I think her name was. She wore a phenomenal amount of wool. It made me itchy just looking at her.

"I think it's best if you two pop home. We'll find Adrian," I said, not entirely sure how they'd manage that, but then I'd never been particularly detail orientated. I wasn't entirely sure how we'd manage our side of the deal either, come to think of it.

"How?" asked the older woman. The last time I'd seen her, she looked like a fisherwoman; now she looked like she should be in a Bond movie. I had to respect the range.

"I'll handle that, leave it to Cherry," said Cherry, the funny little man with the very wide mouth and very red hair.

"Thank you, Cherry," I said, giving him a grateful nod before hurrying away from the witches to catch up with my boys.

"I'm sorry for being a dick about Adrian, we'll sort it out," I overheard Daniel say to Michael as I approached.

"Any guesses where he might have gone, Love?" I asked, wrapping an arm around Michael's waist to give him a quick squeeze as I caught them up. A well-timed squeeze can do wonders.

"What if he doesn't want to be found?" Michael asked rather forlornly.

"In my experience, people rarely want to be on their own deep down, and if you think about it, Adrian's probably feeling lonelier than ever right now. He just needs the right people around him."

"What if we're not the right people though?" Michael

asked, his bottom lip wobbling like it did when he was a little boy and he skinned his knee.

"I don't see any better candidates around, so I suppose we'll have to do. Now, where might that little nymph of yours be?" I asked.

"I don't know. He could be anywhere," said Michael, throwing his arms up.

"Oh, come on, Michael, you and that boy are so close you basically live in each other's armpits. Think, he misses Olivier, where is he going?" I said.

"To her cottage," said Michael, with all the certainty of an idea that had gone straight from gut instinct to vocalisation without getting muddied up by second thoughts and doubts and all those other unhelpful things your brain likes to chuck into the mix.

"Off we go then, lead the way," I said.

"How long will it take to get there?" asked Daniel, whose head had been on a swivel since the moment we walked through that tree. It was much nicer in the forest when you weren't being kidnapped.

"Doesn't take long to get anywhere around here, as long as you've got permission to get there," said Michael.

"Permission?" asked Daniel.

"It's hard to explain. I don't really get it myself to be honest, it's just… You just end up where you're going when you walk on this path and everywhere is on this path. But if you've not got permission to go, you've got to find your own way. Which is a nightmare, cause the only differentiating feature is the path, and the path leads everywhere so... We're here."

Michael gave up explaining, which was probably for the best, as a little cottage came into view. It wasn't tall, only one storey I'd guess, maybe with a little attic, and with two windows on the front, either side of the door. It was off white, with a reddish-brown roof and a chimney just barely peeping out. It looked a bit like a mushroom if you let your eyes go out of focus. Most of it was really a garden, behind a fence that appeared to have grown out of the ground rather than being hammered into it. If anything, the garden inside the fence was wilder than outside, with huge shoots of grass, colourful mushrooms and wildflowers bigger than Michael jutting out at odd angles. Finally, there was a crystal blue pond with a small bench propped up against the house beside it, with a person sitting on it. With skin that from afar looked unhealthily pale, but up close had a charming pink flush. He had a shock of platinum blonde hair the girls on the dye bottles would kill for, and twinkly blue eyes that even I couldn't say no to.

"Michael, do you mind if I have a quick word with him?" I asked, turning my back to Adrian to talk to Michael face-to-face, and hopefully keep him from staring at Adrian for just a minute.

"What are you gonna say?" asked Michael, fidgeting with his fingers as he glanced over my shoulder nervously.

"Probably just talk about benches," I said.

"Benches? Mum, what are you talking about? You can't

Mothers, Witches and Queens

just go over there and talk about benches. Olivier died, I think he might want to hurt... Mum it's important." My god, that look in his eyes. I don't think Michael had ever cared even a tenth as much about anything else as he did about this.

"I know it is, Love. Just trust me, I won't be long," I said, giving him a quick wink before I set off for Olivier's cottage, not giving him a chance to say no. I waved to Adrian as I approached and rather clumsily hopped Olivier's fence, almost falling straight into the pond as I staggered my recovery. He didn't wave back. He barely looked up, barely registered me at all.

"Mind if I sit with you?" I asked, hovering just above the bench. He shook his head silently, and I descended.

"I've got a bench like this in my garden," I said softly.

"David's bench," said Adrian.

"That's right. You know, I got that bench when I was feeling a bit like I think you are now," I said.

"Did it help?" he asked, flashing his bloodshot eyes and tear-streaked face as he looked up at me, just for a moment.

"Not at first, but later it did. You sit on it sometimes don't you, in the mornings, on your own?" I asked. I'd seen him do it, I think he sang on it, but I'd only watched from the window. He just nodded his reply, glancing over at Michael nervously. Guiltily, I expect, Adrian had a great aptitude for feeling guilty.

"So, this was the house at the end of everyone's street

that you mentioned? It's beautiful," I said, patting the cottage behind me.

"It is," said Adrian, almost silently.

"Did you spend a lot of time here growing up?" I asked. I'd got the sense that Olivier had been more of a mum to him than Nimueh ever was.

"As much as I could, Nimueh didn't give me much time of my own, but I spent of most of the time I did get with her," said Adrian. His face seemed undecided between whether that was something to smile about or not.

"I liked her you know," I said, watching a petal land on the surface of the pond, sending a ripple out across the perfect glass surface.

"Me too," said Adrian, a tear tumbling down his cheek.

"You loved her," I said.

"Seems to be a bit of a curse, doesn't it?" Adrian laughed, but not a happy laugh, the kind of laugh someone does when they put diesel in their petrol car. After spilling their breakfast down their work top, or burning their hair off in the straighteners. A sort of self-loathing expulsion of air.

"I don't think she'd see it that way, and I know Michael wouldn't," I said.

"I didn't mean to shout at him like that. I'm not angry at him, I'm just…" Adrian's voice trailed off.

"Full up?" I said.

He didn't speak. Judging from tears rolling down his cheeks, I don't think he could have at that moment. He just nodded.

Mothers, Witches and Queens

"It's a wonder you've got any of those left," I said, wrapping an arm around his shoulder and pulling him into me. Instantly his little arms were around my tummy, and he was sobbing into my lap.

"I don't know what to do with it all. I've got nowhere to put it, she's gone and I've all these feelings and nowhere to put them." His speech was stop-start and shaky, breaking through the sobs and whimpers in bursts.

"I've got somewhere to put them," I said softly, running my fingers through his perfect shiny hair.

"You do?" He looked up at me with those eyes, red and teary and just a little bit hopeful and my God if I didn't almost start crying again, his bloody singing had already got me once today.

"Want me to show you?" I asked him.

"Yes please," said Adrian.

"Okay then, Lovely, let's get a shift on," I said.

He nodded and sat up, then stood up, his eyes lingering on Olivier's door.

"She'd have hated this," he said.

"Hated what?" I asked.

"Us lingering in her garden. She hated lingering, she just wanted people to come in and tell her what they needed so she could sort it out for them. No nonsense," said Adrian. He was crying again, but he was smiling too, which I took as progress.

"Sounds like she was quite marvellous," I said, offering him my hand.

"She was," said Adrian, taking it as I led him out of the garden, beckoning Michael and Daniel to come and join us as we rejoined the yellow path.

"Where are we going?" asked Michael anxiously as he caught up with us. His eyes were on the road ahead, although he couldn't keep them from flitting back to Adrian every couple of seconds.

"I've got something I'd like to show Adrian back home," I said.

"I'm sorry for shouting at you. I'm not angry at you," said Adrian, with all his usual gentle kindness.

"It's okay, can I... Hold your hand?" asked Michael.

"You don't have to ask," said Adrian, and as he grasped Michael's hand in his, they both seemed half a stone lighter. I couldn't tell you how it happened, but before a minute had passed, that grove of giant trees we arrived through was coming into view. Like we'd just rounded a bend, and it was there.

"I wonder when we'll be back here," said Michael, looking around the forest wistfully as we drew close to our way home. It was the sort of look no one ever gave Starkton. Some people got that look on their face when they got to their big fancy university, but Michael didn't. He only looked at this place like that, and all of a sudden it seemed very stupid of me not to have realised that sooner.

"We'll be back. Morgana is out, and I've got a last request to..." Adrian's voice trailed off and his head lowered.

Mothers, Witches and Queens

"We've got a request. You don't have to do it alone," said Michael.

"I think I've had my fill of trying to do things without you," Adrian said, as we stopped before the grove. He took us through in turn.

Michael and Daniel went into the house and I led Adrian to the garden, to David's bench. I sat on the left end and patted the spot just beneath the name plaque, for Adrian to sit.

"It's a lovely bench, but I've seen it before," said Adrian, perching himself next to me.

"Not just the bench. If you look just to your right, you should see a dent, do you see it?" Adrian glanced down and ran his finger along the wood. It was a bit tired and rain-worn now, but it held up fine and had turned a lovely deep brown. It was almost totally undamaged, except for that dent.

"Found it," said Adrian, rubbing his finger against the groove.

"That's where I put my feelings, when David died and I was overwhelmed," I said.

"I don't understand," said Adrian, looking at me, confused.

"It was a few weeks after David's accident. I was back at work, but I wasn't doing very well. I kept dreaming of the police coming to my door, giving me the news that Michael and Daniel had been in an accident too. Daniel was struggling to revise with exams coming up and Michael had turned so inward he was basically a hermit crab, and I couldn't believe I still had to go to work and sell people package holidays to Benidorm, but I did.

"Anyway, there was this man who came into our branch, and he wanted to book a fancy all inclusive, for his family, his sister's family and his wife's sister's family. Three big families. The man was nice enough, had all the dates he needed and all his details on hand, that sort of thing, but as nice as he was, he was driving me completely up the wall. I got so angry I walked straight out of the branch, didn't even tell my manager. I stormed all the way back here, left my car in town, and when I got to this street, I was still furious. I walked right up to the house and just out of the corner of my eye, spotted this bench. We'd just put the name plaque on that weekend. I found myself staring at the name plaque and I was getting angrier and angrier and I realised I wasn't angry at that man. I couldn't be, because I was still getting angrier, and he was back in the branch being taken care of by my manager.

"Then it hit me. I was angry at David, and I sat myself down on this bench and I told him off. I was shouting my head off. The neighbours must have thought I was barmy. Do you know what I said? I said, 'How dare you? How dare you leave me and the boys alone? You're never gonna walk into a travel agents and book me a holiday again. Never gonna give me a foot rub when I get in from work again, never going to cook my tea for me again'. He was never gonna tell me he loved me again. And I hated him for it. I

Mothers, Witches and Queens

hated him so much that before I knew it, I was punching this damn bench of his so hard I left a dent, and my wedding ring cut right into my finger. Had to go to the fire station to get it cut off, still got the scar. But you know what? After I'd shouted and screamed and punched his bench, I felt a bit better. It took me a while to realise it, and a while longer to forgive myself, for hating David. I've forgiven him now too, and that feels better."

"I don't hate... I mean... I'm not angry at her," said Adrian, his eyes firmly cemented to the floor in front of his feet.

"That's okay, you don't have to be, but it's also okay if you are," I said, patting his back slowly.

"I mean, it's not like she chose to leave me... And asking me to look after everyone, well, that's just what she was like. Her mind was always asking what happened next. She'd already worked out the now part, she'd already decided what she was going to do. That she was going to die, saving me. She was just making sure you know?" He turned to look at me and it was there again, that twisted-upness that had exploded after his song.

"She must have trusted you," I said.

"Oh, she must have, mustn't she? Trusted me with quite a lot in the end. I guess that was her last plan. She always had a plan: solve this, fix that, get rid of them, well that means her plan for Morgana was me. Didn't leave me with any clues though, just look after everyone, simple as that. She planned to leave me. I watched her do it now, I think of it. I was barely there at the time, sort of drifting in and out, and she was kneeling and then her head fell. It looked as though she'd fallen asleep, but now it's so clear, that must have been the moment she decided what happened next.

That was the moment she decided to die and leave me behind." Adrian's face was red again, he was just barely hanging onto his words, struggling to carry on ranting rather than start crying. "Didn't bother to include me in the planning of course. Why would she? Why break the habit of a lifetime? Olivier's got a plan, that was code in the forest, code for, you'll do what you're told and you'll like it. Well, I don't Olivier, I hate it, d'you hear me?" he said, shouting now, standing and shouting at the sky, just like I had that day. "I hate your god-awful plan. I hated watching you die, watching the life drain from your eyes whilst you begged me to save everyone. How can you ask that of me? You get to up and leave me behind and expect me to carry on without you." He sank to his knees. "That's not fair." His voice shrinking as he lost the battle to hold on to the anger. "How's that fair?" he asked, turning to me, his eyes full of hurt.

"It's not, Lovely, none of it is, but you know, just because she asked it of you, doesn't mean you have to let it consume you," I said, joining him on the floor and wrapping him up in my tightest squeeze.

"I don't know how not to," he said.

"Leave a bit of it behind, like I did. In the bench, it's not going anywhere, you're not letting her down or giving up on

Mothers, Witches and Queens

her. Just give yourself permission to not feel all of it, all the time," I said, rubbing his back.

"I don't think I want to punch the bench," said Adrian in a small voice. I couldn't help but laugh.

"You don't have to punch the bench, Love, do whatever feels right," I said, struggling up from my knees as I let him out of the hug.

"Okay, I'll try," he said. Without another word, he got back on the bench, closed his eyes, took a few deep breaths, rubbed the dent my wedding ring had left with his finger a couple times and gave a shaky sigh.

5

"So, what do you want to do today? We can do anything you want," said Michael. Linda was heading off for work and Daniel had already disappeared into his room.

"I'm not sure," I said, glancing through the living room window into the front garden, at the bench, where I was supposed to have left some of my feelings. Right now, there was a feeling in my chest, like a pressure, which I was hoping might go away if I ignored it.

"If you want, we can start trying to work out what to do about Morgana. We could get in touch with the witches, or we could—"

"I think I need a distraction, something happy," I said, cutting him off before I caved into the pressure to spend every waking moment trying to honour Olivier. She left me behind. I didn't owe her every waking moment of my life. That's what I was trying to tell myself anyway. To my surprise, Michael's eyes lit up and a broad smile burst across his face.

"What about a feel-good movie? We could make popcorn, cuddle under a blanket, have hot chocolates cause we're out of tea, what d'you think?" he said.

"What's a feel-good movie?" I asked, as I felt a similar smile spread across my face. I couldn't help it. His was infectious.

"Exactly what it sounds like. Come on, I'll show you," said Michael, taking my hand in his as he led me into the living room and started rummaging through the dusty wooden chest they kept their DVDs in.

"You seem excited," I said, perching myself on the sofa arm.

"I am, I get to spend the day chilling with my boyfriend, watching this!" he said, thrusting a little blue DVD box into the air, entitled Mamma Mia! The Movie, sing along edition.

"What's that then?" I asked.

"The greatest feel-good movie of all time, according to Mum, and we're gonna watch it," he said, as he began fervently jabbing at the TV with the various remotes that had to be used in a very particular order to get the DVD player to work. It took me two seasons of Charmed before I got the hang of it.

"So, what happens in it?" I asked.

"Well, this girl is getting married, and she wants to invite her dad to her wedding, but she doesn't know who he is. All she has is her mum's diary from the year she was conceived, and it turns out her mum was sleeping with three men at around the same time. So, she invites them all," Michael said.

"You know, Nimueh did a similar thing with me, only I suspect for different reasons," I said, following Michael into the kitchen where he started the complicated and still somewhat mind-boggling process of creating hot chocolate and popcorn. Whenever I tried, the hot chocolate turned out clumpy, and we ended up with a lot of little hard burnt seed things.

"What d'you mean for different reasons?" he asked.

"Well, Nimueh courted somewhere around ten partners I think it was, to make sure my paternal parentage would be unknown. That way, she was the only one who could ever have a clear claim to my birth. So she'd have total control of my upbringing, and therefore total control over the line of Nimueh. I'm guessing the Mamma Mia lady wasn't trying to control a dynasty," I said, remembering when a few of my potential fathers had turned up in my early life, trying to make an impression. None of them had stuck around for long.

"Oh… yeah, no, she was more sort of having a summer of love. That must have been weird for you, having people fight over you," said Michael. His face had shifted, like my story was chasing away the excitement of the movie.

"It was, but I found ways to hide from it," I said, taking the hot chocolates back into the living room.

"With Olivier?" he asked, in a gentler tone than usual. I just nodded and smiled.

"What's a 'sing along version'?" I asked, changing the subject as my chest tightened.

"Oh, you'll love it," said Michael, his face lighting up again.

6

Adrian was asleep in my bed, in my arms, making the little whistling sound he made, and my chest was finally starting to feel looser. I didn't know what we were going to do about Morgana, or what I'd do about uni or how Adrian would feel in the morning, but right now, as I watched the blazing red numbers on my alarm clock tick over to midnight everything was finally peaceful.

Then a knocking sound reverberated through my bedroom door. I eased my arm out from beneath Adrian, slipped out of bed, and crept across the room. I opened the door only a crack as I was just in boxer shorts.

"Can I come in?" I almost jumped as Daniel spoke through the gap in the door, his normal voice sounding like a yell after all my silent creeping.

"Adrian's asleep," I hissed.

"Can you come out then?" Daniel hissed back.

"I'm not wearing anything," I said.

"You've got your shorts on," came Adrian's sleepy voice from behind me, and with a sigh I dropped my whisper, any attempt not to disturb his sleep defeated.

"Come in," I grumbled, snatching some actual shorts off the floor, and pulling them on as I let my bedroom door swing open.

"Sorry for waking you, Adrian," Daniel said, looking a little sheepish as he hovered awkwardly half in my doorway, half still on the landing.

"It's okay, what up?" asked Adrian, his conversational tone almost comical as he craned out of bed, reaching for my discarded hoodie whilst awkwardly holding my duvet over his chest.

"Here." I handed him the hoodie, and he quickly disappeared inside the surplus of material, his modesty preserved.

"I've been thinking," said Daniel, now stepping into the room, judging that everyone was in an acceptable level of dress. Me in my bottoms and Adrian in my top. "Or rather, I can't stop thinking. I can't get that embroidery out of my head," he said, perching at the foot of the bed.

"What?" I didn't know what I'd expected my brother to be knocking on my bedroom door at midnight about, but I certainly wouldn't have guessed embroidery.

"What embroidery?" asked Adrian, his expression darkening, the word having become synonymous with the image of Adrian draped over a tombstone. The truth that neither of us had ever admitted was that we'd been assuming that image forecast my death, although we now knew it'd foretold Olivier's fate. Or at least in some dark way, I hoped it did, because if not, Adrian was due for even more loss, and he couldn't bear anymore. Not to mention the secret shameful relief that came with it not being my tombstone.

"You didn't tell him about what Penny stitched during the goblin attack?" Daniel asked, looking almost theatrically shocked.

"Funnily enough, it wasn't at the top of the agenda," I bristled, then immediately wished I could muster more patience.

"Well, tell me now," said Adrian, inching towards Daniel, eager for more information, desperation half masked by hope.

"It said something like, Morgana is free and to warn Adrian about a trap which is pretty self-explanatory, but there was another bit. Something about destroying the coven before the seventh in seven wakes, or something," said Daniel, his expression becoming distant as he recalled the embroidery, his words sending a chill down my spine.

"Seventh in seven, where have I heard that before?" I asked. The feeling that I was forgetting something important was palpable.

"I know!" said Adrian, his expression lightening as he scrambled off the bed, my hoodie dropping to just around his knees whilst he rummaged through a pile of clothes in the corner of my room. I caught myself holding my breath as Daniel and I watched wordlessly, a sense of anticipation filling the room.

"Found it!" said Adrian triumphantly, producing Gwen's small wooden chest with its crudely carved pentagram emblazoned on the splintered lid.

"What is it?" asked Daniel, watching as Adrian flipped the latch and grabbed one of the stacks of tarot cards, quickly flicking through them.

"Something the witches gave us. It was Gwen's. It has her tarot cards and stuff in it," I explained.

"What's that got to do with anything?" Daniel asked.

"This!" said Adrian, thrusting a card under our noses, scattering a few more across the floor in his excitement.

"Seventh In Seven" Goosebumps ran down my arms as Daniel read the card aloud. It depicted a round-faced smiley lady with six little stars twinkling around her. "But that's not a normal tarot card, right?" Daniel asked.

"I don't think these are either," I said, kneeling to examine the ones that Adrian had dropped. I was no expert in tarot, but Adrian and I had spent a few restless hours researching dead ends. Typically, tarot cards featured things like cups and wands. We'd never found any reference to cards like the ones in this deck, like The Meditator, The Geomancer and The Gardener.

"I wonder where she got them," said Daniel thoughtfully.

"I think she made them herself. They look hand

Mothers, Witches and Queens

sketched to me," said Adrian, taking the Seventh In Seven card back to study.

"Does this look like anyone to you?" I asked, collecting the pile of scattered cards up and handing The Gardener to Daniel. It depicted a balding man in overalls, tending to a scribble that vaguely resembled a cactus in a plant pot. I watched Daniel's eyes dart from the card to me, recognition crystallising before my eyes.

"Hand me another," he said, all but snatching the cards out of my hands, riffling through them. He gave a snort of laughter before thrusting The Crone card under my nose, a stooped older woman wielding a knife, then The Meditator, a pony-tailed lady, her legs a crisscross scribble beneath her.

"And this one, remind you of anyone?" I asked, my hand shaking with excitement as I reached for another of the cards that had been discarded to the floor. The Geomancer, pictured beneath the title an aproned woman, with a bouncy black ball of hair.

"What is it?" Adrian asked, finally able to tear himself away from the Seventh In Seven card long enough to recognise our shared excitement.

"Remind you of anyone?" Daniel asked, throwing The Gardener, The Crone and The Meditator cards down on the bed in dramatic fashion. I followed suit, adding The Geomancer to the pile. Even in the dull half-light, I could see Adrian's eyes sparkle as they peeled wide.

"Let me see those," he said, grabbing the rest of the cards out of Daniel's hand, shuffling through them at speed, discarding less interesting cards in haphazard fashion. Until with dramatic flair, he added another to the set on the bed. The Weaver, a round-faced girl wielding a crochet hook.

"Well, that makes five," I said, fighting to stifle the tremble in my voice.

"So, we all recognise these, right?" Daniel asked.

"Yep," said Adrian, still shuffling, desperate for a sixth.

"And I can't be the only one who sees the resemblance between this card and..." Daniel's voice tailed off as both of us studied the round-faced smile of the familiar woman, surrounded by six twinkling lights.

"Mum," I breathed.

7

"I'm awake!" I said, jerking forward as a falling sensation froze the muscles in my body stiff. I blinked my eyes, Michael's bedroom steadily coming into focus around me. I didn't remember falling asleep. Which probably explained why I'd woken sitting up on the bed, slumped against Michael's bedroom wall. Gwen's old tarot cards sprawled across the bed in front of me, one of them still in my hand. I groaned at the ache running along my neck as I sat up.

"Join the club," Daniel groaned. He and Michael were on the floor beside the bed, both staring at glowing laptop screens.

"What time is it?" I asked, rubbing my stinging eyes.

"About eight-ish," said Daniel, stretching.

"Have you two slept?" I asked.

"Nope," said Michael.

"Oh... find anything?" I asked, hopefully.

"Nope," Michael yawned and stretched before settling down next to me on the bed.

"That's not strictly true. We've been looking up magic sevens. Like the whole seventh son of a seventh son thing, trying to figure out how Mum could fit in," said Daniel.

"Which she doesn't," said Michael.

"No, but she is a seventh daughter," said Daniel, a little defensively.

"Yes, but Granny was an only child, so she isn't the seventh of a seventh is she," said Michael, his temper sounding a little frayed.

"Well not literally, but obviously Morgana thought someone existed that did. So, I've been thinking that maybe it doesn't have to be so literal. Apparently, when it comes to magic and witchcraft, a lot of its to do with symbolism. Someone doesn't have to be the seventh born of someone seventh born, they could be some other kind of brother or sister," said Daniel.

"Like a sister witch," I said.

"Except we couldn't even find a seventh witch card in the tarot deck," said Michael. It was becoming obvious they'd already had this debate whilst I slept.

Knock, knock!

The sound of someone banging quite loudly on the front door thundered through the house.

"COULD SOMEBODY GET THAT, I JUST GOT OUT THE SHOWER!" Linda yelled, presumably from the bathroom.

Mothers, Witches and Queens

"I'll go!" called Michael, who seemed eager to leave the great debate behind him as he quickly pulled on a vest. Daniel and I followed wearily behind him as he jogged down the stairs.

"Hello, Terrance, bit early for house calls, isn't it?" asked Michael, as he opened the door only for Terrance to step straight through the doorway and into the hall without waiting for an invitation. He had big purple bags under his eyes and looked a little agitated, much like the rest of us.

"Is your mother in? I need to test a theory," he said, kicking his walking boots off as he all but pushed past Michael.

"Of course, she's in Terrance, its only... what time is it exactly?" Michael asked, glancing back at me, whilst flicking his eyes at Terrance. If I could read the look on his face like a book, it'd be titled Does Terrance seem like he's gone a bit mad to you?

"It's 8:15. I've been waiting in my van since seven, but I couldn't wait any longer. Where is she?" he asked, brushing past me out of the entrance hall.

"Oh, hello Terrance, bit early for a house call, isn't it?" Linda echoed Michael from the top of the stairs. She was wearing a fluffy pink dressing gown with a big, splodged bleach stain on it. Her hair was bound up in a big towel balanced on her head, a bit like a banana.

"Could you make me a cup of tea?" asked Terrance. I took another deep breath, ignoring the feeling of urgency spreading down from my throat, tightening my chest again now that I was properly waking up.

"Erm, not right now, I've got to get work, are you alright, Love?" I could see it on Linda's face, vague amusement shifting into concern. Something about Terrance was off.

"It's important, please," he all but begged as he started climbing the stairs.

"Oh, alright then, you're in luck. We just got new tea bags in yesterday," said Linda, switching gears to a gentler tone as she started making her way downstairs.

"Tea leaves would be better," said Terrance. The words tumbled out of him so quickly it was as if he didn't have to think at all. Almost like he'd rehearsed this.

"We're fresh out I'm afraid, Lovely. Will tea bags be okay?" she asked, as she shot Michael a similar look to the one he'd shot me. This book would be titled, Terrance seems to have gone completely mad.

"It's fine, let's just hurry," he said.

"Is everything alright, Terrance?" asked Michael, as Terrance hurried back down the stairs, past him and into the kitchen.

"I've been doing research. I've got a theory," Terrance replied, which didn't really answer the question.

"So have we, but you don't see us barging into your house at eight in the morning," Daniel grumbled under his breath.

"Well, alright then," said Linda, as she followed

Terrance into the kitchen. He watched her make the tea with such intense focus that you'd think she was performing restoration on a piece of fine art.

"Leave the bag in," he commanded, just as she was about to drop it into the bin.

"This is officially weird," I whispered, as the three of us hovered in the kitchen doorway watching Terrance watch Linda make tea.

"Maybe we're hallucinating due to sleep deprivation," Daniel suggested, I think only half-jokingly.

"Oh my God, Terrance, you'll burn your mouth," said Linda, quite melodramatically as Terrance appeared to drain the whole mug of tea in one long draft, at the same time fumbling through his pockets to produce his phone.

"I wonder what his theory is," I thought aloud, the three of us enchanted by the bewildering scene.

"Hello, Liz, how is it looking now? I just had the tea!" Terrance all but yelled down the phone as he clutched it to his ear, still holding fast to his now empty mug. There was a pause as we all watched on in anticipation for an answer we couldn't hear.

"As I suspected!" said Terrance triumphantly as he hung up the phone and almost dropped it, clumsily shoving it back into his pocket.

"Everything alright, Love?" said Linda, with all the delicacy of someone inspecting an expensive antique vase that was threatening to shatter.

"I need you to read tea leaves," said Terrance.

"We don't have any, Lovey, and also, I've no idea how to do that," said Linda, sounding almost desperate now.

"What do you think they put in the tea bags?" he said, fishing his tea bag out of his mug and tearing it open, spilling the contents back inside.

"Terrance, I still don't know how," said Linda.

"Just say what you feel," said Terrance, thrusting the mug into Linda's hands.

"I feel silly. I don't know what I'm doing," said Linda, taking the mug and peering into it. Uncertainty and embarrassment radiating, but with a single breath, a cool focus came over her. Her brows furrowed, and her eyes went steely. "This sounds a bit mad, but I think you're going to be part of a great battle," she said, handing the mug back in a bit of a daze, as if she'd just come out of a trance. My stomach squirmed. For a lady who'd just been staring at the contents of a tea bag, she could be quite convincing.

"Well, that's a bit worrying," said Terrance, as all his urgency melted away and he slumped against the kitchen counter.

"Whys that?" asked Linda anxiously, as the towel banana on her head unravelled and flopped onto the floor.

"Because you're a witch," said Terrance, leaning forward, his eyes sparkling with barely contained tears as a smile broke across his face.

"I'm a travel agent," said Linda, shaking her head as Terrance clasped her hands in his, beaming at her.

Mothers, Witches and Queens

"They're not mutually exclusive," he said with a chuckle.

"What makes you think she's a witch, Terrance?" asked Michael, taking a tentative step forward.

"I noticed it the first time we met, when we shook hands, there was just something about you, something special," said Terrance, answering Michael's question but still talking directly to Linda. From the look on his face, you'd think she was the most beautiful woman he'd ever seen.

"You're pulling my leg," said Linda, glancing away anxiously.

"And then, that night when the goblins attacked us at the community centre. You kept everyone grounded. You helped me open up a portal through a tree, for heaven's sake," said Terrance.

"I just made tea," said Linda, shrinking back, averting her eyes from Terrance's glowing admiration.

"All a witch does is practise rituals, be mindful of intentions, and lend a wise head. Why shouldn't your tea be a ritual? You intended for it to make people feel better, and it did," he said.

"Don't be daft," said Linda, staring at her slippers, her voice sounding choked.

"This was my succulent this morning before I knocked on your door. Look how it's sagging and pale looking? I've not slept for a couple of days, that's why. I needed to stay up for the experiment," said Terrance, showing us all a picture of his sickly, sagging succulent, with his name plaque dangling around it.

"And?" said Linda, struggling for words.

"This is the picture Liz sent me of it, after I drank your tea." He handed the phone around again. It looked like a different plant entirely. Dark green, upstanding, healthy and flourishing.

Knock, knock!

I jumped and almost launched Terrance's phone across the room as the knock at the front door boomed through the house.

"Coming!" called Linda. I suspect she was glad of the excuse for pause in the conversation as she shuffled past us towards the front hall and opened the door.

"Hell—Oh my God!" Linda gasped, stepping aside as to my horror, a bloodied and battered Marshie fell into the entrance hall. I pushed past her, dropping to my knees as I laid my hands on them and let soothing water pour out of me.

8

"Try again, but slower and with more words." Adrian was exhausted, his head rested on my shoulder, eyes closed. He was sitting in the middle back seat of Mum's car. To his right sat a freshly healed, but no less shaken up Marshie. Mum was driving slightly above the speed limit, and Terrance was texting furiously. Daniel was being surprisingly compliant, and quiet, in the boot.

"She's taken Grandfather!" Marshie wailed, which made more sense than the string of jumbled thoughts they'd been expressing so far: red eyes, Mu-Terra, monstrous woman, terrible, taken, beaten, attacked, fallen, doomed, disaster and death.

"You mean Morgana, right?" I clarified.

"Monstrous Woman," Marshie nodded.

"What happened to Mu-Terra?" Adrian mumbled into my shoulder.

"What happened to Mu-Terra?" I repeated, since no one else seemed to hear him.

"Fighting her, his eyes went red, he just... gave up, stood down our defences," said Marshie, with an air of disbelief in their voice.

"We've got to do something," Adrian mumbled, his head drooping forwards as if he'd fallen asleep only to catch himself and jerk awake.

"How did you get out, Marshie?" Mum asked, as she performed a slightly illegal undertake.

"Just because Mu-Terra went all soft doesn't mean I was about to give up. I made a run for it. They spotted me of course, but not before I'd got a good head start. Managed to lose the buggers in Starkton woods," said Marshie, brimming with pride.

"So, what's the plan?" asked Mum.

"Don't have one yet," Adrian mumbled into my shoulder.

"First things first, let's get everyone in one place," I said, stalling for time. Unfortunately, I didn't get much of it before we pulled up to the community centre. We were the first to arrive besides Liz, who'd camped out overnight to keep an eye on Terrance's succulent. Jade arrived next, followed closely by Enid in sopping waders. We'd propped Adrian up in a corner and fed him water by the jugful as the witches trickled in, in hopes of rousing him.

"Alright, Terrance, you said it was urgent. What's going on?" asked Liz as Enid squelched in.

Mothers, Witches and Queens

I looked around the room and a shiver ran across my skin; Mum looked bigger somehow and there was the small matter of the golden rivers of energy pouring out of her. Judging by the complete lack of reaction in the room, I guessed I must be the only one who could see it. With each witch's arrival, she'd swell just a little, the small tracks of light becoming a slightly brighter.

"Is it to do with your theory on Linda?" Enid asked, as if Mum wasn't in the room.

"No actually, although now that you mention it, that did turn out to bear fruit. Well, what I mean to say is—"

"He thinks I'm a witch," Mum blurted out, as Terrance stumbled through his words like someone trying to solve a maze in the dark.

"I think he might be right," I murmured under my breath, watching the golden streams reach out and touch Terrance, Liz, Enid, and Jade.

"Your eyes have turned golden," said Daniel, staring at me as if I had three noses.

"What are you seeing?" Adrian asked, as he sat up, blinking the tiredness from his eyes.

"Mum looks sort of bigger... and there's like, stuff pouring out of her into the witches," I said, watching the strange glittering golden rivers ripple through the air.

"Seventh In Seven!" Daniel sounded excited, struggling to keep his voice low.

"But there's not seven of them," I said, recounting the tarot cards in my head, The Seventh In Seven, The

Geomancer, The Crone, The Weaver, The Gardener and The Meditator, just six.

"Maybe we're missing something," Adrian said, as much to himself as the room, and as he did, two more golden threads peeled off mum. I wheeled around to find the source and found Penny and Jude shuffling in, looking sheepish. My first instinct was to jump for Jude, but Mum's light had already reached him.

"It's Jude," I muttered through gritted teeth, wrestling with my instinct to grab him and shake him and scream at him and maybe put his head through a window.

"Sorry I'm late, I erm, I brought Jude. I hope that's okay." Penny's voice was small and nervous sounding. Jude didn't make a sound at all, keeping his eyes firmly glued to the floor.

"You! You fucking tricked me, you took his stone, do you know what a mess you made?" Daniel bristled, taking a heavy step towards Jude.

"Wait," I grabbed his wrist, probably too tightly, following the river of gold as it flowed out of Mum and into him. He made seven.

"I came to apologise." Jude's voice was smaller than Penny's and cracked as he spoke.

"Just hear him out," said Penny, doing a poor impression of sounding commanding.

"You know what he did to Adrian, what damage he's caused?" I said. Despite whatever the Seventh In Seven

Mothers, Witches and Queens

thing meant, I couldn't just forgive him. It was all I could do not to launch myself at him.

"I'm sorry, I…" For a second he looked up, his red raw eyes shone with tears and then he dropped his face to the floor, his voice trailing off. It wasn't good enough, I didn't feel sorry for him, I resented the idea that I should. I took a step forward, he took one back, he was at the door now, he was about to turn and run, again.

"Keep going," Adrian's voice was soft and somehow less angry than mine. Jude paused. His chest rose, and he looked up again, past me, meeting Adrian's gaze.

"I wasn't myself, not all the time. I didn't mean to cause so much harm," said Jude.

"But she wasn't controlling you all the time. I saw you at the school, when you were with Alex and Jack, she wasn't hovering over you, not like with Gwen," I all but yelled, I couldn't seem to help myself.

"Let him speak," said Adrian, shakily getting to his feet, slipping his little hand into mine before it became a fist.

"It's hard to explain. It's like there were other voices in my head egging me on that I couldn't ignore. Ideas that I didn't recognise, all-consuming urges. Sometimes I don't even think I was there, like I was lost in this red mist and I'd wake up, not sure where I was or how I got there and then the second she stepped through the tree I was in control again," said Jude.

"Sounds like it wasn't really your fault," Adrian

squeezed my hand as he spoke. He was better at forgiving than me.

"And tell them the other thing," said Penny, looking slightly emboldened by Adrian's words. She gave Jude a gentle elbow to the ribs. They'd clearly rehearsed this before they'd arrived.

"Sometimes I heard things I don't think she meant for me to, like her thoughts would slip in between all the voices," said Jude.

"Like what?" I snapped.

"Well... Penny told me about when the goblins attacked the community centre, and the message from Gwen about the Seventh In Seven. I'd heard it before. The memories are all hazy now, but I got the feeling it was scary. That it was urgent Morgana got to the fay forest because of it," he said.

"So that got me thinking, if we can find this Seventh In Seven thing, maybe we can help Adrian and Michael," said Penny, stepping forward, sounding almost excited.

"Way ahead of you," I said, following the lines of light back to Mum, who was glowing so brightly now she was becoming almost painful to look at, although clearly no-one else was seeing what I saw. No one else was squinting.

"Oh, I get it now!" said Adrian, rather loudly.

"Get what?" Terrance snapped. Adrian had made him jump.

"The missing piece is Jude," said Adrian, leaving everyone in the room none the wiser, except for Daniel, who rather dramatically clapped his hand to his mouth.

Mothers, Witches and Queens

"I'm the what?" Jude asked, sounding confused, which was a slight improvement on the impression of a kicked puppy that he had been doing.

"The Seventh In Seven isn't a thing. It's Linda, and you all are the seven," said Adrian, smiling around at the assembled coven, who seemed to be gathering, moving towards Mum. I wasn't even sure if they knew they were doing it.

"Isn't that sort of thing usually a seventh son of a seventh son type thing?" asked Liz, looking sceptical.

"It's symbolic. She's not the seventh daughter of a seventh daughter. She's the seventh daughter and the seventh sister witch," said Adrian, smiling as he gestured broadly to the room.

"I'm not a witch, and I'm certainly not the seventh something or other. I'm just a travel agent. I'm not special!" Mum protested as power poured out of her like she was the source of a river, thoroughly undermining her argument.

"Of course you are!" said Terrance in a surprisingly tender voice.

"Let's just say, for argument's sake, you were. What would that even mean?" I asked, as delicately as possible.

"It would mean Morgana is afraid of her," said Adrian, taking a step towards the centre of the room.

"But I'm not!" Mum protested.

"It would explain why my arm was so much better than it should have been," said Daniel thoughtfully.

"And why her tea did Terrance and the succulent so

much good?" I said and found my words met by Terrance's exaggerated nodding approval.

"It was just a nice cuppa tea, everyone likes a nice cuppa tea. Mum's protests were getting weaker, her voice was shrinking.

"You know this isn't a bad thing, Mum," I said, placing a gentle hand on her shoulder.

"It's daft. I don't want you all getting your hopes up when I know I'm going to let you down. That's all." Mum's eyed turned down.

"You're not going to let us—"

"I see you've awakened The Seventh In Seven." A cruel voice pierced the air, sending a wave of repulsion surging through me.

"Oh my God, Jude, your eyes!" Penny wailed. I swivelled on the spot to face Jude and my muscles tightened as I looked into the scarlet eyes of the shade floating above him, mirrored in his own. Red hair waving wildly above her like dancing flames, arms reaching down, her fingers lightly pressed against Jude's throat.

"She's got him," I croaked. Panic washed through me as I pulled Mum and Adrian out of his arms' reach. Within seconds, everyone in the room had taken a few steps clear of Jude except for Liz, who'd dropped into the lotus position and was muttering something.

"Let him go!" Penny yelled, tears sparkling in her eyes as she took a step forwards. In a flash, Jude lunged for Enid,

Mothers, Witches and Queens

grabbing the knife at her belt. It glinted as it flashed through the air. Before I could move, the knife was at Jude's throat, the shade of Morgana's long thin fingers holding tight to his wrist.

"Ah, ah, ah, would be a terrible shame for poor little Jude to slip now, wouldn't it?" Morgana spoke through Jude's own crooning voice. A single bead of ruby trickling down his neck.

"What do you want?" Enid asked stiffly, her hand twitching around the spot in her belt where her knife should have been.

"Oh, that's quite simple. I'll leave you and your adorable little coven alone, and I'll even give Jude back to you, without a hair on his funny little head out of place." As she spoke, she lifted the knife from his neck, revealing the shallow cut she'd already made, and held it away a little. I supposed this was her way of showing she wouldn't hurt Jude, but I didn't trust her not to put it right back the moment she got what she wanted. Jude's gaze was locked onto Enid's, but the shade's eyes were laser focused on Mum and me. I wondered if she could feel me glaring at her.

"Spit it out," Enid bristled.

"Deliver to me the Prince and The Seven, and the rest of you get to live happily ever after. Agreed?" said Morgana.

"No chance!" Adrian shouted, stepping between Jude and Mum and me before I could get a word out. Around the room, singular defiance showed on the faces of all the witches. All of them glaring into those red eyes.

"If you don't cooperate, there will be consequences," said Morgana, speaking through Jude.

"We don't trade lives," Penny spat, her face twisted up and red, with tears swimming in her eyes.

"I warned you there would be consequences," said Morgana.

The blade glinted as Morgana's shade's arm swooped down, slashing the knife towards Jude's throat. Penny screamed, and I lunged through the air, knowing I'd be too late. Except I wasn't. An incorporeal hand had materialised out of thin air. Attached to an incorporeal arm, wearing an incorporeal Lycra gym jacket. And it had Morgana's wrist in a vice-like grip.

"Damned witch," Morgana snarled as she struggled against the arm. Her furious red eyes found a new focus – Liz. Liz was still in lotus on the floor muttering to herself, her face rigid with concentration and pouring sweat.

"What's happening?" Penny wailed, inching towards Jude, his arm still struggling against invisible forces.

"It's Liz. She's doing something, interfering with Morgana. What's she chanting?" I said. I took a tentative step towards Jude.

"Stay back!" Jude snarled, struggling to kick out at me, although I was out of his reach. When that failed, he began to back away. Morgana was still panting and struggling against Liz's grip.

Mothers, Witches and Queens

"She's chanting, 'hands off, Bitch'," said Terrance quite matter-of-factly. I'd have laughed, were it not for the knife at Jude's throat.

"Very well, you've forced my hand." The voice trickled out of Jude like an alien as the shade grinned and then their unison broke. The shade plunged its free hand down into Jude's head. Jude's face, twisted and contorted let go a scream that was all his own.

"Somebody do something!" Penny screamed as the lot of us froze in horror. My stomach writhed and my muscles tensed. I wanted to lunge, to act, but I couldn't think of what to do and looking around the room, neither could anyone else.

"Ah fuck it!" said Mum, shrugging her shoulders as she marched past us.

"What are you doing?" I asked, failing to keep the fear from raising the octave of my voice.

"Witch stuff hopefully," said Mum as she swiped a grasping hand through the air. I grimaced, expecting nothing, and then my mouth dropped open. Mum's fist was full of auburn red hair. Not transparent and ghostly, but real and clenched between her fingers. The shade had jerked forward violently, her hand slipping from Jude's head, who immediately fell silent.

"You got her!" I said in disbelief.

"Amazing," Adrian breathed.

"I did? I got her!" Mum said, wide eyed fixed on the fistful of disembodied hair. Morgana's eyes were wild and blazing as she stared in horror at Mum as she began winding the hair through her fist, dragging Morgana's translucent face closer to hers until all at once Morgana let out a guttural rage fuelled scream and evaporated like red mist. Leaving Jude to collapse like an old lawn chair. Penny rushed to his side, cradling him in her lap.

"She's gone," I said, struggling to look at Mum, her light leaving my vision dazzled and blotchy.

"Thank god for that," said Liz, flopping backwards exhausted, as she let out a big sigh.

"How did you know to do that?" I asked Mum, covering my eyes from the glow.

"Well, you'd been staring at the space above the lad's head whilst the rest of us were looking at him. I figured it'd be a good place to aim for a fistful," said Mum, whose bravado was melting into embarrassment by the second.

"Well, I think now we know why she wanted Mum to give herself up," said Daniel.

"Does that mean we win?" Penny asked, nervously stroking Jude's hair.

"It means we can fight her," said Adrian.

"I'm not sure about fighting… maybe she'll give up now," said Mum hopefully.

"She can't. Not after this. The reason she wanted you two is because your existence threatens her. She's going to come after you, before you're too powerful to stop," said Adrian, a darkness taking over his features as he began to pace the room.

Mothers, Witches and Queens

"So, what do we do?" I asked.

"We're going to our lake," he said.

"What lake? Why would we go to a lake?" Liz asked, rolling onto her side.

"Because if we have to fight, that's where I want to do it," said Adrian.

9

"Adrian, are you sure about this?" Michael asked in a lowered voice, as all around our lake clearing the witches busied themselves. Liz, Terrance, and Penny were meditating. Jude was resting just behind them at the lakeside with Marshie, some mushroom tea by his side. Whilst Jade placed what looked like little quartz stones around the perimeter, Enid followed with a large bag of salt. Linda was haphazardly chucking some tea leaves that Penny had supplied around the clearing. Daniel was following in her wake, inspecting the tea leaf droppings, I think, trying to feel useful and busy. Linda still didn't seem one hundred percent convinced, but I suppose it's hard to argue when you start plucking angry sorcerous' hair out of thin air.

"We've got to do something, and this is the best I can come up with," I said, looking back at the lake anxiously.

Light played across the surface of the water like fireflies against the night sky. I'd been so sure of everything, when Jude was screaming, when Linda strode through the room like fire wouldn't burn her, when I'd shouted at the sky and raged at Olivier for leaving me. I'd been sure and now I wasn't, but at least that awful feeling was gone, that pressure.

"Well then I'm with you," said Michael, as he placed a comforting hand on my shoulder. Completely unaware that as he spoke, all the confidence he'd poured into me, that I'd never earned, was flowing out like an undammed river.

"It'll work out. I'm going to make it," I said, hoping that if I sounded like I believed it, I would start to.

"What are you going to do?" he asked.

"I'm going to try to live up to the family name. And I need you to just stay safe while I do that. And keep the witches safe too."

"I will," said Michael, as he leaned down and I leaned up and our lips met in the middle. I could have closed my eyes and disappeared into that kiss, into a world of just us, but I didn't. I turned away, towards the lake, and I walked in.

Any old water nymph can connect to water, that comes as naturally to us as breathing but controlling it is another matter. That's about making the water an extension of yourself, and the more you can give yourself over to it, the more you become it, the more it will become you. There are

Mothers, Witches and Queens

legends which speak of a mighty water nymph named Nimueh who could become one with the greatest lake in all the fay forest. So legendary was her power that her name was given to the lake and passed down through generations of water nymphs. Her control of it was such that she became like the moon is to the ocean. It is said that to become one with the water in this way is to surrender something of yourself and become something more.

I thought of that as waded into the water and breathed into my little lake in Starkton woods. With my little banks, feeding my little roots. Grass dancing in the breeze all around me as a gust broke my surface, and I rippled gently, reflecting the warming light of the sun, dancing atop my surface. All around me, people were working feverishly. In a distant, far off way, I knew their names, but they were slipping away. The gardener, the meditator and the weaver, casting shields around me. The maiden resting behind them, in the arms of a gnome. The crone and the geomancer creating barriers of rock and salt, whilst the mother bolstered them all and stood guard over her son. My prince, who in turn, stood guard over me. He had swum in me before.

The hidden queen arrived, as she often does, in the body of another, powerful, dark-skinned, with knots of long green hair. The king of the dryads stepped through worlds into my clearing, followed by a retinue of mirelings and fay alike. None of their minds on their own, but his least of all. He held fast to a glittering silver staff, pommelled by a blazing red stone and as he thrust out his thick, muscled arm his army charged.

He set his dark ruby eyes on the maiden behind the threesome, but as his foot soldiers passed over salt and stone a barrier rippled into being. Milky white light. A flickering dome the witches didn't know they had erected, which permitted her not to pass.

"STOP!" The voice of my prince cried out, piercing past creation, yawning into the realm of the soul, halting the now vacant assailants. The witches looked around in relief and wonder as another command rang out. Stunned by the success of the command, all in the clearing paused before the prince gave another.

"Grab Mu-Terra." But the command came all too slow. Already the roots that had once drank from me were moving at the behest of another, wielded by the kind of dryad, like spears through the earth. They fired out of the ground, piercing through fay and mirelings alike, halting them before the command could be obeyed. Splattering vermillion across my banks and the blanched white shock of the witches. The fangs of the earth stopping just short of them and the prince. All of whom found themselves under the invisible protection of the gardener.

"Poor dears." The gnome wept as familiar faces fell around them.

Everyone hesitated, staring at the menacing, twitching reaching javelin roots inches from their bodies, and then the red stone of the silvery staff flashed. Life blood runes floated up into the air, out of the bodies that littered my clearing.

"Everybody get behind me," the prince called, eyes wild as he counted the creatures being formed of the runes. He'd seen this magic once before, and he feared it.

"Where is Adrian?" The gardener looked towards me in desperation as the witches all began to back towards my edge. The milky white barrier shuddering out of existence as the ring of salt was washed away by fay blood, now animated into living weapons.

"He's in the lake. He's got a plan. We just need to hold on," said the prince, his arms outstretched behind him, shielding the witches from the blood monsters. In his hand, he brandished a large stick. He longed for his shield and his hammer, but they'd been lost to him.

The king of the dryads thrust his staff forwards and the first of the creatures lunged. Where there should have been arms, long needles of blood sailed through the air. The prince danced aside splattering his cudgel through the form of the creature, spreading it across my clearing, but already it was reforming and another had lunged at the mother.

The prince pushed her aside, clear of the creature's path, but before he could defend himself, the creature was on him.

"Oh my God!" the mother wailed in horror as the prince was enveloped in living blood, up to the knee, and then the waist. He turned to me, as the red tide reached his neck, his amber eyes, flickering golden, flashing through the forest, and I remembered. A thought thundering through my mind and chasing all others away.

Protect Michael.

***

It was hot and thick and turned my stomach and held me fast like I was stuck in so much sucking, sinking mud, and it was spreading over me, like the first rush of rain through a river after a drought. I craned my neck, taking one last desperate look over my shoulder at the lake, one great glimmering sapphire. Mum's wailing had blurred into the background. The terrified look on the witches' faces barely registered as I let myself get lost in the lake. Just like Adrian's eyes. There was no way, no way he'd abandon us like this. He'd save me. I knew he would. The blood was at my lips; I clamped them shut tight as the thick, hot liquid crawled up to my nose. Then it happened, the water rippled and for a second I could have sworn it wasn't the lake anymore; it was Adrian's eye, opening wide and shining.

Next second a great wave heaved out of the lake, washing past us from behind, but it didn't push us forward. It didn't knock us off our feet. It wrapped around us like two giant embracing arms, and the blood was off me.

"Impossible." Mu-Terra's voice boomed through the forest as the shade floating above him glowered at the lake. Two more of the bloody creatures lunged, the awful stab-

Mothers, Witches and Queens

bing limbs outstretched towards mum and me. I raised my gnarled club root, but before they even got close two great funnels of water flowed passed us, washing the creatures away.

"He did it!" I said, goosebumps pimpling my skin as water whipped around the nine of us, forming a kind of vortex wall.

"He certainly has a flair for dramatic timing," said mum, flopping into Daniel as she whipped tears from her eyes

"Let's not celebrate just yet," said Daniel, a trembling finger pointing past me. I turned and found he was tracking Mu-Terra's body. It was making a charge past the salt and crystal barriers. This was the first time he'd moved since he entered the clearing. Morgana had been relying on her lackies until now.

"He's going for the lake," said Enid, already pushing through the watery barrier, her filleting knife glinting in her hand.

"He's going for Adrian." I said, hurdling clear of the barrier just in time to splatter a blood creature that had lunged for Enid the second she left the watery walls.

"Protect the lake!" Enid commanded, ignoring the already splattered creature, its legs and body almost half reformed, as she charged, waders squelching.

"Careful Enid!" Jade called after her launching a crystal like a shot put at the place where another blood creature's head used to be, although it didn't seem to miss it once it was splattered. I gritted my teeth and charged shoulder first through the creature just as Enid found her foot trapped in its bloody form. Before I could move it was encroaching on me again. I struggled, panting and sweating, to pull myself loose as another shaft of water arched out of the lake, washing over me.

"I can't get past the buggers!" Enid snarled as another creature formed in front of her like a body blocker in rugby.

"Get back," Penny cried, grabbing her by the waistband and pulling Enid and herself over backwards as one creature jabbed its arm down on the spot where Enid had just been.

"What do we do?" Terrance asked, looking to mum in desperation.

"If only we could control the water." She said, as the barrier stretched to encircle Enid and Penny. The bloody creatures surrounding us, ready to pounce. Mu-Terra was almost at the lakeside, silvery staff in hand.

"I'm not sure Adrian can hear us," said Penny, as an idea dawned on me.

"Everybody get ready to run," I said, lifting Jude and passing him into the bewildered arms of Terrance and Liz.

"ADRIAN, CUT US A PATH TO MU-TERRA!" I commanded, letting whatever it is in me that makes me a prince ring out through the forest. Immediately the barrier shifted, no longer a surging splashing ring of blue. It formed an arch over our heads and stretched forward. Creating a glinting blue sapphire tunnel, like the trees that lead to our lakeside clearing.

I could see Mu-Terra, his glimmering silver staff

shifting to a point in his grasp. I charged, head down, legs pumping, my body felt light and electric, the river stretching out around me, slicing through the bloody creatures that stepped into my path. It was like Adrian was here with me, his perfect glimmering blue eyes watching me.

Then I was there. I was on Mu-Terra, my hands on his staff, forcing his powerful body to the floor, ignoring the shade of Morgana lashing out at me in her immaterial way.

"This is mine," I barked, feeling the staff shift to a shield in my hands, the fiery ruby falling to the floor with a thud. I jammed the shield into his right arm, crushing it into the earth, and pinned the other beneath my knee. I reached down for the gem and chucked it to Jade. All the while Mu-Terra struggled beneath me; he was strong, but I was stronger. The witches had followed me through the tunnel, which had reformed again into a whipping, surging wall of water around us. The bloody creatures had fallen dormant the moment the stone fell from the staff. They were simply standing about the clearing, their bodies vaguely quivering and shimmering.

"Get off me!" Morgana's shade wailed as Mu-Terra's voice boomed through the trees.

"Get out of him," I commanded, but to no avail. She wasn't fay, she was a champion like me.

Her face was all defiance and rage until her eyes focused on something else, over my shoulder. Fury became fear and within a second, the shade had evaporated into the mist.

"Want me to grab her hair again?" Mum asked, leaning forward to peer past me into the recently emptied space above Mu-Terra's now sleeping head.

"What happened?" Said Jude, jerking awake in Liz's and Terrance's rather awkward grasp.

10

I'd pulled my water back into me. My clearing, sodden and muddy, would take time to recover, but she was gone. The gnome tended to the sleeping body of the dryad king whilst the reaches gathered around my banks, staring at me, prying eyes piercing to my deepest depths. I'd known something earlier, something pressing, but it had faded. Now I knew the leaves tumbling through the forest air, coming to rest delicately on my mirror surface. The prince had been staring most intensely of all, his eyes shimmering from gold to amber and then back again. After a time, he pulled off his shirt and dived, splashing me across my bank. He was powerful, each kick and drag of his arms ripping through me, pushing me aside, and then somehow, they were around me.

Somehow, all of me was in his strong, warm arms. I was

being dragged up and pulled through myself, water rushing around me. No, I was rushing around me; I was breaking the surface. Air touching me, my skin, I was apart from myself. I gasped, air filling my lungs as my eyes fluttered open and found Michael staring down at me.

"I knew you could do it," he said, as he leant down and kissed me. I kissed back, breathing him in.

"What did I do?" I asked, wrapping my arms around his neck to pull myself closer to him. Everything had blurred into a sort of haze.

"You saved us, you controlled the whole lake, Adrian, it was amazing, I swear at one point it was like the whole lake was just your eye, winking back at me." Michael was gushing and blushing and his eyes were twinkling, and my smile must have been mirroring his because I was getting an achy jaw.

"I don't really remember. Is everyone okay?" I asked, craning around to catch a glimpse of everyone. They seemed to be in a bit of a huddle.

"Everyone's fine, Jude's even awake, and Mu-Terra hasn't woken up yet, but Marshie is looking after him," said Michael.

"That's good," I said as Michael carried me up and out of the lake, my head nestled in the nook of his neck and shoulder, rested against his beautiful warm skin.

"We won, Adrian," said Terrance, stepping forward to offer me his hand as Michael set me down on the bank. As I looked around, I realised that all the witches were beaming

Mothers, Witches and Queens

at me. Well, not quite all, Enid was holding onto a wry half smile, but otherwise, lots of beaming.

"Not quite, she still has Grandfather... And a lot of foot soldiers..." said Marshie, adding a dissenting voice to the air as they gestured to the bodies littering the clearing. It dawned on me as I turned. The ground wasn't just a muddy brown. Blood was mixing with the earth all around me. I didn't want to look. My stomach lurched, and my legs turned to jelly as I started to recognise familiar faces from the forest among the dead. I didn't want to see the black shorn head of Pendula lying lifeless, face down in the mud. I couldn't stand seeing Ionia's platinum hair dirtied by the earth as she lay among the bodies of goblins.

"We've got to stop her for good," I said, haze and warmth and relief draining out of me, replaced by something hard and cold and pressing on my chest.

"Adrian, don't you want to rest a bit?" Michael's voice was tender and gentle.

"We can't rest. This is our chance now. She'll be shaken. Her plans aren't working." The words rushed out of me with little thought. This was something I knew.

"How are you going to do it?" Enid asked, in a tone of practicality.

"I don't think I am... I think you guys are," I said, turning away from the bodies of the fay I'd grown up with. I should have been sad to do it, but right now I just felt cold. And something in my throat, some choking pressure, pressing on my shoulders.

"Jude needs rest," said Penny firmly.

Jude struggled to his feet. "No, I need her gone. She waltzed straight into my head like it was nothing today," he said.

"She's scared of Linda because she's the Seventh In Seven. That's only true when all of you are around." I said.

"Let's not get too carried away with this whole Seventh In Seven business," said Linda, ringing her hands nervously.

"He's right, Mum," said Michael, hooking an arm around my waist as he held me to him. It was like a deep breath filling me up.

"Listen, I know I pulled some hair out of thin air but—"

"It's not that. It's like you know how I can see things other people can't? Well, when I look at you with everyone else here, it's like you're glowing. Like there are these streams of light pouring out of you and into each of them. You guys must have felt it right?" said Michael, as Linda's mouth dropped open in disbelief.

"This is what I've been saying," said Terrance, standing beside Jude.

"Terrance, you have never once mentioned streams of light pouring out of her," said Liz, standing beside him.

"No, but I felt stronger. You must have felt it too," said Terrance.

"I'll admit, I did feel like I could really reach out and grab someone with my mind when I was meditating earlier. Turns out I was right," said Liz, looking pleased with herself.

Mothers, Witches and Queens

"And my crystals have never projected a real life, honest to goodness light barrier before today, just in case anyone was wondering," said Jade, taking a place besides Jude.

"Nor has my salt, for what it's worth," said Enid, waddling over to stand with Jade.

"Well, since you've all lined up in a row, I guess I'm joining in," said Penny begrudgingly.

"So, what, you all think I'm this super special… I don't know what?" Linda asked, her voice creaking between exasperation and something else, shyness maybe.

"Why shouldn't you be, Mum?" Daniel asked. "I'm just a—"

"Travel agent, we know, and Terrance works in a garden centre, and I teach beginners yoga in a room that smells like feet. We're witches too, just like you." Liz had an impressive way of shifting from berating to encouraging in a single breath.

"Okay fine, say I am what we're saying I am. What's the plan?" asked Linda with a sniffle, turning to me as she quickly rubbed something from her eyes. I'd have thought she was crying, but her cheeks were ruddy, and a smile was fighting its way across her face.

"I need a pen and paper," I said.

"You're not going to write another song, are you? The last one made me cry," said Penny.

"No, I'm just taking a little inspiration from three charmed sisters, Terrance, you start visualising a really big tree," I said, taking the little black diary with purple skulls on it that Jude had fished out of his back pocket.

"Why?" Terrance asked, looking suddenly nervous.

"I have a feeling I know where Morgana is going to be, and we're going to gate crash," I said, as I began scribbling down rhymes and the pressure lifted, just a little.

11

We watched, holding our breath. Well, I was anyway. Terrance plunged his hands into the bark of the biggest tree we could find and began to peel it open. Adrian, Mum, the witches and I all held a little scribbled note from Adrian. And we were all watching, standing by as the dark brown bark curled back, revealing a strange, shimmering, brownish ring and then a ruddy green. Marshie and Daniel stayed back with an unconscious Mu-terra, whilst the rest of us went to finish things, finally. I wanted time to plan and to rest, but Adrian said it had to be now, and he was always better than me at planning. That's what I told myself as I took his hand, and we stepped through the portal together.

"It worked," Adrian whispered as we came face to face with the curtain of leaves and sagging trees and vines that clustered behind Grandfather Tree, with its impossibly wide trunk to our backs. The floor was damp and squashy with moss and veiny with knotted overlapping roots, just as I remembered it, but the light was different. Looking up, the sky spiralled with black clouds, and the occasional flash of red.

"Where is she?" Terrance whispered, as Mum and the witches piled in after us, all huddled in a ball.

"I'm betting, just the other side of Grandfather Tree," Adrian whispered, as he crept to the edge and poked his head out to see what was happening. I followed, staying low, keeping hidden. The clearing had always been bright and green and fresh, with perpetual dew on the moss and beautiful, thick, powerful brown roots, as wide as cars running higgledy-piggledy throughout. Now it had a grey pallor, almost dusty, the roots blackening little by little.

Morgana stood central over a glittering silver caldron, a blanket of red and black smoke spreading out, running through the clearing and out to God knows where. Her hair blew back out of her face, waving wildly behind her as if she had three hairdryers all blasting her at once. Most unsettling of all was the presence of the assembled fay. Normally they filled the air so loud with whispers they'd threaten an avalanche. Today they were truly silent, nymphs and gnomes and elves and sylphs and dryads, perhaps one hundred in total, hunched forward, slack-jawed and red-eyed.

"She's making an army," I whispered, pulling Adrian backwards before he was spotted. Not that I was convinced

Mothers, Witches and Queens

any of them were capable of spotting anything at the moment.

"Are we ready?" Adrian asked, turning as I pulled him clear to face the witches. They'd worked quickly. Enid had already drawn a salt ring around the back of Grandfather Tree and was handing off bags to Terrance and Liz. Jade had done the same with a border of crystals and was handing off more to Jude.

"Are you sure you're up to this?" Penny asked, giving Jude's shoulder a squeeze.

"I want to be a part of it," said Jude, his knuckles turning white as he held the crystals in tight fists.

"And everyone's got their words?" Adrian asked and was met with a unified nod.

"Well, it's too late to turn back now," said Mum, sounding decidedly less convinced.

"Distraction time then," said Adrian, taking mine and Mum's hands in his. Together the three of us ran clear of the shelter of Grandfather Tree. A shiver ran down my spine as an image of Olivier orchestrating Adrian's rescue from Merlin flashed through my mind.

"Hey, Morgana, I brought you a prince and a witch!" he yelled. Morgana stiffened, pulling her face out of her cauldron, her hair falling in loose red curls across her back as she slowly turned on the spot. For the first time I saw the true her, not her shade. Her pale skin, her ruddy cheeks, she was pretty, in a severe kind of way. High cheek bones and thin features, but her eyes were just as they'd always been, angry blazing rubies.

"Finally," she said, scooping a hand through her cauldron, flinging bolts of silvery substance through the air towards us like tiny liquid knives.

"Now!" yelled Adrian, the second she made her move.

My shield sprung into being, splattering the silver concoction across the clearing with a metallic tang as the witches sprang into action. From one side of Grandfather Tree appeared Terrance, the other Liz, carrying the bags, leaving a trail of salt in their wake. Followed by Jade and Jude, encircling the front of Grandfather Tree with crystals completing the barrier, whilst Enid and Penny took up their place in front of Grandfather Tree.

"Seize them!" Morgana yelled, as the smoke that blanketed the floor of the clearing pulsed red. The one hundred vacant fay turned towards the witches, whilst a plume of sickly green arched out of the cauldron towards Adrian, mum and me.

"Last one!" Jude yelled, and just as he placed the final stone, a milky white sheath of energy surged out of the base of Grandfather Tree. Within a second, it'd covered the whole of the great tree and the flashing redness of the clouds replaced with a white light. The enthralled fay faltered.

"YOU'RE FREE!" I yelled, as I tackled Mum and Adrian clear of the smoke, sending us all tumbling over

Mothers, Witches and Queens

roots and moss. Already the red was blinking from the fay's eyes, replaced by vacant, absent looks.

"No!" Morgana wailed and snatched up the cauldron, which became a staff in her hand. I watched as she drove it into the ground, sending flashes of red pulsing into the roots. The weight of my shield shifted in my grasp, becoming a hammer as I charged, swinging it through the air towards her. She ducked and withdrew another shard from her person, which sprung into a glistening silver sickle in her hand. She hooked the edge around my hammer head and slammed it into the floor before kicking me away from her. I sunk to my knee, winded, as she leapt at me, her sickle blade flashing menacingly. My shield again sprung into being intercepting her blow and deflecting her backwards as another pulse of red light reverberated out of the staff behind her and a great yawning groan issued from the giant ancient tree behind me. Her eyes were on me and blazing, unblinking, she wasn't going to let me near that staff.

"What do we do?" Terrance yelled, as the earth beneath my feet started to tremble and I made a leap for the staff, ducking at the last second to avoid her sickle blade.

"Say the words!" Adrian screamed.

"We are all of us in each," Penny's quavering voice issued from behind me, and I saw Morgana flinch. Her singular focus momentarily broken as she looked past my shoulder.

"What?" she snarled.

"We are seven in one," Enid's voice joined Penny's, adding some much-needed steel.

"A spell?" Morgana sneered, but the way her eyes had darted from Penny to Enid was unmistakable. It was fear.

"Our minds she shall not reach," Jude yelled, his voice strained, he sounded like he was almost crying. As he spoke, a pulse of golden light issued from behind me, just like the streams that were pouring out of Mum like a fountain.

"Fools, it won't work, I'll make you suffer as Gwen did, she couldn't stop me and neither will you!" Morgana taunted, looking for an opening, some way to break their focus as panic started to creep into her voice.

"Our home she will not breach." Jade's voice joined the others, and Morgana launched herself at the witches. I leapt forward, grabbing her by the wrists, we collided and suddenly, we were falling. A ball of limbs tumbling into the crowd of stunned fay. As we went, I watched a wave of golden light surge beneath us, forcing the redness back.

"Her spell is undone!" Liz bellowed from out of view as we tumbled.

I landed on my back with a groan, Morgana atop me. Her sickle glinted over head as it sailed towards me, but just as Liz's words echoed out through the clearing, the red in Morgana's eyes dimmed, and she faltered, just for a moment. I took my chance, fighting my hand free from under her knee, slamming my shield into her side, sending her tumbling off me, screaming in pain as she went.

"Morgana, be gone," Terrance roared. Morgana was on her feet again, panting, doubled over. Just behind her someone was pushing through the crowd. Then there was a pulse, another rumbling of the earth, and her staff clattered to the ground, rejected by the forest itself. She leapt through the air like a snake. I raised my shield as it become a hammer, ready to slam into her, but she snagged on something. Her head jerked in mid-air like she was on a bungee cord, and she landed on her back with a grunt.

"You heard 'em, Love, be gone," said Mum, leaning forward so they were face-to-face with Mum standing over her. She'd managed to get a good thick handful of Morgana's hair and had yanked her onto her back with it.

"No, please," Morgana's venom was gone, she was begging.

Can she see it too? I caught myself wondering as I squinted at Mum's glow. So much light was shining out of her, it was like looking directly into the sun. Morgana squirmed for a second before going limp. The sickle slipped from her grasp, becoming a lump of greenish black stone in her hand.

"Is that it?" Terrance asked, looking around the clearing as the black smog dispersed.

"Did you expect fireworks?" Liz quipped. I couldn't help but smirk at the two of them bickering like the first time we met. Then I felt something tugging on my shirt. I turned to find Adrian looking up at me.

"You, okay?" I asked. No. Something was wrong. His

blue eyes were twinkling, set in his perfect face, with his shiny blond hair tumbling, but he wasn't happy. His brows were furrowed, his cheeks sucked in, he might even have been chewing them. He looked almost tight.

"Come with me," he said, beginning to pull me away from the crowd of steadily awakening fay. Little ripples of whispers broke through the crowd as they realised where they were and who was lying in their clearing. I wondered if they could even remember what had just happened.

"We can't just leave her here," I said, glancing back at Morgana.

"Fine," Adrian said as he bent down and scooped up her Excalibur piece and the silvery staff, which popped into another greenish silver stone in his hand. Then scanned the crowd for the nearest dryad he could find.

"Bind her up as tight as you can, cover her mouth and have a gnome make a sleeping draft for her. Keep her asleep," he commanded, before leaving the bemused dryad and returning to me. He seemed cold, almost emotionless.

"What's wrong?" I asked as his little hand found mine and we quietly slipped out of the clearing. Whilst behind us, the crowd of fay converged on Morgana. Someone had even lifted Mum up onto their shoulders like she was some sort of football trophy.

"I don't know what to do," Adrian said, dragging me along as he looked dead ahead down the yellow spiral path.

"You don't have to do anything, Adrian. You've done

enough, we won," I said, trying to infuse as much enthusiasm as I could into my voice.

"I know." Adrian's voice was smaller now and thin.

"Where are we going?" I asked as gently as I could.

"I don't know. I don't feel like I've done it." He choked and my throat felt thick.

"Done what? Just wait a minute," I said, pulling him gently back to me. He turned, his eyes were swimming with tears and his face was reddening.

"I can't just do nothing. There has to be something to do, something I haven't done yet." Adrian turned away, continuing to drag me as tears spilled. It was like he wanted to run away but couldn't be without me all at once. Like he was being pulled in too many directions.

"Adrian, just tell me what's... Wait a minute. Why bring me here?" I asked, as we turned the bend and Olivier's cottage came into view.

"Because I can still feel her!" He almost screamed as he dropped my hand, pointing towards the cottage, then he started running for it.

"Wait, what do you mean, Adrian?" I asked, following him as he crashed through her garden's swinging gate sending a painful echo through the woods before he slammed into her cottage wall. I winced as he pounded his hands against it like hammers.

"What do you want from me?" he bellowed at the cottage, stumbling back into my arms from the impact.

"Adrian it's just a house," I whispered. He was shaking

in my arms and panting, his breath short and ragged. It was the wrong thing to say. I knew it as soon as I said it, but I couldn't think. He was going too fast, and he was hurting himself.

"I thought if we beat Morgana, that'd do it, I'd stop feeling this feeling, but it didn't work. I can't keep feeling like this." His eyes were mad, sweat and tears mixed pouring down his face as he struggled free of my grasp. I didn't fight him.

"What feeling?" I asked, watching as his legs gave way beneath him and crawled into her doorway.

"Every time I get a moments peace, there's this pressure, this endless choking pressure and I can't get rid of it, and then I think of her. Her face, dying and pale, her white sucked in bony face!" He sobbed, his hands scrabbling at his chest and his throat before he pounded his fist against her door. I inched forwards, gently cupping his hands in mine so he couldn't hurt himself.

"And now... Ionia and Pendula and every other person I knew that Morgana killed. They're in my head, they're in here! I see Olivier and now I'll see them too!" he wailed, banging his head against the door.

"Adrian, stop it, you're scaring me." I grabbed him, wrestling him away from the door. He fought me fiercely for a second and then it was like all the strength ran out of him and he melted into my arms.

"It's like she's looking over my shoulder. She left me in the forest that day, but now she won't leave me alone!"

Mothers, Witches and Queens

Adrian's rage had broken. He was speaking through sobs and hiccups as he clung to me.

"It's gonna be okay," I whispered, holding him to my chest and kissing his forehead as he sobbed and sobbed.

"Don't leave me," he whispered after he'd finally calmed his breathing. His voice was so small, and fearful, and it shattered my heart in a second.

"Never," I said, stroking his hair as I blinked back tears of my own.

"Promise?" he asked, rolling over in my arms to look up into my eyes. His were beautiful and blue and bloodshot and exhausted.

"I promise." I smiled down at him and watched his eyes flutter closed.

"Let's get you inside," I said softly as I got to my feet and carried him into the cottage.

* * *

"Put me down, you daft apeths!" I yelled, or at least tried to. It was hard to sound authoritative through a chuckle. I couldn't help but smile as I looked around the clearing, all the once dead-eyed fay now beaming up at me. I almost caught myself staring at some of them now that I'd finally got a proper look. Particularly the sylphs, I was guessing, based on Adrian's description, but they were hard to miss. All of them were a little stooped, but even so, they looked to be about two metres tall, with varying shades of pale blue and lilac skin, with spindly arms that were so long their fingers touched the ground. It was only through my efforts not to stare that I spotted an ebony skinned man with murky green cropped hair who appeared to be coiling vines around Morgana's body.

"No, really, put me down," I said, conjuring all my motherly sternness and slapping the many slightly gropey hands that were holding me aloft.

"Isn't this amazing, Linda?" said Terrance, taking my hand as I was lowered back onto the loamy ground. Already green life was returning to the formerly greying clearing.

"Quite amazing," I agreed, a little rush of excitement or adrenaline, I wasn't really sure which, forcing me into an aching smile as I met Terrance's beaming face. I did my best to politely push past him towards Morgana's body.

"Now, how do you plan to secure her?" I heard Enid's imperious voice before I saw her. Pushing through the crowd, I found the ebony skinned man, who I assumed must have been a dryad standing over Morgana. Enid stood astride the body, with her hands on her hips. Jude was standing just beside her, staring down at Morgana's now closed eyes.

"Everything all right?" I asked, hoping to save the dryad.

"I'm just making sure she's contained properly this time. Can't have her invading anyone else's dreams, can we?" said Enid.

Mothers, Witches and Queens

"No, we can't," said Jude, with no real expression in his voice.

"Of course not," I said, gently laying a hand on his shoulder, hoping I might squeeze a bit of life into him somehow.

"Perhaps I could wrap her in some of my twine," Penny suggested, shuffling up behind us to put an arm around Jude's waist.

"And I'll encircle her in crystals," said Jade.

"And salt!" added Enid.

"All of that sounds like a wonderful idea," I said, hoping I didn't sound patronising. Whatever made them feel safe, that was the main thing, although for my part I couldn't help thinking that none of that would be necessary. I'd felt it when I looked into her eyes, as the lot of them completed the spell. Like something was being burned out of her. I could see it. The grimace turned from painful to empty. Whatever dark power she'd had was gone now. It was frightening really, to think I we could do that to a person. I wasn't sure what of her would remain, if anything at all, when she woke.

"Lor—I mean… Adrian just said to tie her up and give her a sleeping draft," said the dryad, looking a bit daunted by the bickering coven he'd found himself faced with.

"Well, I'm sure that'll be plenty for now, but you wouldn't mind if us witches gave a crack at containing her too, would ya, Lovely? You know, belt and braces and all that." The look on his face suggested he wasn't actually familiar with belt and braces, although I sensed he got the spirit.

"Oh, of course." He nodded, doing a serviceable job of hiding his bemusement.

"Did I just hear you, right?" Liz asked, giving Terance a conspiratorial jab in the ribs.

"Hear what?" I asked, half paying attention as I looked around the clearing, only now realising I hadn't seen Adrian or Michael celebrating with the others.

"You said 'us witches'," Terance said, with such earnest joy in his voice that I found myself getting a touch choked up.

"Well, I'd be looking a bit ridiculous if I kept on denying it now wouldn't I," I said, giving him a quick squeeze.

"More than a bit," said Enid dryly.

"Oh, this is so exciting. I'll text you the calendar for coven meetings," said Penny, grinning. If I hadn't distracted myself looking for Michael, I think all those smiling faces looking back at me might have brought me to tears then. I didn't know much about covens, but I couldn't remember the last time I'd made so many lovely, if a bit strange, new friends.

"Can't wait, Love, but just at the moment I'm wondering, did any of you see where Michael and Adrian got to?" I asked, glancing about the clearing to no avail.

"I think I saw 'em running off down that path," said Jade.

Mothers, Witches and Queens

"Righty ho then, I'd best set off. I've got a guess where they might have gone then," I said, turning for the path, trying to ignore the slightest flutter of nerves that was waking up in my stomach. I couldn't help thinking that Morgana being gone might not have magically snapped Adrian out of his grief. I was so busy thinking that, that I almost didn't notice Terance placing a hand on my shoulder as I started onto the path.

"What is it, Terance love?" I asked, turning around, hoping my anxiousness to get to the boys didn't come off as rude.

"I think you've got a bit of an entourage," said Terance, flitting his eyes to one side, then the other. I followed them and found myself met with about one hundred slightly anxious fay faces, all gathered and looking at me.

"All going the same way, are we? That's nice," I squeaked as my palms started to sweat. I never had been much for the spotlight.

12

Michael was lighting Olivier's fire when my eyes cracked open, the gentle smoky smell reached me along with the crackling of dry logs.

"What are you doing?" I asked, sitting up slowly as I leaned forward, resting my elbows on what I now realised was Olivier's desk. I'd been sleeping in her chair.

"I asked myself what Mum would do," said Michael, turning to me with a worried smile as he put a pot on the fire. He had tear streaks down his cheeks. I'd scared him, and grazed my knuckles if the stinging was any indication.

"Make tea?" I asked.

"Make tea." He nodded.

"I'm sorry for blowing up," I said.

"You don't need to apologise, Adrian, I just... I need you to tell me how you're feeling before it gets that bad," he said, crossing the room to perch himself next to me on her desk.

"I think... I didn't want to acknowledge it. It felt like if I admitted it, it'd be too big, like it'd would consume me," I said, getting out of my chair so we could be at eye level, as I leaned into him a little, placing my hands in his.

"I won't let anything consume you, Adrian, I promise." Michael smiled, leaning forward to kiss me softly.

"Even a feeling?" I asked, a smile breaking across my face as he nodded enthusiastically.

"I'll even learn how to beat up a feeling, but you've got to tell me about it." Michael smiled and I let out a little laugh in spite of myself.

"Okay... well, it feels stupid to say it out loud," I said, already struggling with the lump forming in my throat as my breathing began to quicken.

"Nothing you say is ever stupid. I promise, you're safe Adrian, you can say anything to me," said Michael, pushing my fringe out of my eyes.

"It's like I can feel this expectation, this weight, almost like I owe her something, and I can't be free until I've repaid it. Like there is this feeling in my chest, on my shoulders, in my throat. This feeling, this heavy lump, like I can't breathe, like I can't think. Like she needed me to do to something before she left and if I don't do it, I won't ever be free of this feeling and I don't know what it is I have to do and I thought getting rid of Morgana would do it but it's still there this feel-

Mothers, Witches and Queens

ing, this lump, this weight. I've been pushing it down and pushing it down and saying it'd be gone soon, but it isn't gone. I tried keeping busy to ignore it, but I've run out of busy. I'm scared it might never be gone and I can't keep living with this feeling. I'm going to choke or burst. I can't, I can't," I said. It was there again, the pressure the dragging choking weight.

"How long have you been feeling like this?" Michael asked. He didn't look mad at me or confused or amused. He was just looking at me, just listening. I should have told him before. Why didn't I tell him before?

"I think it's been there since I woke up... and remembered what happened, remembered her face, but it was in the background before. Behind all the pain and the anger and grief, I could ignore it, but I can't anymore. When we decided to find the Seventh In Seven, it felt like I was doing what needed to be done and the feeling, whatever it was, would be gone soon. That made it easier to bear, like a light at the end of the tunnel," I said.

"That makes sense, but you know, I don't think Olivier would want you to feel like this," said Michael, wiping a tear as it tumbled down my cheek.

"I know she wouldn't but—"

Knock, knock!

I jumped and stumbled into Michael's arms as the knock rattled the door. Now I knew why Olivier always answered the door before people had the chance to knock.

"You, okay?" Michael asked, kissing my forehead as he

set me back on my feet and slipped off the table to answer the door.

"Just startled," I said.

"Oh, hey Cherry, what are you doing here?" Michael asked, stepping out of the doorway to give me a view of the fiery-haired little elf.

"Oh well, I wanted to thank you boys, but that can wait for another time," said Cherry.

"Thank us for what?" I asked.

"Never mind about that now, you should probably know, you've got some visitors on the way," said Cherry giving as broad a sweeping gesture as he could manage, with his tiny arm. I hurried to the window and my stomach squirmed. Linda, the witches and what looked like about one hundred dazed fay were making their way down the yellow path towards the cottage.

"They're not here to visit us, they need someone else. We're just here right now," I said, panic washing over me like cold rain. Fay came to this cottage for help. I couldn't help them.

"That's the only place anyone ever is, Adrian, and you've already got the kettle on," said Cherry, giving me a wink as steam started to pour out of the pot in the fireplace.

"Don't panic, they're probably just confused, scared maybe. I bet they just want to talk," said Michael, wrapping an arm around my waist as he came to stand with me by the window.

"N-no, this is what she did. We can't do this. We can't

Mothers, Witches and Queens

be in the cottage at the end of the road," I said. I was thinking a mile a minute, my heart thundering in my chest. I couldn't do this. Olivier did this, and Olivier knew everything. I knew nothing, except that they'd reached the fence.

"Course you can," I heard Cherry say, but when I'd managed to rip my face away from the glass, he'd gone.

"Where'd he go?" I asked.

"Where'd who go, Love?" Linda asked, poking her head through the doorway.

"Cherry," I said.

"Oh, the little elf with the lovely hair? Haven't seen him. Anyway, I know you boys like your private time—"

"Muuuummmmm," Michael groaned.

"Sorry, sorry, embarrassing mothers must be flogged, anyway, you've got a lot of confused people here and I think you might be able to help them, Adrian," Linda said, smiling at me like she hadn't just volunteered my services to half the forest.

"Me? I can't, why me?" I squeaked.

"Hey now, I went along with that whole Seventh In Seven thing. Why not give it a chance, you never know? You might pull an evil sorcerer's hair out of thin air. Terrance is going to take me and the others back before Daniel gets worried. I'll see you boys at home later." Linda shot a wink, which looked like it was aimed at Michael, and stepped out of the doorway. There was an upsettingly short pause and then a knock at the already open door.

"Come in!" Michael called in a singsong voice before a

dark brownish purple-skinned gnome named Gilly stepped into the cottage looking rather sheepish.

"Hey, Adrian, gosh, I don't know what I'm doing here, really," said Gilly, ringing her hands.

"The same as me I expect," I said softly as I pulled out a seat for her almost without thinking.

"What's that then?" she asked, hopping onto it.

"Is it thinking gosh, I'm thirsty? Because I've got tea on the way," said Michael, hastily pouring out three cups and handing one too Gilly.

"Oh, thank you, that's very nice, but no, not quite," said Gilly, sipping the tea gratefully. I'm not sure how it happened, but suddenly I found myself sitting opposite her on the other side of the desk, with Michael perched on the edge.

"It's just, I didn't know what to do, and when I don't know what to do, I used to…"

"Come see Olivier," I mumbled, taking a deep breath.

"Exactly, and then when I saw smoke coming out the chimney, I suppose I just…"

"Miss her, me too Gilly," I said, sipping my tea.

"That Morgana business was terribly scary. None of us even know what happened to Mu-Terra or the others," said Gilly, staring into her steaming teacup.

"Mu-Terra is alright, councillor Marshie has him safe and sound in Starkton wood," I explained.

"Really? That's wonderful. Maybe I'll pop over to check on them," said Gilly, her eyes lighting up.

Mothers, Witches and Queens

"No!" I spoke so quickly I almost shocked myself. The images of the bodies of the other fay in the clearing flashing through my mind. I blinked and realised I'd startled her. I didn't mean to.

"Don't worry about heading over. We'll have him back to you safe and sound. Is there anything I could help you with in the meantime?" Michael asked, swooping into the conversation as words failed me. Gilly's startled look faded as she gazed up at him, and I smiled. I knew what she was seeing, those big warm kind amber eyes.

"She's really gone?" Gilly asked after a moment's hesitation.

"Defeated by the fair hands of my own mother," said Michael impressively reassuringly.

"I mean, I saw her getting trussed up and mushroomed up and all the rest of it, but the way she got into your mind." Gilly shuddered.

"Don't worry Gilly, we beat her, and we've made some friends who can keep her well at bay." I watched Michael reach down, place a hand on Gilly's shoulder, and effortlessly chase her fears away. For the first time in a little while, I thought I might cry for a good reason.

"You boys have been just lovely. Well, thanks for the tea, I'd best be on me way," said Gilly, draining her cup before hopping off the stool and making for the door.

"Any time, Gilly," said Michael, waving her off. Not two seconds after she was out the door, there came another knock.

"We'll be with you in just a second!" I called as I closed the door and stepped back. Taking Michael's hands in mine, I turned and found myself swimming in those amber eyes.

"What is it?" Michael asked, his smile warming me like the morning sun.

"That weight on my chest feels a little lighter." I smiled and Michael's hand was at my back, and his lips were on my lips and my hands were sifting through his hair and he was dipping me and holding me in his arms and my skin was on fire and my breath was short and my hair was standing on end and it was magical.

THE EPILOGUE

I stepped out into the soft breeze and the forest air with moss beneath my feet and sighed. In the fay forest I could really breathe, deep, chest expanding, lung filling breaths. I don't know if I'd never been able to do that in Starkton or if the fay forest had spoiled me. I set off down the yellow path, watching the broken light of the canopy playing across the wildflowers, and stopped to pick one. It was as tall as me, with beautiful blue petals that were soft as silk and reminded me of Adrian's eyes. I took in a long deep breath of it, a mix of mint and lavender, and set off again. My cloak billowed a little behind me as I walked. Mum said the cloak was a little dramatic for her taste, but Adrian liked my uniform, not that he'd told me. I could tell by the way his eyes lingered, and his cheeks pinked, he liked the way it hugged me. I felt like Thor.

As our cottage came into view, I smiled. The door was

open just a little and a wisp of smoke was issuing out of the chimney. I drew close and hovered outside the open window, listening for him.

"Don't worry, Pacifina, we've not got a stopwatch, there is no time limit to this," said Adrian.

"What's a stopwatch?" Pacifina's singsongy voice carried out the window and I had to stifle a laugh. She was one of the new fay being sent out to meet charges. Although things had changed a bit since Adrian had been sent to find me, of course.

"It's a sports thing. Don't worry about it too much," Adrian said, soothingly.

"There's so much I feel like I don't know." Pacifina sounded desperate.

"You know as much as I did, and look how that turned out," I could hear Adrian's reassuring smile without having to see it.

"How did you do it? How did you know with champion Michael?" asked Pacifina, sounding slightly awed.

"I knew it when I saw it, and so shall you," said Adrian. I bit my lip and swallowed a chuckle. For the amount he complained about that line, he certainly used it a lot these days.

"I suppose," said Pacifina, sounding halfway between convinced and defeated.

"And remember, I'm always here for a chat." Adrian's voice was getting louder. She must have been getting up to

Mothers, Witches and Queens

leave, so I took up my position walking down the path towards the cottage as she slipped through the door.

"Oh, hello cham… Michael." Pacifina bowed her head slightly as she spotted me. I'd asked her not to, but I think it was instinct as much as anything.

"Hello, Pacifina, you must be heading to the still world for the first time soon. Good luck," I said, giving her a wink as I passed her on the path.

"I'll do my best!" she called, and waved as she slipped out of the garden gate.

"I'm home. I brought you a flower," I said, pushing the cottage door closed behind me and offering Arian his gift.

"Michael, we're going to run out of space!" Adrian giggled as he took the flower and took a big deep breath of it, before leaning up and planting a kiss on my cheek. He then turned to survey the cottage for a space to put it. It wasn't much changed from Olivier's time here, except now there were fewer papers, more blankets, and giant blue flowers sticking out of every stray vase, watering can and bottle we could lay a hand to.

"I can't help it, I see them, I think of you and suddenly they're in my hands," I said, following him as he made his way to a slightly less cramped vase and speared the stem into it.

"Well, at least I finally get to stop and smell the flowers these days," said Adrian, struggling to rearrange the display.

"I'm glad I'm good for something," I chuckled, resting my hands on his hips as he worked.

"How's Linda?" he asked.

"She's great. Yesterday was her last day at the travel agents. She's officially a full time freelance witch, with tea leaves and an Etsy shop and everything." I chuckled. She missed having Adrian and I around a little, but she could always pop in to see us. Just needed a quick doorway from Terrance, and she was here.

"That's fantastic. We'll have to go round and see her together next time," said Adrian, turning on his heel to look up at me, setting off a swarm of butterflies in my stomach. There he was, hair like silken ribbons, eyes more beautiful than any gemstone, and full of love. Smiling at me.

"Did I ever tell you I'm the luckiest man in the world?" I asked, my hands sliding under his shirt to his back, pulling him towards me. His skin was warm, smooth, and so soft, and once I touched it, I didn't want to stop.

"Every day you tell me," Adrian giggled as he stumbled forwards until I was holding his body against mine.

"That's not nearly enough," I said in mock horror, my hands slipping past his waistband to his upper thigh as I lifted him into the air. Kissing him hungrily as his legs wrapped around my waist. I felt his hand on my chest pushing away and broke the kiss, locking with his beautiful blue eyes.

"Is this okay?" I asked, panting.

"I just wanted to say… I love your cape." Adrian blushed and then a grin burst across his face before erupting into a laugh.

Mothers, Witches and Queens

"Then the cape stays on!" I chuckled and then shuddered, my breath catching as one of his delicate hands slipped under my tight shirt, brushing across my chest.

"The rest can go," he whispered, eyes half lidded as he attacked my lips anew, his other hand twisting fingers into my hair.

Goosebumps raised along my body as I let out a shuddering groan. One hand tracing up his body, feeling his slight form until I found the back of his neck and held him close to me. The other squeezing his thigh as I carried him into the backroom and kicked the door closed behind us.

AUTHOR'S NOTE

Although this is the third book I've written, I think in some ways it was the book I always wanted to write.

In this story I finally worked out how I wanted to celebrate some of my deepest obsessions. Witchcraft and powerful women; without putting them on an unattainable pedestal. When we fall in love with someone, we fall in love with their foibles, their strange habits and even their mistakes. Without those wrinkles, it's not really love, its admiration or some idealised imagining.

Through Adrian and Michael we meet and get to know these witches, and these women, and I hope you fall in love with them, as I did writing them.

A personal favourite moment of mine happens late in part 1 (spoilers) when Michael sees with his own eyes that these witches and their magic really are real. It was the witch's joy, in being seen and being believed in, that never

Author's Note

fails to bring a tear to my eye (although those who know me know that, that is no great feat). I think because deep down, we all want people to see the magic we have inside us is real and believe in it. If for no other reason than to remind us that it really was there, all along.

SIGNUP PAGE

Hey there! It's me again, the author. I just wanted to let you know that I have a website! If you liked this book and think you might enjoy reading some more, you should check it out.

I have a mailing list and everything (very high tech I know) but don't worry I won't spam you. I occasionally have giveaways ran through there though, signed copies and so forth.

Also, I have all sorts of social media, so you can see little clips of me being silly/having an existential crisis/with bad hair. Best of all, they're also all on my website, with handy dandy clickable links that someone else set up for me because I'm useless with everything of that nature.

If that sounds like something you're interested in, you can find me at this link:

https://www.albertjauthor.com/

Printed in Great Britain
by Amazon